WEDDING NIGHT

He'd had lovers, had known passion. But what he was feeling tonight wasn't to be compared to past experiences. Prudence was his wife. The word formed images in his mind, but none that matched the look on his bride's face as her head came to rest against the pillow.

She reminded him of a newly awakened flower, soft and sweet and fragile. He smiled, then reached out to trace the curve of her lower lip. A living fire seemed to spark from his fingertips, and she flinched.

Not wanting to rush her, he chose a more coaxing game and sat on the bed next to her.

"Do you know how many times I've imagined you in this bed? How many nights I've thought of nothing but seeing every sweet inch of you?"

<u>BOOK YOUR PLACE ON OUR WEBSITE AND MAKE THE READING CONNECTION!</u>

We've created a customized website just for our very special readers, where you can get the inside scoop on everything that's going on with Zebra, Pinnacle and Kensington books.

When you come online, you'll have the exciting opportunity to:

- View covers of upcoming books
- Read sample chapters
- Learn about our future publishing schedule (listed by publication month *and author*)
- Find out when your favorite authors will be visiting a city near you
- Search for and order backlist books from our online catalog
- Check out author bios and background information
- Send e-mail to your favorite authors
- Meet the Kensington staff online
- Join us in weekly chats with authors, readers and other guests
- Get writing guidelines
- AND MUCH MORE!

**Visit our website at
http://www.kensingtonbooks.com**

HE SAID NEVER

PATRICIA WADDELL

ZEBRA BOOKS
KENSINGTON PUBLISHING CORP.
www.kensingtonbooks.com

ZEBRA BOOKS are published by

Kensington Publishing Corp.
850 Third Avenue
New York, NY 10022

All Kensington titles, imprints and distributed lines are available at special quantity discounts for bulk purchases for sales promotion, premiums, fund-raising, educational or institutional use.

Special book excerpts or customized printings can also be created to fit specific needs. For details, write or phone the office of the Kensington Special Sales Manager: Kensington Publishing Corp., 850 Third Avenue, New York, NY 10022. Attn. Special Sales Department. Phone: 1-800-221-2647.

Zebra and the Z logo Reg. U.S. Pat. & TM Off.

First Printing: October 2004
10 9 8 7 6 5 4 3 2 1

Printed in the United States of America

CHAPTER 1

London, 1867

Opinions differed when it came to the vices and virtues of Benjamin Edward Exeter, Viscount Rathbone, but there was no denying his charm.

Having just enjoyed his favorite vice, that of making love to a beautiful woman, Rathbone was putting on his trousers. As much as he enjoyed sex with the lusty Lady Ainsworth, he was glad the Season was drawing to an end. The pause in London activities would adequately conclude their brief affair.

"Must you go?" Millicent asked. She lay posed against the satin pillows that had added an erotic touch to their lovemaking. Sated, but insatiable, she ran her fingertip invitingly around the pink areola of one breast.

"Can't stay, luv. His Grace is expecting me."

The viscount's relationship with the Duke of Morland was well known among his peers. The duke was an intriguing old gentleman possessed of prodigious generosity and a fairy-godfather tendency to meddle in the lives of those around him. The effect he had on Rathbone's life resulted not so much from the duke's actions as it did from his reaction to the young viscount's all-too-often uninhibited behavior. But no matter how fierce the ensuing lectures might be, Rathbone enthusiastically continued on, wielding his charm among the ladies.

"The Duke of Morland?" Millicent's smile changed from one of inviting sensuality to one of curiosity. "I've heard about your infamous card games. Do you really appear on command at Brooks's each and every Wednesday night?"

"Yes," Rathbone said, unabashed. "It's a matter of honor."

"How like a gentleman to speak of honor *after* he's bedded a lady."

Rathbone's gaze flared for an instant. "I'm never a gentleman in the bedroom, luv. And you're certainly no lady."

Millicent smiled, certain the remark was a compliment. She left the bed to study herself before a full-length cheval mirror while slipping her arms into a red satin robe that she didn't bother to sash. "Will I see you later this evening?"

"Perhaps." He moved to stand behind her, then fondled her generous breasts until the nipples stood erect. She moaned with delight when his hand moved to stroke more sensitive flesh.

"You are a scoundrel," she said, the pleasure on her face reflected in the polished glass. "At least stay long enough to finish what you've started."

Lifting her hand to his mouth, he kissed it with all the flare of a courtly gentleman before placing it over the damp curls between her legs. "Finish it for me."

"Damn you."

Rathbone watched as her fingers began to move, lightly teasing the treasure he'd so expertly aroused. Smiling, he turned and left the bedroom.

Upon reaching the street, his steps hastened toward a waiting carriage. It was a brisk evening with a hint of chill left over from the day's earlier rain. A small patch of spring flowers captured his eye. Bathed in the subtle swath of a pearlish twilight, the delicate blossoms seemed out of place in a street lined with lavish brick and mortar homes.

"Home, Thaddeus. I'm in need of a hot bath and a change of clothes."

Groggy from his own nap, the carriage driver, a lean man of questionable years with the discretion of a priest, smiled down at his employer. "Home it is, milord."

A few moments later the carriage was moving along Pall Mall, passing St. James's Palace on its way to Belgravia. It was at the corner of Constitution Hill near a copse of trees that marked the perimeter of Green Park that Rathbone called for the horses to be halted.

"Bloody hell!" he swore in the tone of a man taken completely by surprise.

That couldn't be Prudence Tamhill standing beneath the limp branches of a rain-drenched oak. Not *the* Prudence Tamhill.

Most people knew life from bouts of compromise, judicious decisions, and financial necessity. Miss Tamhill knew it from the perspective of having the Duke of Worley as her guardian. She had been ensconced in His Grace's blanket of wealth and security since her twelfth year, thus making her inapproachable by all but the very elite of Society.

To see her without a chaperone, unless one counted the squirrel perched on a nearby branch, was as unthinkable a thought as any Rathbone could imagine. It was growing late. The lamplighters were beginning their rounds, walking from post to post with their long-handled poles, setting the gas lamps ablaze with a practiced touch as the mist began to roll in from the Thames. Most young ladies, at least those considered respectable and acceptable, were home, tucked away behind closed doors.

Rathbone stared at this particular lady, taking in the rich walnut color of her hair and the dark brows that framed even darker eyes. If London possessed one female of unquestionable, untarnished virtue, it was Prudence Tamhill. She did not willfully flirt or brag of her prosperous circumstances, but conducted herself with honesty and compassion. That said, her presence in the park was puzzling.

"Miss Tamhill," Rathbone said, having crossed the street to stand in front of her. "Are you in distress?"

He couldn't help but notice that her dress, a color once known as "the King's blue," was damp at the hem. That, in addition to the wilted condition of her bonnet feathers, presented another question. Just how long had she been in the park?

"Miss Tamhill?"

She blinked as if refocusing both her sight and her thoughts before replying, "I wouldn't use the word 'distress,' my lord."

"Lost, then?" he asked, inspecting her with a connoisseur's eye and seeing a great deal more than blue mousseline and damp lace. The tiny pearl buttons on the bodice of her dress drew his eyes. Beneath them, small breasts rose and fell in a slightly faster rhythm than normal.

She returned his gaze, her dark eyes made even darker by the approaching night. "Lost? In Green Park? I think not."

"Then what are you doing here?" he demanded, feeling like he always did whenever he encountered Prudence—provoked by her beauty, resentful of her inapproachability, and grudgingly envious of the man who would one day claim her for his own.

Unfortunately, that claim would have to be made with a wedding ring. There'd be no having the lady any other way.

"I am minding my own business, my lord. May I suggest you do the same."

Her unexpected curtness took him by surprise. It said wonders for his forbearance that he did not take to his carriage, leaving the lady where he'd found her. He reached for her hand instead. "I'll escort you home."

"No." She pulled away from him, leaving behind the lace glove that had once encased her left hand. It now hung loosely from the viscount's fingers.

"You can't stay here. With any luck you can sneak back into the house without anyone seeing you." He supplemented the remark with a dashing smile that more than one London lady had compared to that of a grinning tiger.

Prudence gave his expression no notice. "I do not need to *sneak* anywhere, my lord. I am old enough to do as I please."

If only that were true, Rathbone thought. Prudence had always sparked his secret interest. She was young and pretty, with eyes that held a promise they shouldn't. Innocent or not, she wasn't completely naïve of the effect she had on men.

Unfortunately, dallying with the ward of the Duke of Worley was tantamount to defying God.

Realizing the direction of his thoughts, Rathbone gave her a scowling glance. "Does Worley know you're wandering around in the park? Alone?"

"I am not wandering, my lord. I thank you for your offer of assistance, but having no need of it, bid you a good evening."

Rathbone wasn't used to being snubbed, but Prudence was doing an excellent job of it. Her tone was dismissive, and she was staring over her shoulder as if she'd left something or someone behind. He surveyed the park for any sign that she might not be alone. All he saw was damp greenery and an empty park bench.

"Come along. I'll see you home."

"Oh, do go away, my lord. I am not a damsel in distress."

Determined to do the right thing—he wasn't a complete loss as a gentleman—Rathbone gripped her wrist and, holding tight, forced her to walk alongside him and across the street.

"Are you mad? Let me go this instant."

He continued walking.

"I shall scream."

"Then scream," he said. "A constable will come running. You'll be rid of me and handed into his care. I'm sure your guardian will find the subsequent explanation most interesting."

"I insist that you release me."

The look he gave her ended her resistance. "Excellent," he murmured, propelling her across the street to where Thaddeus had the carriage door open and waiting. "I'm in no mood to debate propriety."

"Propriety," she scoffed. "You have no comprehension of the word. A gentleman does not manhandle a lady."

"I'm rescuing you."

"Against my will!"

He glanced over his shoulder again. "There's always the constable. Would you care to scream now?"

Her chin lifted imperiously, but she didn't make a sound.

The Duke of Worley maintained a residence in Holland Park. Rathbone made Thaddeus aware of the address while tucking his reluctant guest into the carriage. Pulling the door shut behind him, he settled into the opposing seat.

"May I assume Worley is unaware of your whereabouts?"

"You may assume whatever you wish," she replied stiffly.

Rathbone's resentment was stirred again. What did it matter that the hoity-toity Miss Tamhill was wet and bedraggled and acting more like a spoiled brat than the heiress to a small fortune—which according to rumor, she was to inherit on her wedding day or her twenty-first birthday, whichever came first.

The longer Rathbone lived, the more diamond-cut his cynicism became. His thoughts quickly formed questions. What had Prudence been doing in the park? Did she have something to hide? And if so, was it a secret or a sin?

It was a stretch of even his creative imagination to think of *the* Prudence Tamhill engaged in a sinful activity. An emblematic example of the desired purity of the times, she was the scale by which other young ladies were measured. Even the Queen was said to have suggested that the royal daughters should take notice, thereby increasing their own quality and consciousness.

"I don't suppose you want to tell me what's so intriguing about Green Park?" he asked, the tone of his voice compelling her to stop staring out the window and look at him.

"I have always found nature intriguing, my lord."

"So intriguing you're willing to risk your reputation

in order to enjoy an outing among the trees and flowers?"

She smiled, or rather, she smirked. "Were I you, I would not speak of reputations, my lord. Yours is beyond scandalous."

"That it is," he agreed all too lightheartedly. "But then, I am a man, and you are a woman. The difference permits me much."

"Too much." She withdrew a small jeweled watch from her pocket and studied the time before glancing out the carriage window, ignoring him once again.

Reluctant to admit that he was intrigued by her put-off attitude, Rathbone slanted her a quizzical glance. "You have yet to explain yourself."

"To you!"

"If not to me, then to your guardian, the Duke of Worley."

She appeared unimpressed by the mention of her guardian's name. Rathbone waited her out with a smile on his face.

"Oh, very well. I went to the park to meet someone. That someone was delayed. I was returning home when you accosted me."

"A lovers' tryst!"

"A business meeting."

"I must remember to ask my solicitor if he'd care to stroll among the daffodils and daisies the next time we have matters to discuss."

Obviously angered by his cavalier tone and the suggestion that she'd been doing anything inappropriate, she replied most deliberately, "Need I remind you, my lord, that *my* business is none of *your* business."

Rathbone didn't rise to the bait. He knew women far too well to let this one gain the advantage.

"Point taken, Miss Tamhill. However, if anyone other

than a discreet gentleman, such as myself, had seen you standing alone in Green Park, rumors would soon be tiptoeing about. By morning the entire adult population of London would know of your rendezvous."

"It was a matter of business."

"So you say."

Her retort was drowned in a cacophony of jingling harnesses and creaking wheels as Thaddeus maneuvered a sharp corner. Twilight was descending heavily upon the city, blurring the roofs and blackening the windows with shadows. A soughing wind rustled the trees, a soft reprise after the hurly-burly activity of a London business day.

Prudence gave her skirts a flick, then concentrated on putting them in a satisfactory position, all the while avoiding any direct eye contact with her escort.

Rathbone smiled to himself as he regarded the young woman sitting across from him. He thought her amusing as well as endearing—or did he mean challenging? People did not endear themselves to him easily, but they could certainly challenge him, especially women. He let his eyes dwell on her face as she gazed out the window, and beneath the cover of his clothing, he felt his body quicken as if he hadn't had a woman in weeks.

He studied the delicate planes of her face, the brows firmly arched without a hint of heaviness, the chiseled nostrils and perfect mouth cast in the softest feminine mold. With all its purity of outline, the face was neither severe nor coldly statuesque, but rather superbly classic. Added to its glory was a pink coral tint that flushed faintly through pale cheeks, while the lift of long, trailing dark lashes revealed magnificent dark eyes.

Rathbone had a sudden memory of how Prudence Tamhill had looked the first time he had seen her, at a soirée given in honor of her eighteenth birthday. He hadn't asked her to dance, since he hadn't wanted to give anyone the misconception that he had turned his attention to virginal young ladies. Funny, he could still remember what she had been wearing, a white dress with a dark pink sash that had called attention to the slimness of her waist.

It was easy to see why a large number of young lords had tried so diligently to win her hand since then. Not beautiful, but still very pretty, Prudence had an air of quality about her that even a damp gown and one missing lace mitten couldn't harm. She drew the eye in much the same way a work of art demanded its viewer's appreciation.

Silent, her attitude conveyed a wealth of information to Rathbone's watchful eyes. He had, within the past years of his life, established a certain expertise when it came to women. The eminently respectable Miss Tamhill was hiding something.

His mind moved between speculation and suspicion as he settled himself more comfortably against the cushioned seat.

"I will take my leave here," Prudence said when the carriage rolled past Kensington Gardens, nearing Holland Park.

"It's late," Rathbone replied, stating the obvious. "The streets aren't safe at this hour."

She surveyed him with a slanted brown-eyed look, half amusement, half shrewd assumption. He grinned at her.

"There's more than enough light for me to find my way home."

Something flickered in her expression, disappearing as quickly as it had arrived—a shadow of excitement, as if she had only just realized that they were alone in the carriage.

"The longer I am in your company, Miss Tamhill, the more you surprise me. While I have always found you intriguing, I had never thought you unreasonable."

His voice, too calm to be called argumentative, carried more weight than his words. Slanting a glance in his direction, his passenger finally realized he had no intention of setting her down anywhere but her own doorstep. This was one of the rules that kept their little corner of the world intact.

But then their entire encounter was about rules, the chief of which was not to be caught doing anything unseemly if one could prevent it. It was hypocrisy, to be sure, but Society offered no apology for its attitude. One obeyed the rules or paid the consequences, especially if one was female.

Satisfied he'd heard the last of her protests, Rathbone asked, "What were you doing in Green Park? How did you get there? Surely you didn't walk."

"I hired a hansom."

His smile curved into an ironic smile. "No lady hires a hansom when she has a ducal mews at her convenience. Not unless she has something to hide. I must say, I'm surprised. Never thought you the type to invite scandal."

"What I am, sir, is angered by your interference in matters beyond your jurisdiction. Now, kindly halt the carriage."

"Can't." His gray-blue eyes met her dark ones with candor. "As a gentleman, I cannot abandon a young lady to the dangers of the street. What would His Grace think of me should I act so disrespectfully toward his ward?"

"His Grace will think nothing because he will not learn of our chance meeting or this conversation. Should he, neither would be viewed in a noble light, and well you know it."

"Are you challenging me or warning me?"

A curious look of anger crossed her face, as if she were dealing with a simpleton who refused to understand. "Should we be seen together, alone in a carriage and at this hour, my guardian would demand that you repair my reputation with a proposal of marriage. Are you prepared to propose, my lord?"

For a brief moment, Rathbone was tempted to order Thaddeus to stop the carriage. Even the most inconsequential things took on serious proportions when they involved marriage.

It was well known that a strong fraction of mothers were intent on making this his last bachelor Season. The aura of Society combined with the parading of young innocents, just down from the country or newly commissioned from some obscure finishing school, made for a calculating, and often enjoyable, campaign of wills, but Rathbone had no desire to make it more than a game. Still, his pride wouldn't allow Prudence to have the last word.

"Should I tremble in trepidation of your guardian? Alas, what if I don't, Miss Tamhill? What if I relented to his demands? Would you find being my viscountess so disagreeable?"

Bloody hell, he'd just proposed marriage to the chit!

Blessedly, Prudence brushed his words aside as easily as one flicked lint from a sleeve. "I am not inclined to marry, my lord. Which is why His Grace would be all the more adamant should we be seen together. He wants me settled, you see. Properly married and presumably content."

"How very boring."

"I couldn't agree more."

Rathbone purposely allowed the conversation to end.

It wasn't until the carriage turned onto the main boulevard of Holland Park that Rathbone's companion showed her true nervousness at being deposited on her guardian's doorstep by a man of notorious reputation. She moved to the edge of the seat, her posture growing more stiff. Taking pity on her, Rathbone called for Thaddeus to stop the carriage.

Prudence sat silently for a moment, her profile framed in the waning light. Rathbone had to restrain himself from reaching for her. He wanted to touch the delicate features of her face, to outline the contours of her mouth with his fingertip. It would be the next best thing to kissing her. The thought quickened his blood.

Instead of giving in to the impulse, he reached out and opened the door. Holding out his hand, he waited for Prudence to accept it. "The front door or the rear entrance?"

"Through the garden."

They left the carriage and began to walk. Dark clouds were blowing in from the east, presaging rain. The wind picked up, and a sudden bolt of lightning streaked above the tree tops with a flash of searing white. It would rain again, and soon.

As Prudence moved beside him with soundless, graceful steps, Rathbone was conscious of a luxurious pleasure in her nearness. Everything about her was enticing, from the upward sweep of her stylish hair to the graceful curve of her neck. She was also of a very nice height, not so short a man had to stoop to kiss her, and not so tall that he felt diminished by her size.

Rathbone couldn't keep from thinking about what it would be like to get her into bed, her body exposed for his exploration, her mouth swollen from his kisses, her breath coming in short, excited gasps as he moved over her. Into her.

Something else mingled with the vivid impression in his mind—less specific, but still strong—suggesting that a sexual encounter with Prudence would be found lacking unless the lady's heart were surrendered as well.

The contradiction of the two was so alarming that Rathbone was forced to wonder if he'd lost his mind somewhere between Millicent's boudoir in Trafalgar Square and the fashionable houses of Holland Park.

"The gate is there," she said, pointing toward a shoulder-high, wrought-iron fence threaded with an overgrowth of climbing roses, the stalks full-leaved and rowed with thorns.

Beyond it lay a house of classical stucco with stained-glass windows and elaborate ironwork on the second- and third-floor balconies. A small cluster of chestnut trees shaded the front walk and the wide stone steps while their brawny branches prevented anyone from seeing the garden gate through which Prudence meant to enter.

She hesitated for a moment, her gaze focused on the lace mitten tucked into the breast pocket of his jacket.

"I'm keeping it," Rathbone said.

"Why? It's hardly an identifiable means of blackmail, my lord. I'm not the only woman to purchase lace mittens from Madam Vicente's boutique."

"I shall keep it as a memento of our time together."

She accepted his meaning with an unsteady breath. He wasn't going to let her forget their chance encounter, or the fact that she had yet to offer an explanation. With a smile, he reached around her to open the gate. It gave way with a ghostly creak.

She turned, unconsciously lifting her face toward his.

It was exactly what Rathbone had hoped she would do. He reached out, framing her face with his hands, and before she could stop him, he kissed her.

Rathbone told himself it was the young lady's exquisite reserve that fueled his need to kiss her, that and his bruised pride, but his body was telling him something else. Something far more elemental.

Unprepared and inexperienced, Prudence was momentarily lost in his actions. Rathbone took advantage of her shocked acquiescence to deepen the kiss. His arms went around her, directing her body the same way he would lead a dance partner into a waltz, drawing her into the intrinsic warmth of a lover's embrace.

He could taste her pureness, but more surprisingly, he felt a warm spilling of pleasure, something he hadn't been prepared to feel. The unprecedented feeling came over him and through him in small waves, strong and sweet and unflawed, like heat from the sun.

"So sweet," he whispered against her lips. The words were said with slow and passionate emphasis, his eyes intent upon her face. "So very sweet."

When she didn't move to leave his embrace, Rathbone kissed her again, knowing the second kiss was far more dangerous than the first. The lady could become addictive.

After a third kiss, he drew his fingertips over the curves of her face, lightly caressing the rise of her cheekbones, then touching the lips he had kissed so thoroughly.

Again, her only movement was to stare at him, her expression suggesting an even greater naïveté than he'd first imagined. Her gaze was mute astonishment, eyes wide, moist lips parted—and for a moment, he stared down at her in equal wonder.

His lips touched hers again. It was the gentlest of

kisses, and yet it carried more importance than the ones that had come before it.

"Good night, Miss Tamhill."

He turned her slowly, aiming her toward the gate.

She hesitated, but only for a second. Then, presumably regaining her senses, she suddenly gathered up her skirts and hurried toward the house, leaving Rathbone with the odd feeling that Fate had just tapped him on the shoulder.

CHAPTER 2

"Hurry," Prudence said, encouraging her maid, a girl of eighteen with unruly blond hair that routinely insisted on escaping its pins by mid-morning. "Oh, why did Uncle Horace have to invite guests for dinner tonight of all nights?"

"The blue gown, then," Fiona suggested. "And the pearls."

"Anything will do," Prudence replied impatiently. "Blue, green, it doesn't matter."

There were few people to whom Prudence could reveal her true feelings. Fiona was one of them. In the years since becoming the Duke of Worley's ward, Fiona had been there, first as a companion who had slept in a bed across an enormous bedroom from the shy little girl newly arrived at North Hill, then as a lady's maid.

Acting in the latter capacity, she removed the blue evening gown from a tall clothespress and draped it over the end of the bed. The silk had been purchased in Paris, a present from Lionel, the Duke of Worley's second son.

Prudence removed her hat and the lone lace mitten. She tossed them onto a nearby table, not having the time to properly examine the feelings Rathbone had aroused with his unexpected kiss. Lord and Lady Wallingcroft were due to arrive within the hour.

A domed pendulum clock on the white marble mantelpiece began to chime, confirming the need to push any and all thoughts of the viscount to the back of her mind.

"Did you meet with Mr. Sauer?" Fiona asked, making haste to gather all the things Prudence would need before presenting herself downstairs.

"No. He was delayed for some unknown reason. I waited as long as I could."

There was no mention made of the viscount. As much as Prudence trusted Fiona, some things were better left unsaid.

Despite her resolve not to think about him, Prudence knew she shouldn't have allowed Rathbone to kiss her.

While the venue had been romantic, the circumstances were not. The kiss didn't signify anything beyond her own inability to have gauged the man's boldness.

It was doubly annoying to know that the viscount suspected she had been up to no good. While men blamed the spreading of gossip on the female tongue, Prudence knew London's clubs were a steamy caldron of information. The members spoke freely about everything from politics to which shrew mother was trying to trap what eligible young man into proposing marriage to her daughter.

"I'll carry a note to Mr. Sauer tomorrow," Fiona offered, unaware that Prudence had momentarily lost track of her original objective.

Taken out of her musings by the remark, Prudence shrugged her shoulders. "Possibly. Then again, it might serve best to visit his shop a second time. I did admire the topaz necklace he crafted. Perhaps purchasing it would resurrect his memory and loosen his tongue."

Prudence sat down, staring into the mirror over her dressing table. She resisted the urge to touch her lips, still slightly swollen from the impact of her first kiss. Kisses, actually. There had been three. Or was it four? Succumbing to the knowledge that she'd been too befuddled to count them, her mouth curved into an unconscious smile.

Since childhood, when sorrow had come down on her at the loss of her mother, she had learned to go still on the inside. The inactivity had allowed her to cope, to center on something inside herself rather than the confusion of the outside world. Over the years, the childhood practice had become habit. When there was too much to feel, she refused any but the most carefully guarded emotions.

The viscount had gotten past those defenses.

She had been spellbound by the exquisite shock of his touch. The result was a splintering blow to her innocence, one from which she might never recover.

She hadn't realized until now what a kiss could do, how much fuller and brighter it could make one feel.

"We'll need to do your hair," Fiona said, coming toward her with an ivory-handled brush in hand.

Thrust back to reality by the necessity of playing hostess, Prudence forced her reveries aside. It wouldn't do to give Rathbone's outrageous behavior too much importance. The man was not given to fixing his attention upon a lady for long, and she had far more important things on her mind.

To the ordinary observer, her life might seem as carefree as a butterfly's, for ordinary observers were apt to overemphasize the benefits of wealth. The average person might fail to realize that when one is rich, one can cease to value money, making room for other concerns to intrude.

It was still difficult for Prudence to imagine her mother, the sterling Rachel Tamhill, being the source of an indiscretion so strong it had produced a child—her.

The fact of the matter was that Prudence had no earthly idea what the unvarnished circumstances of her birth might reveal should she be able to uncover the truth. She was assumed to be the daughter of Sir Archibald Tamhill, one of the Tamhills of East Sussex. The Tamhill family had owned a lucrative shipping business for several generations, the profits of which were now being held in trust for the last of their line, a daughter who might or might not be a legitimate heir.

It was Prudence's quest for the truth that had taken her to Green Park. She was to have met with a jeweler, Mr. Sauer, who, according to an observation made during a casual visit to his shop, had fashioned the ring she now wore. The ruby had belonged to her mother.

The ring had not been a present from a husband to his wife. In fact, when Prudence had inherited her mother's jewelry, an impressive collection of gems that included a diamond tiara, her father had specially asked that she never wear the ring in his presence.

It hadn't been difficult for Prudence to honor the request. She had been only eight, much too young to flaunt a blood-red ruby on her finger. Her father, following her mother to the grave some four years later, had never seen the ring again. It had remained locked away until the last Tamhill had come of age.

As a child, Prudence had been as awed by her mother's appearance as she had by Sir Archibald's indifference.

She knew now that her father hadn't been intentionally cruel; he was simply uninterested in anything that involved the little girl in the upstairs nursery. After her mother's death, he had continued to do his duty, appearing in the schoolroom from time to time to inquire dispassionately about her studies or to tell her that he would be away on business, the latter being the majority of the time.

There had been the occasional Sunday dinner, with him at one end of the table and she at the other. Nothing of substance was ever spoken and there had been no demonstrations of affection. There had been only rigid rules and lessons in etiquette.

The four years separating Rachel Tamhill's death from that of her husband had been sterile ones for Prudence. Years spent wondering what she'd done to displease God so much that He would take her beautiful mother away, leaving her no one but a silent, stone-faced father she couldn't seem to please.

In retrospect, Prudence now realized the first eight years of her life had been spent as if perched on the edge of a slippery brocade chair, fingers clutching and feet dangling. Discovering her mother's diary had been a blessing in disguise. Finally, after years of looking inward, as if there were a flaw that, once found, could be cured, she had come to understand why Archibald Tamhill had treated her so coldly.

She wasn't his daughter.

"There," Fiona said, putting aside the brush. "The duke will never guess you were up to no good this afternoon."

"Let's hope not," Prudence said, knowing that was exactly how her guardian would view things.

Horace Delmont, the fifth Duke of Worley, implemented a strong will and rigid discipline in his personal life. His actions were governed by fixed principles of good sense, practicality, and propriety. That betrayal was not to be rewarded was one of those rules.

It wasn't the thought that the duke would blame her for her mother's sins that kept Prudence from telling him of her suspicions. She simply wanted to sort out the details first, to discover who she truly was, and with that discovery, to take charge of her own life.

More than a little exasperated by the day's events, Prudence took a deep breath before going downstairs. As expected, she found Griswold, the family butler, waiting in the foyer. The man had an uncanny knack for being in the right place at the right time—obviously the reason he had been employed by the duke for almost forty years.

"Have Lord and Lady Wallingcroft arrived?" she asked.

"They are in the parlor with His Grace," Griswold told her. "Lord Wallingcroft's nephew is with them—a scholarly young man by the name of Titus Counce."

Prudence grimaced. "Is it my imagination, Griswold, or has His Grace suddenly discovered a fresh flock of friends, each endowed with a nephew or grandson of good character and no matrimonial entanglements?"

"It isn't my place to say, miss, but there does seem to be an abundance of young gentlemen about these days."

It was no secret, especially to the staff, that Prudence's guardian wanted her married off as soon as possible, especially with a fortune as sizeable as the Tamhill inheritance on the horizon. The very idea of a young woman managing countless coffers of money boggled the male imagination.

It wasn't that Prudence didn't keep abreast of current affairs. On the contrary, she took a keen interest in them and read any pamphlet that came her way. It was simply the duke's ingrained philosophy that life was divided into those responsibilities that fell upon a man's shoulders and those that flowed to a woman.

"I suppose I shall have to resign myself to the evening's entertainment," she said, hiding her irritation.

"It would seem so," Griswold agreed. He opened the door to the parlor, his expression alerting Prudence to the fact that she'd find Titus Counce as unimpressive as his name.

Mentally preparing herself for several hours of social chatter and parlor whist, Prudence put a smile on her face before sweeping regally into the room.

This particular parlor was ostentatiously welcoming. The windows were heavily curtained in gold velvet. A large silver bowl had been filled with yellow chrysanthemums and white daisies and placed on the center table in front of the settee, adding a touch of spring. The chandelier provided a soft glowing light that called attention to the elegant seventeenth-century furnishings, accented by an Italian marble mantelpiece that displayed an expensive collection of porcelain figurines.

"Prudence, my dear, do come in," the duke said, rising to his feet.

Seeing his warm smile, the reality of Prudence's life warred with her admiration for the man. It was impossible to think of anyone getting the better of the Duke of Worley. He was a formidable man, both in size and influence, who ruled supreme under his own roof. Beyond his home, he was a trusted confidant of Queen Victoria, the chairman of several Parliamentary committees, and a successful businessman. His guardianship of Prudence had come by her father's request, based on a distant family relationship.

"Come," he said, taking her arm and guiding her

across the richly colored Oriental carpet to where Lord Wallingcroft and his wife were seated. "You've met before, I'm sure."

"Yes, of course," Lord Wallingcroft said, coming to his feet with a brisk huff of breath. "Only last week at the Stonefield soirée."

"A pleasant party," Prudence replied, remembering their guest as a man who enjoyed the sound of his own voice. He was the sort of gentleman one tried hard to forget, pious and obnoxious, with a narrow mind and inflexible attitudes, his chief obsession being himself.

"Lady Wallingcroft," she said, acknowledging the thin woman with dull brown hair and nose glasses. "Please, forgive me for keeping you waiting."

"Nonsense." This from the duke, who was still holding onto her, his thick hand firmly anchoring hers to his arm.

Prudence knew he was doing so because Worley was afraid she would run from the room after being introduced to Titus Counce.

Wallingcroft's nephew, who was in his mid-twenties and had thin brows framing eyes the shade of weak tea, shoved his spectacles up the bridge of his nose before bending into a bow that sent them right back to where they'd started.

"Miss Tamhill," he stammered self-consciously. "I've looked forward to meeting you."

Prudence felt sorry for him. He was tall, big-boned, loose and awkward under his black coat. It was apparent he'd been coerced into coming by his aunt and uncle. Griswold's description fit the young man to perfection. Titus Counce belonged in a room with moldy manuscripts and dusty scrolls, deciphering some obscure ancient text.

"The pleasure is all mine, Mr. Counce," she replied, slipping effortlessly into the role of the perfect hostess.

The evening progressed very much as Prudence had envisioned it. Lord Wallingcroft, a staunch conservative, quickly drew the duke into a political conversation that left no room for comment from either herself or Lady Wallingcroft.

Titus ate slowly, saying little, until Prudence happened upon a topic that allowed him the confidence to speak.

"You've been to China. How wonderful!" she remarked.

"I've only just returned," he said, letting her know why she hadn't encountered him before. "I spent a year in Peking. The city has the most intriguing history. Did you know . . ."

While Titus regaled her with details of the Khitan Mongols, who had established a capital on the site of present-day Peking after invading the North China Plain, Prudence recalled an event more recently recorded in history—a kiss at the garden gate.

An odd anticipation, a feeling without focus, swelled inside her as she thought of seeing Rathbone again. She should, by rights, cut him most severe. He had overstepped all bounds of propriety by kissing her so shamefully, and yet she couldn't help but wonder if he would be attending Lady Winthrop's ball at week's end.

What would it be like to waltz with him? Though they often attended the same parties, the viscount was one of the few men in London who had never sought her favor. She supposed it was because he was a known rake and scoundrel and she an overprotected heiress. He didn't need her money, nor, did it appear, was he in any hurry to fulfill the obligations of his title and take a wife.

The soft chime of a fork meeting the edge of a gold-rimmed dessert plate brought her attention back to the business at hand: fulfilling her obligation as hostess.

"The Chou dynasty is most fascinating," Titus said, continuing his dissertation. "It can be traced back to 256 B.C. Imagine that. The British Empire is in its infancy when one considers the longevity of the Chinese culture."

Prudence smiled, agreeing with feigned interest. She couldn't get her mind off the viscount. The shocking intimacy of his kiss had aroused more than curiosity.

The sum of her excursions into the adult world had been strictly supervised by her guardian. Until this evening, she had presumed women responded to men with the detached tenderness and introspection peculiar to a true lady. But nothing about the viscount's kiss had brought tenderness to mind.

Scandalous sensations had coursed through her, deep and intense, starting at the base of her spine and fanning outward until her toes had tingled. Thinking about it made her tremble inside, even now, but it was the deeper feelings that confused her. Unconsciously, she licked her lips.

An attentive footman refilled her water glass. Prudence sipped at the cool liquid, but it didn't quench her thirst. Her curiosity had been aroused and, once awakened, she knew it would take another kiss from the viscount to satisfy it.

The thought of comparing his kiss to that of another man didn't enter Prudence's mind.

It was several hours later, after Griswold had closed the door behind Lord and Lady Wallingcroft and their nephew, that Prudence had an opportunity to voice some of her frustration.

Following her guardian into the library, she confronted him by saying, "You've become quite impossible, Uncle Horace."

"Whatever are you talking about?" He sat comfortably behind his desk, a brandy and cigar nearby.

"You know very well what I'm talking about." She had gotten over her fear of the duke years ago. Underneath the craftily painted veneer that accompanied his title, he was a very nice man. A bit stolid in his attitudes, but not unkind. "Titus Counce! Do you actually envision me marrying such a man?"

"I can envision you marrying one of several men, all of whom you have turned down without a moment's thought," he said, not so benignly this time. "Since none of them appealed to you, I thought young Counce might. No harm done if you don't take to the lad. I grant he's a bit too studious for my liking. Can't see him managing Tamhill—too much responsibility."

"No harm done!" She was angrier than she should be and it showed. "I won't be forced into marriage."

"No one is *forcing* you into marriage," Worley replied with rising sharpness. "I'm your guardian. It's my responsibility to see to your welfare."

"And if I choose not to marry?"

"Don't be ridiculous. What else would you do?"

"Live my life as I please, accountable to no one but myself and God."

"Where are you getting these foolish notions? Has that maid of yours been collecting pamphlets again? Outrageous ideas floating about the city nowadays. Anarchists spreading moral decay like farmers spread manure."

Prudence looked at him with a mixture of impatience and affection. "My feelings about marriage have nothing to do with political ideology," she assured him. "I simply want the satisfaction of marrying for love."

The duke's expression didn't change. "Balderdash. How can you expect a man to love you when you refuse to give one so much as the time of day? You brushed Lord Caulfield's proposal aside like a maid gathering dust off a parlor floor. And St. Ives and Lord Brisbane. All decent, respectable men."

"You think I'm being stubborn."

"Aren't you?"

The change in her mood was imperceptible until Prudence smiled. Her anger deflated, she sank into a chair. "My stubbornness isn't deliberate. I simply dislike having men paraded about the house like thoroughbreds circling an auction ring."

"Who is he?"

"Who is whom?"

The duke looked at her with concerned curiosity. "The man who has you thinking about love?"

"No one in particular," she said a little too quickly.

The topic turned her thoughts. Perhaps marriage, that distant thing which she had always put aside to consider later, was the goal she should be seeking.

Prudence knew the reason for her continuous procrastination wasn't fear. On the contrary, she had always considered marriage one of the accepted elements of a woman's life. But when she thought of marriage, the men who had passed in a continuous succession through the parlor seemed a ghostly series, all with the same face and voice, the same manners and mundane way of looking at life.

But suddenly there was a face. The lure of Rathbone's stark, daring sensuality had been the ruin of more than one tender heart. It wouldn't do to reveal her encounter with him. The duke was certain to think the worst. As for falling in love with the viscount . . . the idea was preposterous. He'd kissed her, nothing more.

"I know you better than that," the duke remarked, his expression changing from one of altercation to one of bovine tenderness. "Someone has gained your attention. Who is he?"

"No one," she repeated, continuing in the tone of one imparting some ordinary bit of information to a friend. "And why must there be someone? Why do men presume that a husband is all a young lady thinks about? There are other things in life that are just as meaningful in their pursuit."

"You're becoming totally unmanageable," Worley grunted good-naturedly. "The sooner I get you married off, the better."

"I've always been unmanageable."

"Only in private." His expression changed, turning serious again. "I don't suppose you'd reconsider Caulfield's proposal?"

"No, Your Grace."

"Off to bed with you then."

Prudence kissed him good night, then quit the room, only to meet up with the duke's younger son in the foyer.

"The Honorable Mr. Delmont," she said. "We didn't expect you back until tomorrow."

Lionel was a robust young man with sparkling green eyes and unruly black hair. His chronic escapades and quicksilver refusal to conform had been the cause of more than one interview between himself and his father throughout his young manhood. Every summons to the library had been alike: his father stomping up and down the room, more baffled than angry, and Lionel, impeccably deferential in his bearing, being entirely reasonable and adamant. It invariably ended in tacit victory for Lionel, but the duke never ceased trying to reform the waywardness of his youngest son.

Prudence adored him. The household was different when Lionel was about. His zest for life rubbed off on everyone, including his austere father.

Both of the duke's sons had gladly taken up the reins of brotherhood, teasing and taunting Prudence from the first day she'd arrived at North Hill, the duke's family home. Frederick and Lionel had immediately protected and accepted her as if she were a misplaced sister who had finally found her way home.

Prudence loved them both dearly, but it was Lionel who had taken a shy, confused girl under his wing and taught her how to laugh again.

"Prudence," he said earnestly, "I do believe you've gotten prettier since the last time I saw you."

Laughing, she took his arm, guiding him toward the smaller of the two downstairs parlors.

"The last time you saw me was two months ago, and I haven't changed one whit since then. How was Paris?"

"Boring."

It struck Prudence then just how much Lionel resembled the Viscount Rathbone. Not in appearance, but in attitude. Like Rathbone, Lionel displayed a flagrant disregard for Society and its rules. Prudence was certain he engaged in all sorts of debauchery when he wasn't in residence, but she preferred to think of him as a childhood playmate who had grown older, though not terribly wiser.

Lionel kissed her on the cheek. "Griswold told me Lord and Lady Wallingcroft carted their nephew along for dinner this evening. What do you think of Titus?"

"Not you, too!"

He gave her a sympathetic smile. "Father's only doing what he thinks best."

"I know. It's you joining the ranks that surprises me."

"It shouldn't. Your birthday isn't that far away. If you're not married by then . . ."

Prudence let go of his arm to give him a scalding look. "Will the world come to an end? I think not. And what is so wrong with me managing my own affairs?"

Lionel removed his jacket and tossed it over the back of a chair before helping himself to a drink. "The Tamhill estate isn't your normal realm of affairs, Pru. It's a bloody fortune. Once you come of age, you're no longer under Father's protection. Every fortune hunting bastard in England will be sniffing around your skirts."

"I know a fortune hunter when I see one, Lionel. Just as I'll know the right man when he comes along. If I'm to marry, it will be then, and not one moment sooner."

"Stubborn chit," he grumbled.

"Tell me about Paris," she insisted, nestling into a comfortable chair. She was done talking about marriage. "Do the women really wear net stockings and show their legs when they dance?"

"You *are* in need of a husband." He gave her a long, hard look, seeing beneath the properly dressed young lady to the young girl he had once chased through the orchard because she'd put salt in his tea instead of sugar. "Something's happened. You've never inquired into my travels before. They're mostly business, you know."

"Mostly," she mused sweetly. "As for questions, why shouldn't a lady be curious? We live in the same world as men."

"Not quite the same," Lionel countered seriously. "Something has happened. What? Tell me, or I'll question Fiona until she spills all your little secrets."

Having every faith that Fiona would hold her tongue

under any threat, Prudence smiled. "Nothing out of the ordinary. I simply dislike having other people make my decisions for me."

"There's always Freddie. He's very fond of you. And Father would be delighted to keep you in the family."

Prudence laughed again, the soft, rich sound rising to the vaulted ceiling where plaster cherubs danced around a glass-globed chandelier. "While I adore your older brother, he's much too serious minded. Besides, Frederick doesn't want a wife."

"Be that as it may, you'd make a good match. Liven up the old boy's life a little. God knows he needs it."

"Enough," she said, leaving her chair. "No more talk of prospective husbands. It's giving me a headache."

"Shall we ride tomorrow morning?"

"Yes. You can tell me all about Paris."

"Only what I think acceptable," he scolded. "Father would have me drawn and quartered if he thought I was leading you down the wrong path."

"No chance of that. You're just like him, determined to protect me from everyone and everything. Pity. It makes for a dull life."

"Upstairs, you little scamp." There was a teasing light in his eyes as he set aside his drink to kiss her on the forehead.

It wasn't until she was alone, lying in her bed, staring into the dark, that Prudence allowed herself to think of the viscount again. Recalling how it had felt to be in his arms, she was forced to admit curiosity.

Maybe it was because her polished existence, so carefully fashioned for so long, had recently begun to seem empty. More often than she liked to admit, while following the long-familiar pattern of social activities, she had stopped with a sudden blank shock and asked herself: What does my future hold?

Even if she managed to avoid a marriage of convenience, she still had a lifetime in front of her. Managing Tamhill Shipping would consume her time, but could it consume her heart?

Prudence doubted it. She enjoyed the few aspects of the business in which Uncle Horace and Frederick allowed her to dabble, but she had no great desire to spend her entire life pouring out the endless energy required to keep a business the size of Tamhill Shipping afloat and profitable.

She wanted a family—a loving family. She wanted a home filled with laughter and evenings spent in a parlor where children feuded and played, where her husband sat reading while she rocked a baby in her arms.

A frown knitted her brow as Prudence found herself wishing the viscount had kissed her just one more time.

CHAPTER 3

The Winthrop's ballroom was ablaze with light. The massive crystal chandelier, which had to be secured within the ceiling by special iron beams, glittered. Servants had worked throughout the day, festooning the banisters of the mezzanine above the ballroom with flowers from the greenhouse. Streamers fluttered from white satin bows and furbelows sewn with silver beadings caught the light and reflected it back like captured fireflies. The room rivaled any to be found at Buckingham Palace.

In the minstrel's gallery, black-coated musicians played softly, the mellow tones of their violins mixing with the animated conversation of the crowd. Champagne flowed from long-necked bottles into fragile glasses handed out by liveried servants who passed among the guests with practiced anonymity.

A momentary silence fell over the room as the musicians ended a lilting Mozart sonata. On cue, the dancers left the floor in a colorful migration that took them to the refreshment tables, where a lavish buffet of cold meats, spiced fruit, and tiny iced cakes were waiting.

Prudence, with Lionel as her escort, arrived stylishly late, but her entrance drew no fewer stares. Entering the room, she seemed oblivious to the collective sigh of admiration that came from a group of young dandies standing near the door. She had made her debut two years ago, but she was still very much on the market.

The Tamhill fortune, Rathbone decided as he watched her gracefully maneuver about the room to greet their host and hostess. He continued watching her. It was still early in the evening, but there had been several late nights since his previous encounter with the lovely Miss Tamhill. He was still puzzling out his reaction to her; she was pretty and enticing, very probably the most intriguing young woman he had ever met.

In his mind he held the vivid image of dark, dark hair piled under a small, feathered bonnet, of delicately flushed cheeks, and of her warm, spicy mouth. The reverie made not a ripple on the surface of Rathbone's outward appearance, but inside, the memory added itself to a succession of fantasies, each dominated by Miss Prudence Tamhill.

"I hear you bought the stallion I was bidding on last week. Hope you paid more than he was worth. It would serve you right."

Rathbone switched his gaze from the crowded room to Lord Granby. Besting his best friend always made him smile. "Three-fourths Arabian, as fast as the wind, and worth every shilling."

"You could at least look remorseful. I had plans for that stallion."

"And I have a stable full of needy mares. Can't go disappointing the ladies."

"Why do I get the impression we're talking about two different things?"

"Are we?" Rathbone let his gaze wander leisurely

about the room until it came to rest on a young woman in a ice-blue satin gown. Her back was to him, but he could see her escort. "I thought Delmont was in Paris."

"Just got back," Granby said. "Had a few words with him at the club earlier today. It seems the French court is uncertain what will happen since Palmerston's death."

"Our new Prime Minister will keep the Queen informed and hopefully averse to becoming too involved with her Continental cousins," Rathbone replied. "I, for one, don't like the rumblings in Prussia. Greedy monarchs make for nasty wars."

"Couldn't agree more. Ah, there's my lovely wife." Granby handed off his glass, minus the champagne. "Duty calls."

Rathbone acknowledged the earl's departure with a smile. All of his closest friends were married now, lost to the world of wives and children and family obligations. He'd stopped counting the christenings he'd attended in the last five years. Not that he begrudged his friends their happiness. He didn't. It was simply that he couldn't imagine one woman making him equally content. Not for long, and certainly not until "death do you part."

Sighing, he wondered if he'd made a mistake in attending the ball. Admittedly, curiosity had drawn him. What would the prim and proper Miss Tamhill do when they came face to face? How would she react if he kissed her again?

Curiosity seemed little enough, but why should it matter? He'd kissed more women than he could count. One more made little difference, even if she had tasted sweeter than he'd expected.

* * *

"Would you care to waltz, Miss Tamhill?"

Prudence looked up to find Titus Counce standing in front of her, his evening attire already wrinkled, as if he'd been dozing in some secluded corner.

She accepted his hand, groaning inwardly as she looked at the swarm of assembled guests and recognized a good many of them as gentlemen who had vied for her attention in the past. Her patience for such gatherings was growing thin, but it would have been rude not to have come after accepting Lady Winthrop's invitation.

Privately, Prudence was surprised she had any toes left by the time the music ended. Smiling despite the discomfort, she accepted the glass of lemonade Titus offered her.

"I had hoped to see you again," he said. "I just acquired the most magnificent manuscript from an antiques dealer. A journal of sorts, written by a man who claims to have accompanied Marco Polo on his first journey to the Orient."

"How intriguing," Prudence replied, as her gaze swept past a small knot of matrons gossiping in a corner and came to rest upon a lone figure standing between two white Corinthian columns. Her attention was caught by the blondness of his hair. As her gaze traveled lower, she found herself staring into the most disconcerting pair of blue eyes she'd ever encountered.

Rathbone.

So he had come.

Prudence's breath caught in her throat. She was unnerved by the intensity of his slow, lazy smile. The man was openly mocking her, and yet as the thought took form, she got the distinct impression that the same blue eyes had been watching her all evening.

While Titus rambled on about the implications of Marco Polo's discoveries and the subsequent opening of the Eastern trade routes, Prudence returned Rathbone's stare. His stance was almost a slouch, his arms crossed before his silk-covered chest. His expression was just as insolent, his casual attitude declaring that he recognized no authority higher than himself.

Aware that they were studying each other much too closely, Prudence looked away. Like a wild animal sensing danger, she knew Rathbone would mark this evening with their first dance.

A few minutes later, a sea of expectancy shivered around Prudence as her suspicion was confirmed. The musicians were preparing to play another waltz when Rathbone made his way across the room, heading right for her.

"Miss Tamhill," came the deep, now-familiar voice. "May I have the pleasure of this dance?"

The words were naught but a formality, but it was on such formalities that Society existed. A man extended his hand and a woman accepted, if they had been formally introduced, which she and the viscount had been several years ago. It was having him ask her after so long a time that gave the event significance.

Prudence passed her lemonade to Titus, who appeared totally surprised that the party hadn't ceased to exist the moment he'd mentioned Marco Polo.

An indrawn gasp swept through the ballroom as Rathbone drew her onto the floor for their first waltz. Prudence grimaced inwardly, then fixed an angelic smile on her face as the music began.

"You're holding me too close."

"Not close enough," he whispered in return. His eyes gleamed as he intimately tightened his hold about her waist. "I didn't realize you were a student of Chinese history."

"Do not think to mock Titus, as you have mocked me," she said in a brisk, businesslike manner. "Mr. Counce is a scholar."

"And I but a lowly viscount."

"A viscount with the devil's own reputation," she countered, refusing to meet his gaze because she knew what she'd find—a triumphant look, because she, like so many other young women, had been taken in by his charm.

"When have I mocked you?"

"You kissed me."

"Several times."

Prudence deliberately stepped on his toes.

A smile spread to his lips, becoming a subdued chuckle. "That's no way for a lady to behave."

"You are the last one to speak to me of behavior, my lord. And stop grinning like a goat. Everyone is watching."

"I take offense, Miss Tamhill. I never grin like a goat."

"But you are gloating."

"At the moment, I'm simply enjoying the feel of you in my arms *again*."

She looked up at him, trying to discern if he was speaking anything close to the truth. The look he gave her was more disturbing than his touch, as if he knew that she'd done little but think of him since that night.

"Your necklace is most unusual," he said, letting his gaze slide from her eyes to the pale hollow of her throat, where six perfectly matched gems lay warm against her skin. The necklace's setting was silver and very delicate, taking nothing away from the iridescent play of color that characterized opals.

"Thank you." The necklace was one of three she had purchased from Mr. Sauer, hoping the expenditure would increase his memory.

It hadn't.

The only thing he'd been able to tell her about the man who had purchased a flawless blood-red ruby twenty years ago was that he had been tall, with dark hair and impeccable manners, certainly a gentleman. There had been no name given—only a hefty deposit, followed by payment in full when the customer had returned to the shop several days later to pick up the ring.

Since the description applied to over half the men in London, Prudence was no closer to identifying her real father than she had been the day she'd first read her mother's diary.

"Is something wrong?" Rathbone asked.

"You're holding me too close. People are watching."

"Let them watch."

The same intriguing smile she had seen in the carriage played over his lips, and Prudence thought again that she had never met a man so arresting. Despite the fact that she was a gentlewoman, and well aware of all the niceties of feminine conduct, she was also capable of admitting unpleasant truths to herself.

It was insane, of course, to recall that day . . . to seek out another adventure with the notorious viscount, another kiss. But he had filled her mind from that evening on with enticing question marks that refused to be erased.

"What are you thinking?" he asked in a low, lazy whisper that set her heart to hammering again.

"That I should cut you, end this dance, and walk away."

"Honesty," he said. "One hears it so rarely."

Her gaze quickly swept the ballroom. So many people, so many secrets, she thought. Her attention to Rathbone dimmed a little as she thought of her father. Was he here tonight? Amid the crowd, concealed by a respectable name?

Not knowing if he was alive or dead, she clung tenaciously to the belief that one day she would be able to know him, if not publicly, then privately.

Following her thoughts, she looked at the man who was waltzing her around the room and said, quite seriously, "Wouldn't it be wonderful if we never spoke anything but the truth to one another? Not just us, but everyone. For all our lives, nothing but the truth."

"What brought that on?"

"Nothing," she sighed. "It was just a thought."

The music stopped, but they continued dancing a moment longer, as if revisited by the momentum of their first kiss.

Realizing what his actions were revealing, Rathbone stepped away from her. "Thank you for the dance, Miss Tamhill."

With that, he turned and walked away, melting into the crowd. Slightly dazed, for she too hadn't noticed the music stopping, Prudence made her way back to the refreshments table, where Titus was waiting.

"Would you care to take a breath of fresh air?" he inquired solicitously, and she wondered if he had noticed the blunder she had made by not stepping free of Rathbone's embrace the moment the last note had been played.

"Yes, thank you."

The doors to the terrace were open, and they stepped outside. Several couples were there, some talking in whispers, others simply standing near the stone balustrade and enjoying the coolness of the evening.

Titus said nothing as Prudence composed herself.

What kind of man was Rathbone to have such an effect on her? More importantly, what kind of woman was she to allow it?

"Prudence?"

It was Lionel, looking concerned. He'd seen her dancing with Rathbone, and there was no mistaking the look in his eyes. He *had* noticed her gaffe.

Prudence smiled despite the turmoil flowing through her. "The ballroom grew overly warm. Mr. Counce suggested we take advantage of the evening air."

"Sir," Titus said, obviously discomforted by the expression on Lionel Delmont's face.

"Would you like to go home?" Lionel asked, looking directly at Prudence.

"Don't fuss," she said playfully. She took Lionel's arm and turned him toward the ballroom. "If Mr. Counce would be so kind as to excuse me, we shall dance."

Lionel took her inside and onto the dance floor. Prudence forced herself to act as if nothing had happened, keeping her eyes on her partner instead of scanning the room for the viscount.

It was a welcome relief when the musicians took a short break around midnight and she was able to flee Lionel's protective presence. Unnoticed by anyone, she escaped into the garden.

Turning her head, Prudence glanced back at the house where the silhouettes of whirling dancers passed the tall French windows. The sound of laughter and gaiety drifted to her on the night air, evidence that the guests were enjoying themselves.

As for her, she'd much prefer to be home at North Hill, surrounded by endless green woods and whispering streams, the stuffy social whirl of London a hundred miles away.

Finding a small gazebo, Prudence swept up the steps and into the shadowed solitude. She gasped as a tall form materialized in front of her. The faint moonlight glowing from a star-studded sky fell full on his face, revealing his aristocratic features. It was impossible not to recognize the mocking glitter of his steel-blue eyes.

"You!"

"Yes, me," Rathbone chuckled. He tossed the cheroot he'd been smoking over the wooden railing and into a small fish pond. The red-gold arc of light quickly disappeared with a short sizzle. "Running away from Chinese history, are we?"

"I will have you know that Titus is a very nice man."

"I'm sure he is." The lips that had kissed her so devastatingly not four days ago curled into a cryptic smile. "If you know what's good for you, Miss Tamhill, you'll return to the festivities."

When she didn't move, he took a step toward her.

"You're a stubborn little thing, aren't you?" he remarked, with a devilish grin that might have disarmed her completely if she hadn't been prepared for it. "And here I thought you as straitlaced as they come."

"Pity I can't say the same for you, my lord. But then, everyone knows your reputation."

"Oh, yes, my reputation. I'm to be feared by virtuous young ladies. But you're not afraid of me, are you?"

Prudence was old enough to recognize sexual interest in a man's eyes, yet what she saw in Rathbone's was even more intriguing. The palpable ferocity of his gaze made her uncomfortably aware of just how much she wanted to be kissed again.

She turned away from him to look into the darkness, all too conscious that he'd seen the need in her eyes. How could he have missed it? It was tangible, making her heart pound and her skin tingle, flowing though her more strongly than the champagne she'd sipped before leaving the ballroom.

When he put his hands on her shoulders, she felt a tremor pass through her. There was a tension between them, a current that wasn't anger anymore, but something stronger, more primal, and less easily ignored than either wanted to admit.

"I told you to go inside," he whispered into her ear, a scant second before he encircled her waist with a strong arm, pulling her back against his body. He held her that way for what seemed liked an eternity. She was immobile against him, trapped and unsure of his intentions.

"Please," she finally whispered.

"Please, what? Hold you closer, or let you go?"

She reached to push his arm away. Catching her hand, he brought it to his mouth, kissing the back of it before gliding the tip of his tongue along the grooves formed by her clenched fingers.

"You're not at all what I assumed you to be," he said, the husky sound of his voice sending shivers through her. "Soft and warm. Spirited and spicy. I like that in a woman."

Her brown eyes went wide as he twirled her around to face him. His gaze questioned. Hers answered.

"I've been called a dangerous man," he said, issuing what she knew would be the last warning.

"Have you?"

She reached up to touch his lips, shocking them both.

The world retreated, the pageantry of the ballroom forgotten, the laughter and gaiety unheard, the brilliance of chandeliers and glittering jewelry unseen. All were miles away. Life was confined to this very spot, to this very moment.

"If you keep looking at me like that I'm going to kiss you again."

"Promise?" she whispered, amazed that she'd spoken so boldly, but unable to regret it. She was being swept along by a wildness beyond any she'd ever felt, caught up in feelings that were older than time. An agony of need opened inside her, an emptiness that needed to be filled.

Rathbone did as she asked, claiming her mouth without hesitation.

Prudence shivered at the texture of his tongue moving past her lips, at the way he used it to taste her. It was too carnal, too wicked. His touch called to forbidden impulses, personifying all the fears used to keep a young lady firmly rooted within the boundaries of propriety.

Nothing had prepared her for the ferocity of physical passion. It was hot, like a flash of uncontrollable fire, and like a fire, it melted her opposition into nothingness.

Never had she dreamt that her body knew more than her mind. Never had she imagined that being out of control could be so right, so inordinately necessary.

"My God," Rathbone hissed, lifting his mouth away from hers only to place it over the pulse beating wildly in her throat. He was careful not to leave a mark, but he wanted to; oh, how he wanted to. The tension spreading through his body was centered hard and heavy in his groin. It was primitive and powerful, the need to mate as elemental as the night.

In truth, he was as shaken as Prudence was by the intensity of the passion that sparked unexpectedly between them. He had meant only to scare her away, to make her angry enough to return to the party so he could brood in peace.

Now he found himself an unwitting victim of his own

game, the tables turned so explosively that he could think of nothing but finishing what he'd begun days before.

He kissed her with a passion that had been left cruelly unsatisfied the last time. The beating of his own heart rose in his throat as he touched her, his hands roving possessively over her now-willing body, seeking to lay bare the skin he so desperately needed to touch and taste.

An expert, even when his mind was dazed, he had no trouble freeing her breasts from the confines of the gown. Her nipples were already hard, awaiting his mouth.

Hungrily, he sought them, licking each crown before taking it into his mouth and sucking so hard he caused her to moan.

Prudence didn't understand what was happening. The heat of his mouth caressed a consciousness beyond her body. Her own hunger swelled in an urgency that stole her breath as she felt his hands on her back and hips. Through the welter of agitated feelings she realized a strange hardness was pressing into her belly, a hardness she hadn't felt before.

After tormenting both breasts equally, Rathbone lifted his head. They stood looking at each other, their bodies pressed in an intimate embrace, her breasts bared and flushed, an age-old wildness pounding in their blood. He knew well enough what would happen next.

Prudence didn't, but she wanted to know as she had never wanted to know anything in the world. She'd seen horses mate despite the grooms' attempts to keep her ignorant. She'd seen the wild, fierce vigor of the stallion as he mounted the mare. Yet never, never before tonight, had she been able to imagine the same process between a man and a woman. But now, she was filled with a strange new awareness—male and female, the ultimate match, the ultimate puzzle. Propelled by those feelings, she reached up and touched Rathbone's mouth.

"My God, woman, you're playing with fire!"

He grasped both her shoulders this time and held her away from him, his eyes searching hers as if she somehow held his salvation. He stared at her naked breasts in the moonlight. Finally, deliberately, he spoke again, the urgency of his voice almost frightening. "I need your honesty. Do you want more of my touch?"

"Yes."

He held her gaze for a moment before allowing his to drift lower, down to where pale flesh lay exposed to moonlight, to the vulnerable curves and hard little nipples that told him she was being honest. She wanted him.

And he wanted her.

Though he was called a seducer, he'd never actually seduced a woman. He'd never had to. His looks and title and wealth did it for him. Even now, there was no seduction, no whispered promises that would fall flat come sunrise, no vows of undying devotion, nothing but the heat of passion and the echoing madness that came with it.

Prudence felt the gentle marauding of his hands, the heat of his open palms against her stocking-clad calves, then higher, smoothing first over the silk of her pantaloons, then under the gauzy cloth to her bare skin. Her body began to warm again, growing tight as her abdomen contracted in an involuntary spasm.

"Easy," he whispered, his voice heavy with emotion. "I'm not going to hurt you. Never that."

His hand moved higher, circling her thighs, his touch as light as air. Then he was there, at the center of her, his open palm pressed intimately over her mound, his fingers teasing the soft private curls.

The shocking touch of his hand exploring her inside and out was the most intimate contact Prudence had ever had with another person. The feeling was profound, both emotionally and physically.

He took his time with her, stroking her with one finger, then two, teasing the swollen nub of her womanhood until she writhed and pressed her hips forward, demanding more.

Holding his own desire under control, Rathbone slowly transported her from one world to the next, from complete innocence to the edge of womanhood.

For Prudence, there was no reprieve from the pleasure, no escape. Each movement of his hand struck fire within her; each kiss kindled an ongoing communion between male and female. When the pleasure peaked, it was unexpected and unbelievable.

He covered her mouth, absorbing her soft cry of alarm as her body tensed, then relaxed, only to tense again. She was wet and wanting. Who could have imagined she'd feel like this?

Rathbone had imagined it, more than once since their first kiss. All it would take was a toss of her skirts, the undoing of a few trouser buttons, and he could be inside her where it was wet and warm and tight, sheathed in hot pleasure. He'd dreamed of it and wanted it, and now it was happening. Except he couldn't allow it to happen.

Damn! When had his cock developed a conscience?

Prudence was a virgin. Despite the pleasure he'd given her, the proof was at his fingertips. Soft and yielding, but still intact. Collecting himself with a sheer force of will, he withdrew his hand, then kissed her ever so gently.

"Go back inside, Miss Tamhill. *Now*. Before I forfeit the right to be called a gentleman."

His voice was heavy with emotion, his touch as gentle as moonlight. Then there was no more touching, no more anything.

Prudence opened her eyes to find herself alone. Silence reigned through the first moment of disbelief. Then, realizing where she was, what she'd done, she quickly righted her clothing.

Looking out into the shadows, she sensed Rathbone was there, waiting until she reestablished herself enough to return to the ballroom. Her face red with shame, Prudence closed her eyes and tried to concentrate on something besides her body. Several deep breaths later, she was still aching, still wanting, but the fever was cooling.

She could think again.

Regrettably, all she could think about was what would have happened had anyone seen her in Rathbone's arms. Had they been found in a compromising embrace, the gossip would have gone home with Lady Winthrop's guests to be spread anew come morning. The end result was too terrible to think about. While men gained a certain prestige by flirting with scandal, a woman's reputation could only be repaired by marriage.

Unsure whether the empty sensation she now felt was one of relief or regret, Prudence allowed herself one last glance into the darkness before leaving the gazebo.

It was past time to put an end to the evening.

CHAPTER 4

The hands of Leicester Square's tower clock were pressing midnight when Rathbone placed his wager on the table. Behind him, a footman was handily posted by the door to fetch anything he or the other guests might request. The servant was employed by Willard Ramsbury, a baronet who frequently indulged his extravagant tastes by opening his London residence for a night of cards and sexual entertainment.

It had been over a week since Rathbone's encounter with Prudence in the gazebo, eight days of discreetly keeping his distance. For the lady's sake, Rathbone told himself, though he didn't believe it.

He took a sip of the Irish whiskey he preferred when playing cards. The last few days had taught him that the strong drink would do little harm. He was uncommonly lucky, even when he was drunk. Under his unpredictable but polished manner he possessed an infallible business sense and a profound liking for playing a game for its own sake. Then again, he'd always had the extraordinary capability to devote himself to pleasure so totally that nothing else was permitted to interfere.

Unfortunately that devotion was beginning to waver. Like it or not, he was acutely aware that Miss Prudence Tamhill had affected him in a most peculiar way. If he allowed himself, he could still feel the silky softness of her skin, still smell the light fragrance of lavender soap, still taste the spicy sweetness of her mouth. When would the effects of their last meeting begin to fade?

Rathbone's thoughts were momentary disrupted as several well-paid whores came winsomely tripping into the room. They were chattering gaily, as bright and beautiful as actresses upon a stage in their low-cut gowns, calling out hellos, pursing lips to exchange a kiss here, smiling a vivacious greeting there, until each was claimed by a gentleman.

To say that the women were the center of attraction was to say no more than was obviously true, for although they might often be observed entertaining at one of Ramsbury's little parties, tonight was the first time they had been seen as an ensemble in several months.

Melody, a few steps in the lead and on the gallant arm of a young lord, was the most poised of the sisters. Behind her, Matilda conversed animatedly with Lord Butterwick, a man three times her age, but one known to bestow lavish rewards upon any woman willing to bed him. The last of the sisters, Minerva by name, was wearing a crimson gown and holding tightly to another gentleman's arm to keep him from straying. Nevertheless, the major share of attention was inexorably directed to the hefty stack of coins in the center of the table.

"Feeling lucky tonight, are we?" Ramsbury asked as Rathbone placed his bet.

"Not necessarily." He tossed another coin onto the

stack. "Are you going to play cards or entertain the lady?"

"Get on with you," Ramsbury said, gently nudging a raven-haired beauty off his knee. "I need to concentrate."

The girl tossed her pink skirts, exposing silk stockings fastened with gold garters, before prancing off across the room to fall into the lap of a middle-aged man who eagerly accepted her attention. His bony hand was thrust down the front of the girl's bodice. She responded with a giggle.

Rathbone ignored what was going on around him. He played out the hand, winning it as he had been doing most of the evening.

"Egads, I'm to be made a beggar in my own home!"

"Deal the cards."

"Not bloody likely," Ramsbury retorted. He looked around the room. Though he hadn't been drinking nearly as much as Rathbone, he was twice as drunk. "It's time to let the ladies entertain us. What say? It's been a long time since you and I enjoyed all of them."

"I'll pass on that pleasure."

"What! You, saying no to a good fuck? Is Lady Ainsworth that good? I've heard she has a fondness for keeping a man on his back."

Rathbone didn't comment. He reached for his money instead.

Ramsbury's hand came down over his, scattering the stack of coins. "Can't have you running out when the night is still young. What kind of a host would I be if I let one of my best friends leave unsatisfied?"

"I am satisfied. I'm richer by five hundred quid."

Ramsbury smiled a cunning smile. "If you won't have a go at the ladies, then perhaps another game might interest you?"

"I thought you were done with cards for the evening," Rathbone said. His head was beginning to ache. Hopefully a walk in the night air would clear the dull pain.

"Not cards." Ramsbury lifted his hand away from the center of the table to reach for a glass of port. "A wager of a different kind. Something more worthy of a gentleman of your reputation."

"That reputation being?" Rathbone asked, as Minerva did her best to distract him by kissing the back of his neck.

He avoided a grimace as her hands came around his shoulders to move slowly down his chest, over the pristine silk of his ruffled shirt, to the polished buttons of his waistcoat. He stopped her before she could go any farther.

"What's wrong, luv?" she whispered into his ear.

Rathbone chose to ignore her rather than answer, and after several silent seconds she moved on, realizing she wasn't wanted now, nor would she be later.

"Isn't Minerva enough of a challenge?" Ramsbury asked. The mischievous glint in his eyes turned more devilish as his mind went to work. "Yes, that's exactly what you need. A challenge. Women come too easily to heel around you, my friend. I must think of a lady who wouldn't, or rather couldn't, allow herself to be spellbound by your notorious charm. A challenge in itself."

He got up and began pacing the room, his finger posed beneath his chin as though he were contemplating the very essence of life.

The room quieted, its occupants suddenly aware that Ramsbury was about to offer one of his notorious wagers, the sort that usually ended up spelling trouble for the loser.

"It's difficult for a name to come to mind." The baronet held out his arms and two of the sisters flocked to his side. "Rathbone's charms are undeniable. Wouldn't you agree, my lovelies?"

Both sisters nodded their heads.

Rathbone showed no outward sign of caring one way or the other. He knew Ramsbury, had known him since Eton, where they'd lost their virginity to the same woman only a week apart. Rathbone had been the first, and had continued in that fashion, always a step ahead, his rank higher, his fortune larger, his future just a tad brighter. It had brewed a jealousy he sensed was finally about to erupt.

"The wager will be a lady, then," Ramsbury continued, obviously enjoying the suspense. "A lady of good standing and perfect breeding, a lady fair and virtuous."

One of the sisters laughed at the last, since any woman who lost her virginity to Rathbone was sure to gain more than she gave, and what was the wager in that?

"Ah, my sweet, but it's not the lady's virtue that will be the challenge. Rathbone could seduce the Queen herself if he put his mind to it. Nay, it's not to be a wager of a sexual nature, though more's the pity, for I'd love nothing better than to hear about the deflowering of one of London's best."

"Then what?" Lord Butterwick called out. He staggered across the room to lift a glass of port from the footman's tray before turning to watch the evening's little drama.

"A wager of friendship and trust, I think," Ramsbury said. "What say you, Rathbone—can you forsake your cock long enough to charm a lady into thinking herself a chaste confidante? Someone with whom she can share her most secret thoughts?"

It was Rathbone's turn to laugh. "What would you

have me do? Tote chocolate bonbons and a bouquet of flowers to woo the fair maiden?"

The room erupted into laughter.

"As you will," the baronet declared. Disengaging himself from the sisters, he returned to the gaming table. "I will give you ten days. Ten days in which to gain a favor from the lady and return it to this very room."

"What favor?" one of the women asked laughingly. "A lock of hair?"

"If it's hair, you can be sure it won't be coming from her head," someone else snickered.

"Something more substantial," Ramsbury declared. "A ring. They say she wears it every day. Woo her properly and she will give it to you as a token of her friendship. Bring it to me in the allotted time and receive five thousand pounds. Return without it and lose twice that sum."

"Name the lady." The demand came from a strutting, vexatious man by the name of Emmet Martindale.

"What lady?" The cry circled the room, the guests all in a fever to know which of London's beauties was about to be subjected to Rathbone's unfailing charm.

"Remember, I'm a gentleman," Ramsbury said. "Thus, the lady's name will remain between Rathbone and myself."

He motioned and a footman came forward with a small tray that held pen and paper, the kind used to leave a marker when a man's luck had run out. The baronet wrote down a name, then folded the paper before passing it across the table.

Rathbone opened it and fought down the urge to double up his fist and break Ramsbury's nose.

"So, Rathbone, do you accept the wager?"

The room turned silent.

"I accept," Rathbone said, his pride allowing him no other choice. His smile was enigmatic as he placed the square of paper in the brass ashtray on the table and set his cheroot to it. He didn't look up until there was nothing but a mound of ashes to testify to the lady's name.

It wasn't until he was collecting his hat and gloves from the butler that Rathbone was allotted a few minutes of privacy with Ramsbury. The baronet ambled into the foyer, pausing just long enough to send the black-haired Lilly upstairs with a firm swat to her bottom.

"Are you sure you won't stay? Lilly's talented enough to satisfy both of us."

Rathbone's tone was censorious. "Why Miss Tamhill?"

"It was your doing," Ramsbury said, laughing. "Saw you dancing with her the other night. Made a right fine couple, you did. Got the idea then."

"I figured as much. Remind me to repay the favor."

"I fully expect you will. Now, if you'll excuse me, Lilly isn't known for her patience."

"One more thing," Rathbone said, bringing the baronet to a halt with the tip of his walking stick. "If I'm to procure a ring, shouldn't I know what sort of ring it is? And how do you know she wears it every day?"

"It's a ruby. As for knowing her habits, I don't. But I do have eyes, and I've never seen her without it."

With a final invitation, telling Rathbone he could watch if he wasn't in the mood to participate, Ramsbury made his way upstairs.

Rathbone stepped out into the night air. He glanced around the lavish neighborhood, knowing that a few scant miles away, the borough of St. Giles was alive with gin-numbed whores and myriad criminals. The contrasts of the city never failed to amaze him. On a clear day the towers of St. Paul's and Westminster Cathedrals could be seen lording over the grimy walls and soot-blackened rooftops of the East End, reinforcing the premise that London had both saints and sinners.

Gesturing for Thaddeus to follow with the carriage, he turned up his coat collar and began to walk. His mood was pensive, his mind slowly clearing of the whiskey he'd consumed, but not of the things he'd been drinking to forget.

Prudence Tamhill, blast her lovely little hide.

And now he couldn't forget, wouldn't be able to put that night behind him, because Ramsbury's wager was forcing him to confront her again.

Ten days wasn't an abundant amount of time, but Rathbone wasn't worried about finding a way to meet Prudence again. A mirrored twist of fate had made the arrangements for him. The Duke of Morland would be celebrating his birthday in eight days. There was to be a party at his estate north of London. Worley was sure to attend with Prudence under his wing.

Eight days to the party, a night or two to get his hands on the ring, and another day to return to London.

He could do it.

Since gaining, or rather, regaining Prudence's trust was doubtful, he'd *borrow* the ring, making sure it was returned as discreetly as he planned for it to disappear.

That decided, a satisfying picture of Willard Ramsbury forfeiting five thousand pounds soothed Rathbone's conscience as he signaled for Thaddeus to halt the carriage. He climbed inside with an order to be taken directly home, Lady Ainsworth forgotten.

CHAPTER 5

It was a crystalline morning, everything sharp and distinct. A morning cut from soothing gold and cool blue. Prudence sat next to Lionel in the ducal coach, the fugitive fragments of a daydream drifting through her mind: the soft melody of a waltz, a starlit sky, the passion of a kiss.

Then, in the confusing way of dreams, the music ended, the sky darkened to nothingness, and the heat of the kiss turned cold. From dream to reality: only a moment in time, yet how long a passage, Prudence thought.

A sound disturbed her reverie, and she looked out the window. Ahead of them, between a tavern's slanted roof and the towering spire of a church steeple, lay the village of Aylesbury. She could see a cluster of neatly painted cottages and redbrick chimneys. It was market day, and the village was filled with people. Children dashed willy-nilly, laughing and calling out dares to their friends. One youth spanked a wooden baton along a picket fence. Dogs barked, babies cried, and mothers gossiped while their husbands talked business over tall tankards of cold ale.

In all the activity, there was no way for her guardian or Lionel to know that Prudence's heart was pounding wildly, no way for them to imagine that she had been forever changed by a kiss.

Looking back on the night of Lady Winthrop's ball— the waltz with the viscount and the sensual assault he had launched in the gazebo—Prudence found it hard to give credence to what had happened.

Their second encounter had ended every bit as strangely as their first had begun. Since then, she had had plenty of time for thought. Reviewing the facts, she was now convinced that she had no one to blame but herself, and she was determined to profit from the lesson. Hopefully her resolve would hold, for it was soon to be tested. It was a certainty that Rathbone would be among the Duke of Morland's guests.

The line of carriages waiting in front of the ducal estate, each with driver and footman, bore testimony to the importance of the stately people who owned them. There were polished broughams, sleek landaus, victorias, and finally, wagonettes for the retinue of visiting servants—for every woman had brought her personal maid and every man his valet. There was also a fleet of wagons for the mountains of luggage without which no self-respecting guest would travel for even a weekend.

Rathbone frowned as he made his way across the lawn. He had, by adroit scheduling, managed to arrive ahead of his quarry. The view from a second-floor window had allowed him to witness Prudence departing Worley's coach. Unfortunately, he hadn't seen her since.

There! A flash of blue among the snapdragons and

delphiniums. It was Prudence, strolling along the path that ended near the pond. She was walking with another young lady. It was an advantage, Rathbone supposed. A chance meeting chaperoned by a close friend wouldn't arouse any undue suspicions.

Knowing Morland's estate nearly as well as he knew his own, he selected a different route, one that would ultimately take him to the same destination.

"But you must meet him," Prudence insisted. "He's a perfectly charming young man and you have so much in common."

"Will he be joining the party?"

"Yes. I asked the butler. Did you know his name is Darling? Josiah Darling. A strange name for a butler, don't you agree? It's most uncanny to hear His Grace shouting about the halls for him. But I digress. Lord and Lady Wallingcroft are expected to arrive before sunset, and a room has been set aside for Titus."

Her friend paused, causing Prudence to stop as well.

Hattie was the youngest offspring of the Marquis of Corry, a small birdlike creature with a homely but enthusiastic face, her cheeks perpetually blotched by either heat or cold. Though her voice lacked elegance, it possessed its own Yorkshire flair. Prudence thought her endearing, with a grand sense of humor once she abandoned her shyness.

It was assumed that since Hattie lacked the passable prettiness of her two older sisters, she would reside on the shelf, growing old while she ran her father's household.

"I've had my Season," Hattie reminded her. "And it was disastrous."

"Don't belittle yourself. I will not allow it. You are the

kindest person I know, and there is no reason to think that Mr. Counce will not agree with me."

"But what if he doesn't?"

"He will," Prudence assured her. "Now, come along. There are so many guests, they're sprouting out of the shrubbery. I need some peace and quiet before everyone descends on the dining hall."

A few steps farther along and Prudence found herself wondering if Rathbone hadn't been hiding in the bushes listening to her every word. He stepped out onto the graveled path, appearing like a genie summoned from some magical bottle.

"Good afternoon, ladies," he said, sounding much too pleased to have stumbled upon them for Prudence to think it coincidental.

The current of excitement she had felt since arriving at the Duke of Morland's estate reached a nearly unbearable pitch when she looked into Rathbone's eyes. They virtually sparkled with anticipation. Though she struggled to maintain a subdued demeanor, she was bathed in a rich awareness that bewildering events such as these were quickly taking hold of her life.

"My lord," she said, praying she didn't sound as nervous as she felt. "May I introduce my friend, Lady Henrietta Corry?"

Rathbone smiled his best smile. "Lady Corry and I have met before. A soirée, was it not?"

"Yes," Hattie stammered, clearly amazed that a man of Rathbone's reputation would remember her. When she moved to step back, Prudence held tightly to her hand.

"We were just discussing how lovely the gardens are for so early in the spring," Prudence said, hoping to bore him into leaving. "I don't believe I've ever seen alstroemeria blooming this time of the year."

"We had a mild winter. If you enjoy flowers, you'll find the maze near the pond to your liking. There's a striking display of stargazer lilies and purple iris."

Men like Rathbone weren't supposed to know a lily from a rhododendron.

"You like flowers?" Hattie asked.

"Yes. Does that surprise you?"

It certainly surprised Prudence.

"It is unusual," Hattie remarked, her gaze darting about as though she were looking for a rabbit hole in which to hide.

If she found one, Prudence swore to follow.

"I'm an unusual man," Rathbone replied, turning around and offering an arm to each of them.

It would be a rudeness to cut him in front of Hattie, who knew nothing of why Prudence wished to avoid the viscount at all cost. Gracefully bullied into it, she accepted his arm, and they began to walk.

Hattie was normally too timid to speak so augustly to a gentleman, but Rathbone had no trouble drawing her out of her shell. "What think you of that peony, Lady Corry?"

Prudence glanced toward the flower. With its many side buds opened at once, it created a whole bouquet on a single stem.

"The color is lovely," Hattie said. "Prudence has a dress nearly the same shade of pink."

"It is lovely," Prudence agreed, not wanting to seem too standoffish. If Hattie suspected Rathbone was up to something, she'd be certain to mention it to her brother, Barnabus, who would make haste to tell Lionel, who, if he suspected Rathbone had been anything but a perfect gentleman, would turn into a Trojan, thirsting for blood.

As Prudence struggled to still her inner turbulence, the threesome came upon the summerhouse. Its remote site made it a perfect place for a romantic assignation, or so Lord and Lady Granby must have thought, because they were kissing each other most passionately.

Rathbone cleared his throat in a theatrical tone. Lord Granby reluctantly released his wife. Greetings were exchanged, and, to Prudence's dismay, Hattie excused herself, hurrying back toward the main house.

"Oh, dear, I'm afraid we've embarrassed her," Lady Granby said. She was extremely beautiful, with auburn hair and dazzling hazel eyes, while her husband was so much like Rathbone that the two men could pass for brothers.

"It was only a kiss," Granby said, sounding put out that he hadn't been able to continue as he'd started.

"It is the middle of the day," Rathbone chided good-naturedly.

Finding herself abandoned, and desperately needing to change the subject from kissing to something less volatile, Prudence inquired into the health of Lady Granby's children.

"They're an exhausting delight. This is the first time I've been away from them, and I miss them terribly."

"It's only for a few days. Little hellions, both of them," her husband added, speaking to Rathbone this time. "I'm paying the piper, just as Morland warned me I would."

"*My* children are adorable," his wife remarked, laughing indulgently as she disengaged his arm from around her waist and took his hand.

The mention of children brought a fresh flood of thoughts for Prudence to ponder. Children were a gift, the world's most remarkable wonder. But she had difficulty fitting such thoughts alongside her desire to venture forth independently—for how could a woman successfully become her own mistress with a nursery full of babes and a household to run? And, of course, there was the matter of a husband. One could not think of children without giving thought to the man who would provide them.

"Shall we?" Rathbone said, choosing that very moment to offer her his arm again. His hair shone silverblond in the sunlight, and his heavily hooded eyes lent a curious, prophetic air to his words.

Prudence was hard-pressed to explain the strange feeling that surged through her as she accepted his arm. Any thoughts that filled her mind in that moment fled, her need to avoid Rathbone becoming far less important than the imminent need to be with him again.

Now two couples, they began to stroll back to the house, this time taking a path that was bordered by waist-high bayberry bushes and small patches of gerbera daisies. Lord and Lady Granby took the lead, their heads close as they exchanged intimate whispers.

Rathbone couldn't have been more pleased. The ruby ring twinkled like a drop of red sunshine on Prudence's delicately sculptured hand. So, she did wear it often.

Why hadn't he noticed it before?

Because he'd been too busy noticing other things: her sable-soft hair, the pink hue of her mouth, the way her eyes sparkled when she was angry, the creamy smoothness of her breasts bathed in moonlight. Not that he'd seen enough of her that night. Not nearly enough to satisfy his curiosity, and certainly not enough to satisfy his desire.

"I hope you are as glad to see me, Prudence, as I am to have stumbled upon you," he said, keeping his voice pitched low. The remark was intended to be amiable, but they both knew it had a darker side.

Realizing he was wooing the lady on one hand while, on the other, he was planning to pilfer her ring gave whatever system of philosophy Rathbone possessed a start. He glanced toward the heavens, half-expecting a terrible blow of retribution—a fitting rebuke for his current lack of decency.

"That remains to be seen, my lord," Prudence replied with anticipated honesty. "It is an embarrassment."

He purposely slowed his pace, allowing a discreet gap to form between them and the couple walking ahead. "What happened is nothing that should shame you, Miss Tamhill. The transgression was mine alone."

"I allowed the kiss," she said. "That makes the transgression a joint one. And yes, I am embarrassed."

Despite her serious tone, Prudence wanted to laugh at the two of them speaking so formally about something so intimate. Their words said nothing, but at the same time, they uttered a wild torrent of meaning. *I have not even addressed him by his given name,* she thought; *I will not.* And because she would not, it thundered through her mind.

He moved, blocking her path for a moment. There was a naked tenderness in his eyes as he addressed her. "You are embarrassed only because you have been told that you must be."

The memory of the last time they had met came instantly to Prudence's mind. Vivid and touching, like the first rays of morning sunshine, it calmed Prudence's mind for a moment. A faint smile came to her lips, but she had no reply to his words.

Since the remark was rhetorical, Rathbone expected no reply. He rested his hand lightly over hers. The ring pressed into his palm, reminding him that he could avoid stealing it by gaining the lady's trust.

"Will you waltz with me tonight?"

The look on her face indicated that she wanted to say no. She intended to say no, but when the word came out, it was a soft-spoken "yes."

Rathbone smiled. There was no further attempt at badinage on his part. Rather, he continued walking with Prudence at his side. From time to time he glanced down at her to see an expression that was almost a smile.

As they neared the house, he couldn't help but wonder where their next waltz would lead them.

Fiona came bustling into the room at twenty minutes past six. A ball gown, freshly pressed, was draped over her arm. Shoes and stockings dangled from her fingertips. "I'll draw your bath," she announced, taking charge as any good lady's maid would. "There's plenty of time to wash and dry your hair."

Yawning from a late-afternoon nap, Prudence allowed herself to be fussed over. After all, she was attending a ducal birthday party, and she should look her best. The *why* of it didn't seem nearly as important as it had earlier in the day.

Walking to the window, she looked out over the lawn. The nimble air carried the scent of a fair English day. The sunlight was fading, turning the sky that peculiar shade of gray that identified twilight. She often enjoyed this part of the day best, the stillness lying soft about the landscape, the lull between the day's business and the night's approaching activities.

"Will it be the pearls or the opals or the sapphires?" Fiona asked as she unlocked the small trunk where Prudence's jewelry case was packed.

"The diamonds, if you please."

"Diamonds! Well, I'll be knowing what dandy has you thinking that way," Fiona said, a faint smile turning up the corners of her mouth. "The last time you wore diamonds, it was Buckingham Palace and the Queen you were off to visit."

"My gown is pink. Pearls will tone it down, not dress it up. The opals will accomplish the same, and the sapphires aren't the right color to pay the fabric a compliment," Prudence said, thinking the explanation quite logical even though the real reason had little to do with her gown and everything to do with wanting to be seen in a more mature light.

Fiona set the jewel case on the vanity table, then leaned down, using the small key she wore on a chain around her neck to open it. A black velvet case was removed. "The tiara, too?"

"No. We'll save that for Buckingham Palace."

With the water for her bath bubbling into a claw-footed tub in the other room, Prudence moved away from the window.

Viscount Rathbone . . . she'd never allowed a man to occupy her thoughts so thoroughly, with the exception of her real father, of course. If only she could explain what she was feeling, and why she was feeling it.

There was no logic to the buoyancy that had lifted her above the normal routine of her life since that night by the garden gate. How much of it was owing to the romantic notions of being young, to the mood set by moonlight and shadows?

It was mostly curiosity, she supposed. Passion was an adventure beyond the norm. A dangerous adventure, if one wasn't careful.

"Oh, Miss, I've learned something," Fiona said, sounding as though she was surprised that she hadn't boasted of it the minute she walked into the room. "One of the maids mentioned that her mother worked for Sir Archibald."

Prudence's attention immediately diverted to the quest she'd begun the day she'd found her mother's diary. "What was her name?"

"Maude Holman. Her daughter's name is Audrey. She's been here with the duke all of her service."

"How do you know her mother worked at Tamhill?"

"Audrey spoke up about it. Said she remembered seeing you when you was a little girl. Remarked on what a lovely young lady you'd become. All prim and pretty."

"She lived on the estate?"

"A year or two. It seems the master wasn't impressed with her mother's skills in the kitchen. She weren't the cook, but a scullery maid. He let her go with references, else she wouldn't have been able to come work for the duke. Audrey said she was eight or nine when her mother left Tamhill."

"How old was I?" Prudence wondered out loud.

"Not more than a baby toddling about, from what she said to me. Still with a nurse."

"Do you think she knows anything? Could she be questioned without arousing suspicion?"

"We've a day or two to find out," Fiona answered. "I'll put a few words to her—nothing direct, mind you, but enough to set her talking. She's a likeable sort with a tongue for chit-chat. If there's anything to be said, I'll hear it."

"What of her mother? Is Mrs. Holman still alive?"

"No."

The answer put a damper on what Prudence had hoped was a fresh trail of clues. It was unlikely that Audrey knew anything, having been so young and not a servant herself at the time. Still, she might be able to re-member some tidbit of gossip her mother had brought home.

"There should be a servant ledger," she said, won-dering why she hadn't thought of it sooner. "I could hire a Bow Street Runner to find the servants who were employed when my mother was alive. Surely, someone saw something. Heard something."

"The ledger would be at Tamhill Hall," Fiona said. "It's yours, right along with the house and the land."

"I could write Mr. Craddock, the steward. I'll ask that he send it to me, but under what guise?"

Fiona gave it a moment's thought. "There was Miss Hunnicutt, your governess. She'd be in the ledger right along with everyone else."

Prudence dashed across the room to give Fiona a hug.

"You are brilliant. I will write Mr. Craddock the mo-ment we return to North Hill, saying I have recently had thoughts of Miss Hunnicutt and wish to inquire into her welfare, along with some of the other servants I remember. He will send me the ledger, and we'll begin the search."

"It won't be easy. Having a household shut down puts the four winds to those working inside it. They could be anywhere. And some are surely dead. Old Piper was near ancient when Sir Archibald died."

Prudence refused to have her hopes dashed a sec-ond time. "I'm certain an experienced investigator could find most of them. The solicitor would have paid their final wages and provided references. There's cer-tain to be a record."

"Aye, from what you've told me, your father was a tidy man when it came to business."

"He was meticulous," Prudence said. She pulled her chemise over her head and tossed it to Fiona. "I remember one of the cooks grumbling that he counted everything, even the potatoes that went into the soup pot."

"Well now, I can see you've something to keep you busy." Fiona followed Prudence into the dressing room, where the tub sat steaming. "No more brooding, then."

"I haven't been brooding."

Prudence stepped over the rim of the tub and sank into the scented water with a sigh.

"Brooding, daydreaming, staring into your teacup as if it held a fortune-telling gypsy instead of tea—whatever it is you've been doing, I'll be glad to see the end of it."

"I'll be of legal age soon," Prudence said, defending her recent moodiness. "I'm to inherit what Lionel refers to as a 'bloody fortune.' The responsibility is heavy at times."

"I'm not saying otherwise. It's just that you've been different. Sort of melancholy-like, gazing out the window at nothing you haven't seen a hundred times before."

Prudence lathered the sponge Fiona gave her. She had been melancholy of late, and for good reason. Passion was upsetting.

Just thinking of Rathbone set shivers moving up and down her spine, like the chills that so often preceded a fever.

When she recalled that night in the gazebo—relived a thousand times already—it was with a flush of heat. Rathbone had said she had nothing to be ashamed of, and while she admitted embarrassment, she couldn't in all honesty admit regret. It had been so very wonderful, that feeling.

Seeing him today had set her to dreaming again, dreaming of strong arms that could carry her aloft, out through the open window, across the still grass and over the treetops, above the meadows, up and away to—to where? Some fairy-tale world that didn't exist?

Prudence couldn't say, for in her dreams, she never left the viscount's arms.

CHAPTER 6

Rathbone normally thought of birthday parties in the same way he thought of other social functions: as obligations to be attended, if not otherwise avoidable. But tonight was different. In spite of the lectures he'd received from the Duke of Morland over the past years, he was sincerely fond of the old gent.

Whatever disagreements they had had were a variation of the same ones he would have had with his father, were the former viscount alive. The authority of both men had become one and indivisible to Rathbone's way of thinking, since Morland had stepped into his life shortly after he'd graduated from the university.

"It's going to be a grand party," Rathbone said, strolling into the second floor library, where his friends had gathered to share a few minutes of conversation before their wives took up their dancing slippers and forced them downstairs. "Morland's in fine form. He's been bellowing for Darling. Poor sod's been running up and down the steps like a madman for the last hour."

"You know he hates having birthdays. Reminds him

that he might not live long enough to see you married off like the rest of us," Granby said, passing a glass of brandy to the viscount.

"Bollocks! The old fool is going to outlive us all. And I won't be getting married just to please him, you can be damn sure of that."

Neither Lord Granby nor the Marquis of Waltham paid any heed to their friend's declaration. It wasn't the first time it had been voiced, nor, did they imagine, would it be the last.

"Then why the interest in Miss Tamhill?" This came from the Earl of Ackerman. Fitch was the most recently captured bachelor, now the father of two: an adopted daughter by the name of Lizzie, and a new son by the name of George Morland Minstead, in honor of the duke.

"What interest?" Rathbone chortled. He sank into a chair, drink in hand.

Sterling chimed in. "A waltz, the first since her coming out two years ago, and a walk in the garden. All within a fortnight." The viscount was the oldest of the "lads" with three robust children of his own, each of them with a godfather in the room. "Rebecca noticed straightaway."

"Your lovely viscountess is jumping to conclusions. One waltz and an unexpected encounter in the garden do not insanity make."

"By the way, did you know your mother is here? Arrived this afternoon with Lady Forbes-Hammond."

"I suppose they shared the same coach." Although Rathbone adored his mother, he couldn't think of a more stifling event than her arrival.

"Birds of a feather," Fitch said. "So what of Miss Tamhill—are you pursuing her?"

"No."

"There is the Tamhill fortune," Granby inserted. "A tidy sum to go with a lovely lady."

Rathbone grinned amiably before recommending that his friend depart for Hades.

The room came to attention as the Duke of Morland entered, looking fearfully proper in evening black. His silver-white hair and piercing eyes gave him the appearance of a wily old wolf, seasoned and tested, and still leader of his pack.

"Good evening, Your Grace," Rathbone said. "May I be the first to wish you a happy and prosperous birthday."

"You may not. All this bloody festivity has my gout acting up. Damn nuisance is what it is. Ought to send the whole lot of you packing."

Fitch poured him a brandy, knowing full well the old man would be just as bad-tempered if no one had accepted an invitation. "Happy birthday, Your Grace."

"How's that son of yours?" Morland asked. "Thought perhaps you might bring him along." He glared around the room. "Haven't seen any of the little ones. Don't suppose this sort of thing is for children."

The men all smiled. Since none of their own fathers were living, Morland had taken it upon himself to play grandfather to their various offspring. He also used the excuse of "looking in on the little ones" as a reason to appear on any given doorstep at any given time.

"Georgie's a walking piece of deviltry," Fitch told him. "He's into everything, including my desk inkwell. Hilary scrubbed until I thought the boy's skin was going to come off."

"Should have anticipated he'd be curious," Morland said, always defensive of anything his *grandchildren* might do. "Children naturally get into things they shouldn't. Georgie's a good lad. He'll grow up to make you proud."

"Yes, Your Grace."

Fitch sat down, and the inquisition began. Each of the "lads" delivered their expected report, detailing the most recent shenanigans of their progeny.

Morland laughed out loud when Sterling confessed that his oldest son, Emanuel, a bare five years of age, had kidnapped his newest sibling, Amelia, thinking to sell her to the gypsies. When asked why, the young boy had simply shrugged his shoulders and said, "She looks like one."

"She is a pretty little thing," Morland agreed. "You'll be paying your dues when the lassies get grown, mark my words."

Not a father in the room doubted him.

The duke turned toward Rathbone. Throughout the recital, the viscount had remained where he was, sitting easily in a chair, legs thrust out in front of him, eyes atwinkle, waiting his turn. Now he said easily, "I've no brood to report upon. Will a recount of my latest seduction do in its stead?"

The duke had his retort prepared, but before he could deliver it, Darling eased open the door. The butler looked recuperated from his hectic day, having changed into a fresh set of black for the evening, his white shirt as perfectly pressed as that of his employer.

"The guests are arriving downstairs, Your Grace."

"Very well," Morland said, using his cane to push himself free of the chair. Casting a look in Rathbone's direction, his gaze warned that the young lord's reprieve was only temporary.

As expected, the main floor of the house was flickering with light, gas lamps illuminating the staircase upon which dozens of fashionable ladies descended on the arms of their escorts. No miserable faces here; only gaiety, as they set out to enjoy the evening. And no Prudence. Not yet, at least.

Taking his disappointment with him, Rathbone went in search of his mother, Lady Augusta. Love her as he did, she was becoming tedious in her pursuit of a daughter-in-law and grandchildren.

Entering the downstairs parlor, the formal gathering place of matrons prior to the dinner bell, Rathbone found his mother seated next to Lady Felicity Forbes-Hammond. The blue plume his mother had pinned in her hair bristled like the tail of a fighting cock when he entered the room.

"There you are," she said, her voice barely heard above the rustling of her satin skirts as she turned toward him and extended her hand.

Rathbone kissed both it and her left cheek. "Good evening, Mother. Had I know your intentions, I would have greeted you earlier."

Augusta, Lady Rathbone, was an attractive woman in her middle fifties who carried herself as though she were much younger. She dressed most fashionably, but also with the utmost sense of who and what she was: a widow with a full-grown son. Her finely featured face showed traces of satisfaction as she smiled up at him now. "Had you known my intentions, Benjamin, we wouldn't see each other for another fortnight."

Rathbone gave her a wicked wink before turning to greet Lady Forbes-Hammond with equal ease.

The matron tucked in her chin, lifted her lorgnette, and gave him a sharp looking-over. "Excellent timing, young man. I was just proposing a question to your mother. Your opinion would be valued."

Just as long as it agrees with yours, Rathbone thought.

Lady Forbes-Hammond was a law unto herself when it came to voicing opinions. Rathbone admired her backbone, her gallant manner, and her high-nosed British loyalty, although she had become, by reason of her close friendship with his mother, a proverbial thorn in his side. Like Morland, she seemed determined to see him married off at the earliest possible moment, no matter how inconvenient he considered her meddling.

The lady continued to speak brusquely. "Being a friend of the family, I've been asked to render a judgment as to young Mr. Mansell's worthiness. Do you think him a fitting match for Lord Aberdyne's daughter, Rosemary?"

A felicitous smile preceded Rathbone's answer. "I've never seen him drunk, or lingering too long at the tables. If he has any peculiar habits, I'm unaware of them."

"Excellent. It does occasionally serve some good to know a scamp such as yourself."

Rathbone laughed. "Never change, dear lady."

"As if I would," she said, lifting her chin so emphatically that her own hair plume threatened to become dislodged.

He spent the next few minutes conversing with his mother while he waited for Prudence to come downstairs. It was still a good half-hour before the guests would be chimed into the dining hall.

The passage of time filled Rathbone with a restless uncertainty, and with what he knew was the dishonesty of the whole weekend. Few would call him conservative, but none, until now, could have labeled him dishonest.

In those wretched moments when his conscience was asserting itself, Rathbone tried to calm it by justifying to himself that he'd be doing no one any real harm. It was a ring, nothing more, and would be returned as promptly as possible.

It wasn't until the guests had been seated at an extraordinarily long table, in an extraordinarily large dining room with plum-colored draperies and a Bohemian glass chandelier, that Rathbone finally saw Prudence.

Prudence sat midway down the table. Lord Welbeck, a mature man of forty and unmarried, sat to her right, while Lord Allphin, just as mature and equally unmarried, was seated to her left.

As expected, and no doubt as planned, she held the attention of the men around her. The bodice of her gown was modest, but fashionably cut to complement the diamonds around her slender throat. Her hair, rich and dark and given to soft curls, was adorned with two matching diamond hairpins.

The meal progressed, course after delicious course: a tureen of turtle soup, lobster mousse, oysters in creamed asparagus sauce, fresh-baked pastries, a soufflé, puddings, and brandied peaches were all served. Rathbone ate and drank, observing whenever he could the young lady who had promised him a waltz.

Prudence was just as aware of his presence. Amid the excited babble of the dinner table, she endured, upholding her image of social distinction, dress, and etiquette, but with her mind focused on the viscount. Sipping her champagne, she darted a nervous glance down the length of the table.

The dancing would begin soon.

Two hours later, she watched with a satisfied smile as Titus Counce led Hattie onto the dance floor.

"I see you've taken up matchmaking."

Prudence caught Rathbone's commanding smile, but only for a moment, before her gaze skimmed across the room. It wouldn't do to act as if they were engaged in more than the most casual of conversation, a mere exchange of words.

"The next waltz," Rathbone said.

"I promised it to Lord Allphin."

"I'm to wait my turn then, is that it?"

His tone gave no indication of the irritation he felt at being put on a list of partners for the evening.

"Please don't be offended, my lord," she said, suddenly finding the common sense that had abandoned her earlier in the day. "But I'm certain you'd agree it wouldn't be wise for us to engage in any activity whatsoever."

Rathbone blanched, but not so that anyone could notice. He forced a practiced smile to his face. "You think me a careless good-for-nothing concerned only with pleasure, a man who spends his time in gambling halls and the indulging company of obliging ladies."

"Am I wrong?"

He looked into her eyes, into the jet beads of her pupils, which were boring through him, and smiled.

"There are all sorts of pleasure, Miss Tamhill. The quietness that comes over a person when he watches the sunrise, the satisfaction one obtains from seeing a rose in bloom. Substance of character is distinct from appearance. A scoundrel has one, a gentleman both. There is quite a lot to know about me."

"I have no doubt," she replied, determined to remain on the path she had chosen. "But you are wrong if you think I do not know you, my lord. While I may lack sufficient knowledge in some areas, I have more than enough in others to form an opinion."

"And that opinion is . . . ?"

"You are poised, articulate, and invitingly interesting. Humorous, when you wish to be, and devastatingly attractive, no matter your mood."

"I see you haven't lost your honesty. If so, then answer me this. Would you like me to kiss you again?"

"No," she said, trying her best to sound as resolved as possible in her desire to see the last of him.

"Liar."

Smiling, he took her hand and led her onto the dance floor. Prudence didn't resist him. Something in his voice when he'd called her a liar coaxed her back into his arms. Now, in more propinquity than before, she found herself completely deserted by both common sense and resentment.

The party seemed to take on the same tenor; the laughter more bubbly, the candles brighter, the music more animated. Outdoors, along the lighted garden paths and exposed terraces, women moved and mingled, engrossed in conversation with their spouses or beaux, while Prudence felt suspended in time.

The part of her that could still think straight wished Rathbone hadn't asked her to dance. But he had, and now, some wordless message was passing between them, an acknowledgment that there would be no pretending that he hadn't kissed her, hadn't touched her so intimately she couldn't imagine another man ever taking the same liberty.

"Where shall we meet?" Rathbone asked, smiling when she drew in a quick breath that caused her breasts to rise and fall most charmingly. He could feel the ring on her hand, concealed by her gloves, but most definitely there. "The garden is ablaze with Chinese lanterns. There are some secluded spots, though I cannot think of one with a gazebo."

Prudence drew back, her irritation apparent in her expression. Saying nothing, her mouth turned down in a tight line and her eyes blazed.

"Miss Tamhill!" he said when she stepped on his toe in a display of irritation. "If you persist, I shall be forced to recommend a dancing instructor."

"Let me go!"

"Not until the music ends. To do so before that would cause a scandal, and that's the last thing either of us wants."

"What do you want?" she demanded.

"One last kiss."

It was a bold request.

She avoided a reply as the music ended.

Rathbone watched Prudence turn her back and walk away, painfully aware that if he couldn't get her alone for a few minutes, he'd be forced into the role of a common thief.

Prudence made a point of walking about the room, stopping to chat here and there with those she knew. If she dashed out as she wished to do, Lionel or Uncle Horace would be sure to follow, assuming her sudden disappearance had something to do with the waltz that had just ended.

When Lord Allphin found her, claiming the dance she had promised him, Prudence managed him with practiced ease, then made good on her escape. She knew the house well, having visited it several times. Deciding upon a small parlor far enough away from the ballroom to prevent detection, she entered the room in hopes of gaining a few minutes in which to compose herself.

One last kiss, she thought as the door shut softly behind her. With her heart pounding unmercifully, her cheeks flushed, and her mouth dry, she managed two words: "I can't."

What had happened to bring her to this scandalous

pass? Here she was, hidden away in a lonely little parlor. The room was suffused with hazy silver moonlight that flattened objects into a confusion of vaguely familiar shapes. As her eyes grew accustomed to the dimness, she made out pieces of furniture, a divan covered in dark fabric, a table, and several chairs.

Knowing she had to put her mind on something else, Prudence began to move about the room, counting her steps in an effort to concentrate. She paused by a small bookcase to withdraw a novel and study its title. There was just enough moonlight to make out the words *The Warden*. Further investigation produced the author's name, a Mr. Anthony Trollope. It was easy to see that the book was newly printed, having nothing about it to indicate that a single page had been turned.

"It's rather dark to be taking up a book."

The voice made her jump back and drop the novel on the floor. Turning in astonishment, she found Rathbone standing just inside the closed door. She hadn't heard him enter. Or had he already been inside the room, seeking his own privacy?

"Sir! Have a care how you startle a person. It cannot be considered good manners."

"I apologize for taking you unaware," he said. "And for keeping you waiting."

"I wasn't waiting."

He gave her a modest smile, then, instead of stepping closer, he began to move about the room, very much as she had, opening a drawer only to close it again, adjusting the draperies to admit more light. Prudence found herself unable to speak. When he paused to regard her again, she returned his gaze.

The frankness of the silent exchange was an intimate thing. There was nothing impertinent about it; it was simply a look of recognition, as if he were saying, "Remember."

Yes, she remembered. All too well. Before coming downstairs, she'd told herself that, knowing the game, she was now strong enough to resist playing it—but was she?

"I should return to the ballroom," she said. "Lionel will be looking for me."

"He's in the billiard room."

With a thrilling shock, Prudence realized Rathbone had made sure they wouldn't be disturbed before following her to the parlor. Her eyes remained fastened on him as he picked up something from a small desk and studied it. It was a cunning miniature hourglass. He turned it upside-down before returning it to the desktop.

"Well, here we are," he said, flashing her a scimitar-like grin. He stepped nearer—too near. His gaze browsed over her. Accented by the moonlight, his eyes were unlike any Prudence had ever seen—opaque, almost colorless. They didn't blink, but captured her own with a steadfast, unwavering gaze, as if they were trying to read not merely her expression, but her very soul. She felt even more disconcerted when he spoke.

"Well, then, how must we begin. Shall I kiss you? Or would you prefer to kiss me?"

He spoke in a light, earnest voice, not at all seductive. It hadn't entered his mind that she might refuse him.

Prudence said nothing, trying to sidestep him instead.

He moved as gracefully as a cat—a hungry cat all too eager to go on the prowl—and blocked her path.

"Do you believe in Fate, Miss Tamhill? The Greeks

did. They believed Fate had three faces: Clotho, who spun the thread of life; Atropos, who wove the cloth; and Lachesis, who, when mortal man least expected it, cut the threads. Three unpredictable females who ruled the destinies of men."

He paused to gaze at her, and in the depths of his eyes, Prudence saw a flame come to life. She had a sudden impulse to reach up and brush aside the boyish lock of hair falling across his brow, to touch his cheek, to caress the strong line of his jaw and chin. She wanted to speak then, to say that she should surely go, that if she didn't there would be trouble, but she didn't.

A moonbeam fell across his features, and for a instant, she was back in the dream. The endless, mesmerizing dream that had kept her company since their first kiss.

Behind her the sand was trickling through the waist of the hourglass, but for her, time had ceased to exist. There was nothing, no measurement of minute or hour, nothing but an ecstatic current that seemed to leap, to arc in the air between them. Even the room seemed unreal, an enchanted place bathed in eerie, magical light.

Nothing was as it should be; everything had been touched, altered by that same miraculous power. It was as though a silken veil had been lowered over them, the two of them together, shutting them away from the outer world, sharpening the effect of their being alone together.

She blinked, hoping to break the spell. "I really must go."

The touch of his hand restrained her. She could feel his strength, the warmth of his palm, and the current leapt again.

"What if I won't let you go?"

His face caught the light, and she could read his expression: a look of such earnest intensity it stole her breath, a look without mockery or falsehood.

Then, blindly, without thought to reason or consequence, she kissed him—achingly, greedily, as if everything in her life had led only to this moment, to this kiss.

Her blood raced, her heart pounded, and her lips clung to his. When she tried to pull away, he held her fast. The one kiss quickly became two, three, four . . . She felt his hands pass over her body with a soft, intimate knowledge of where and how she needed to be touched. Soon she could feel the coolness of the air on her arms. He was pushing down her gloves, caressing her from elbow to wrist, then wrist to fingertip.

His fingers intertwined with hers. He pulled away then, for a moment, giving her time to breathe, to savor all that was happening, but a moment was all she needed. The magic was gone, replaced by the frightening fear that she was about to do it again—forget herself completely.

"I can't," she said. Glistening tears sprang into her eyes as she pulled away, then ran from the room.

Rathbone called after her, but Prudence kept running, down the corridor and into another room. This time, she locked the door.

CHAPTER 7

Rathbone glanced at the hands of a lantern clock sitting atop an inlaid serpentine table. It was early in the morning, much too early for the majority of Morland's guests to be anywhere but asleep in their rooms. Finding Prudence's chamber wasn't the problem. It was finding the ruby ring when it was residing in her jewelry case rather than on the young lady's hand.

He'd certainly botched it last night. Truth be told, he'd almost forgotten about the ring by their second kiss. Not completely, mind you; ten thousand pounds was a considerable sum, even to a man such as himself. And there was the little matter of his pride, which would be noticeably bruised were he to lose the wager to Ramsbury.

Not that Prudence hadn't done some bruising of her own. He'd never had a woman run away from him before. For all its brevity, the small amount of time he'd had with her had stayed with him through the rest of the evening. It was with him now and, as always, having a staggering effect on his mood.

Deciding there was little good to be served by loitering about in the hallway, Rathbone took himself downstairs and outdoors. Pale light was beginning to add color to the land, obliterating the last of the stars. He continued his passage across the red clay tiles of the veranda and onto the graveled drive that wound toward the stables and mews. By the time he had selected a mount, long rays of light were spreading out to caress the burgeoning splendor of the day. He turned the saddled roan toward the game reserve and gave a nudge of his heels.

Eager for a good run, the gelding responded with a hearty snort and a toss of its russet mane. Empathetic, Rathbone let the horse have his way. He rode for almost an hour, enjoying the sting of the brisk morning air against his face and the solitude that was impossible to find when riding on one of London's many greens. It wasn't until he had turned back toward the manor house that he met up with the earls, Granby and Ackerman.

"You're up early," Granby remarked.

"What of you? One would expect a contented husband to keep to his bed."

"It's enough that I left a contented wife."

Rathbone responded with a sly smile. "Remember the last time all of us were here together? Five lads with nothing but mischief on their minds."

"And Morland knowing all our games before we played them," Fitch added with a chuckle.

The three friends continued reminiscing about their misspent youth as they rode back to the house. Rathbone was glad his companions made no attempt to plumb his private thoughts. While he presented a calm exterior, he was concentrating on the coming day and night.

Time, like fate, was not aligned on his side. In order to win the wager, he had to have the ring in his possession no later than tomorrow morning. To wait any longer before departing for London was storing up trouble.

"You're in a melancholy mood this morning," Fitch remarked as they dismounted and handed their reins over to one of the stable boys. "Too much champagne last night, or a solitary bed?"

"Both."

"That's one of the benefits of being a married man." Granby's eyes flashed with humor. "If you drink too much, your wife tucks you into bed, and if you aren't too deep in your cups, she stays there."

"I can manage a night or two of celibacy," Rathbone assured him, although he'd had the devil's own time falling asleep last night.

He looked toward the house and saw the very lady who had caused the dilemma. Elegantly turned out in a riding habit of rich brown serge, she was sporting a crisp white blouse with starched front pleats and a perky little bonnet with gold feathers. Her brown boots had been polished to a fare-thee-well. She wore gloves of kidskin, buff in color and snuggly fitted, but not so snug that they revealed what the viscount wanted to know: Was she wearing the ruby ring?

"Good morning." Granby was the first to greet her.

"My lords," she replied, giving both him and Fitch a glance and a cordial nod.

Rathbone sensed as much as saw the slight stiffening of her posture, a warning that she hadn't forgotten their last encounter. Nor was she likely to.

The stablemaster, apparently familiar with her preference in mounts, led a springy little mare from the stable.

"Enjoy the sideboard," she said, speaking to the

three men as though they were one. "Cook served some delicious scones."

With that, she was gone, riding down the drive until she reached the lawn, where she put the mare into a speedy trot that took her toward the riding trails.

Rathbone was sorely tempted to take to the saddle again.

Miss Tamhill was becoming much too adept at dismissing him.

By contrast, he was entrenched in his attitude toward her. His reaction to her formed a more than disturbing oddity within him. That was the real irritation. He couldn't think of the ring without thinking of the lady, and he couldn't think of the lady without thinking of what it was like to kiss her, and he couldn't think of kissing her without thinking of what it would be like to . . . Damnation, but he had to get his mind out of his breeches and about business.

"Hungry?" he called over his shoulder as he headed for the house. His friends followed.

The clock in the hall was striking the hour as Rathbone entered the breakfast room. If luck was with him, he'd be able to satisfy at least a portion of his hunger, have a cup of strong coffee, and then take to the upstairs. It was time to have a look-see at the lady's room. Perhaps he'd find the ring.

If not, if circumstances forced him to go lurking about tonight, he needed to know what furniture to avoid. A stubbed toe, followed by the customary grunt or groan, could turn his planned sleight of hand into a disaster.

Prudence was surprised to find herself seated directly across the dinner table from the viscount. She'd managed, quite admirably on her part, to avoid him since their brief encounter that morning.

For a drawn-out moment, she was tempted to plead a headache and excuse herself from the table. Giving a quick glance to where the Duke of Worley was sitting, she decided against it. Both her guardian and Lionel had already commented upon her preoccupation, asking if there was something on her mind. It wouldn't do to give that something a name.

Employing her customary manners and charm, Prudence engaged Titus Counce in casual conversation, and the talk quickly meandered to philosophical realms. Hattie was seated to Rathbone's right, across the table from Titus. It was easy to see that the two young people, whom she'd introduced the previous day, had taken up a friendship.

Prudence was both surprised and impressed when Rathbone joined the discussion. His questions were logical, his replies wryly humorous, and his understanding of Greek and Roman history impeccable. Often, however, he simply listened, his expression that of a man truly intrigued by what was being said. Had she perhaps misjudged him?

No. He was only doing what he did best—charming people into believing him harmless. Prudence knew better.

While most young ladies lusted after titles and properties, often wishing to assume a rank higher than what had been allotted them, she was from a sensible and more wisely reared line. Respectful of money, and as frugal as any Scot, her family had accrued the good things in life gradually, and while not blatant opportunists, the former Tamhills had made the most of those opportunities. Prudence planned on doing the same.

She was not of a mind to marry, and while she admitted a fascination with the viscount, she wasn't foolish enough to become his plaything. The situation would result in nothing but misfortune, last night being the perfect example.

She'd made of a fool of herself again!

Her reward, if any, was a forced admittance that she could not allow herself so much as a private exchange of words with the man.

"Have you traveled abroad?" Titus asked Rathbone.

"Somewhat," he replied. "France, of course, and a short excursion to the south of Italy."

"I've always wanted to see Egypt," Hattie inserted.

"Then you must speak with Lady Ackerman. She's planning a trip to Cairo next spring," Rathbone announced. "Talked Fitch into it somehow."

"Having met Lady Ackerman, I do not think she had to put much effort into the convincing," Prudence said, speaking in direct reply to the viscount for the first time. "She is an energetic woman, one whom I like very much."

Their eyes met, but the previous night's embarrassment kept Prudence from responding with anything more than a cold stare, while Rathbone smiled as handsomely as a newly fallen angel. When his reply came, it was offhanded but sincere.

"Takes this independent female business a bit far, if you ask me."

His smile stayed in place as she turned her head toward Titus, who was remarking on the quality of the soup.

"Prudence is *very* independent," Hattie said, speaking her own mind with more vigor than was customary. "After she inherits her fortune, she's going to run her own affairs, aren't you?"

"Yes. Uncle Horace predicts doom, of course."

"And what do you predict?" Rathbone asked of her.

"I, sir, predict that women will master a great many things in the years ahead. Before another generation fades into oblivion, our voices will be heard around the world."

An older lord, sitting to Hattie's right and within hearing distance, had trouble keeping his jaw from succumbing to the law of gravity. Prudence's remark infringed upon the ideas that had guided the world since Adam's day. Men were husbands, fathers, and masters of all they surveyed; women were wives and mothers. To think beyond that was to be guilty of blasphemy.

"Does that include the men in their lives?" Rathbone countered in a wry style.

"That depends on whether the men in their lives support them or oppose them," she replied, giving him another glimpse of her personality.

"Don't say that to my uncle," Titus cautioned goodnaturedly. "He dislikes progressive-thinking females who stir up intellectual dust. Insists it isn't good for the digestion."

Too refined to cast aspersions at Titus's uncle, Prudence looked down the length of the table to where Lord Wallingcroft was seated, her gaze effectively reducing him to the consistency of rice pudding, before glancing directly across the table to where her current nemesis was seated.

Rathbone replied with another of his wicked smiles, leaving Prudence to wonder if beneath all that charm, he wasn't furious with her for walking out on him last night.

Then again, why should his mood concern her? Tomorrow would bring an end to their odd association. She'd return to North Hill, and the viscount to his estate in Herefordshire. When they next met, she would be of legal age, her own guardian, and all this would be a memory.

After dessert, the women abandoned the dining room for the parlor. The gentlemen stayed behind while the footmen removed the tablecloths and the butler circled the table with a humidor that contained fine Turkish cigars, followed by a selection of Madeira, port, and brandy.

Prudence entered the parlor, crossing the Persian carpet, richly woven with an elaborate pattern set against a crimson background, to the far corner of the room, where an overstuffed, tufted, and tasseled divan faced the mantelpiece. A few seconds later she found herself seated next to Lady Rathbone.

While she had met the viscountess on previous occasions, this was the first time they had engaged in more than a few cordial words.

Augusta, Lady Rathbone, sat with erect posture, her alert blue eyes missing nothing. Her hair, impeccably coiffed in the latest style, was a burnished blond that showed only a miniscule trace of gray. Her face, while slightly lined by the years, retained its clarity of beauty.

Prudence was hard-pressed not to give in to her curiosity and ask about the lady's son. It wasn't like her to be flighty—to make a decision, then change her mind at a moment's notice. It was bewildering. Her emotions were mixed. She knew she had to stay away from Rathbone, and yet, she wanted to be with him.

She'd escaped him last night, avoided him all day, and now she found herself hoping he would ask her to dance—one last time.

During dinner she had felt particularly vulnerable to his charms and his unrestrained masculinity; the sheer physical fact of having him across the table from her had been disarming. For all his swagger and conceit, his reputation and his idiosyncrasies when it came to collecting women by the score, she sensed there was more to his armor.

What lodestar attracted him, beyond the obvious?

He spoke of things Greek and Roman as casually as other Englishman spoke of grouse hunting and the flavor of a bread pudding. Had he once possessed a secret desire to become a lord of the classics, to devote his life to scholarly endeavors as Titus was now doing? There was so much she didn't understand about the man, yet she was discovering things about him that chimed deliciously with her own personality.

"Benjamin is sure to brood," Lady Rathbone was saying to Lady Felicity Forbes-Hammond. "He's come to dislike the country. Roams about the house as if he's misplaced himself. It borders on irritating."

Hearing the personal remark, Prudence's curiosity peaked, then overflowed. "London doesn't seem to bore him."

"Yes, well, a man can't spend all his time doing what my Benjamin does so well," his mother replied, none too happily. "It's time he took things more seriously. I talk, but of course, he doesn't listen."

"He'll find his bearings soon enough," Felicity said, dismissing the worry with a wave of her Viennese fan. Being a bit eccentric herself, she had a high tolerance for the idiosyncrasies of others, as long as those oddities didn't do irrevocable harm. "Be patient a while longer, Augusta. Your son will see the light soon enough."

Several hours later, Rathbone's patience ran out. He silently cursed fate and its integrated links, small as they might be. One thing hinging upon another, he was now forced to do something he would rather not.

The corridor was dark, excluding the small glow of the gasoliers that had been turned down to show only shadows of the hallway tables and the portraits hanging above them. The ancient, historical house on the out-skirts of Aylesbury was quiet, as soundless as the stars. It was nearly four in the morning, the hour when most slept soundly, lost to dreams.

Rathbone felt the night encircle him, oddly alive and vivid. Clad in dark trousers and the white shirt he'd worn under his dinner jacket, now unbuttoned at the throat, he made his way toward a closed bedroom door. He'd left his shoes behind, not wanting to make any un-necessary noise as he moved stealthily toward his desti-nation.

A thorough inspection of Prudence's room had left its image in his mind. Possessed of a singular grandeur, with a high Jacobean ceiling decorated with elaborate plasterwork, tall leaded windows, a blue and gold Savon-nerie carpet, and walls painted a soft primrose, its im-posing detail matched the other rooms of the duke's country estate. The furniture was just as imposing: a Chippendale armoire, a vanity table and mirror, the ex-pected writing table and chair, and of course, the bed. A grand affair with carved posts and thick fluffy pillows.

Hopefully, he'd find Prudence's pretty head resting on one of those pillows, her eyes closed, her body cap-tured by slumber.

He paused just outside the closed chamber, listening intensely. When no sound returned to him, he twisted the knob, and, holding his breath lest the door squeak like an irate mouse, he pushed it open. His breath was released when the door made nary a sound. So far, so good.

The draperies that would normally be drawn had been left open. A stream of pale moonlight revealed his chosen path. There was a silver bowl of red roses on the bedside table. Their scent filled the room.

Rathbone paused for another moment, taking in the atmosphere of complete peace, which was in direct contrast to his current state of mind.

He looked toward the bed. The shape of the coverlet told him Prudence was sleeping beneath it. His footsteps were soundless on the soft carpet, so he couldn't resist a closer look.

She lay with her head turned toward the door, her shoulders covered with waves of dark, silky hair. *How innocent she appeared,* he thought. How breathtakingly fragile in her white nightgown with its soft lace and tiny buttons, like a child. But she wasn't a child. She was a grown woman who, if awakened, would scream at the sight of a man lurking in the darkness.

Get the ring, and get out, Rathbone told himself.

He surveyed the vanity first, carefully searching the mirrored tray for the ring. It wasn't there. The jewelry case was where it would normally be found, resting on a lowboy within reach of the vanity. As quiet as smoke, Rathbone made his way to it, lifted it gingerly, then set it down on the carpet.

He knelt in front of it, prepared for the lock. Taking a small slip of wire from his pocket, he inserted it into the brass mechanism. It took some time, but eventually it gave way and the lid opened.

With moonlight to guide him, Rathbone silently inspected the box's contents. Diamonds, emeralds, opals, an onyx and gold brooch—each impressive, but none the glittering jewel he sought.

Was she wearing it even now? In her sleep?

He looked toward the bed, but all he could see was the rounded shape of Prudence under the rose and white coverlet. Closing the jewelry case, he returned it to the lowboy, then went about the room, looking at each tabletop, hoping to find the ring resting on a lace doily, easy pickings for a thief.

When nothing was found, he reluctantly turned back to the bed. Step after careful step took him closer, until he was peering down at Prudence. He studied her face, with its dark lashes and pale skin. Her lips were parted, as if she anticipated some imagined prince to offer up a kiss.

Rathbone was tempted—sorely tempted—but he didn't dare test fate. To kiss her now would be to guarantee she would awaken, for it would be no light brush of lips but a deep, rousing kiss, one meant to rekindle the fire that sparked so easily between them.

Forcing his gaze away from her mouth, he looked down to find the ring where it always was, gracing her pretty little hand.

Having come too far to stop now, he reached out and let his fingertips rest lightly against her own, a whisper of a touch that would hopefully be absorbed into the illusion of her dreams.

Uncertain if she was suffering from a nightmare or reality, Prudence jerked upright, then opened her mouth. A hard hand clamped over it, and she was forced back down on the bed.

"Promise not to scream, and I'll take my hand away."

Prudence nodded, then gulped a breath of air before twisting around to look at her assailant. "Is this how you dazzle the heart of a lady, my lord, by sneaking into her room and scaring her out of her wits?"

"Believe it or not, I've never had to sneak *into* a lady's room. Out of one, I'll admit, but that's another story."

The reference to his jaded exploits was the match that set fire to Prudence's temper. She lunged at him, taking the bedclothes with her.

Rathbone reacted as any man not wanting to have his eyes clawed out would react. He gripped her wrists and, holding them firmly, forced her back onto the mattress. The movement brought one of his knees atop the bed, then the other.

"Stop it," he said, keeping his voice low as he fought against laughter. The circumstances weren't humorous, but it did his pride a world of good to know he could make the woman jealous.

"Let me go!" she snapped, struggling to get free.

He pinned her more firmly. "Ten thousand pounds," he mumbled as he lowered himself full-length on top of her. "This has got to be the most expensive kiss in history. But I'll be damned if I'll leave without it."

The moonlight offered her a clear view of his face, of the irresistible features that had won the hearts of countless women. His gaze was slanted and mischievous, like that of a guilty schoolboy, but in no way repentant. Except that he was no longer boyish. His shirt was open and she could see hair, crisp and curly and as golden as that on his head, about his upper chest and collarbone.

Prudence turned her head. The kiss landed on her temple. "Please, let me go."

The words, delivered with far less enthusiasm this time, only served to do the opposite. Rathbone kissed her again, letting his mouth glide over the ridge of her eyebrow, then down to her cheek. She tensed under his touch.

"Kiss me back," he urged, forgetting the wager, the ruby, even the ten thousand pounds and his soon-to-be humiliation at losing his first bet to Ramsbury.

Prudence struggled, not with her assailant this time, but with her own conscience. The man she had been thinking about before falling asleep was here now, this very minute, and he wasn't a dream. He was real. Very real.

Her hesitation was her downfall.

Rathbone released one wrist just long enough to reach up and turn her head. His mouth found hers and the kiss began.

With a helpless sigh, Prudence let her head fall back against the pillow. He tasted of tobacco and whiskey, of wild pleasures and forbidden dreams.

With an abandonment like none she'd ever known, she kissed him back, offering her mouth to him, offering anything that was within her power to give. When he took it, the result was like thunder and lightning, an instant storm of passion.

Rathbone plunged his hands into her hair, tangling it around his fingers as his tongue eagerly invaded her mouth. It was the most tormenting, most exciting kiss he had ever shared with a woman. He turned, taking her with him, rolling them both in the coverlet, cocooning them in a world that shouldn't exist, but did.

In a sudden, sure movement, his hands made their way to her body, pressing her against him. As he held her close he could feel the wild beating of her heart, the panicky strain of her breathing. Their mouths merged, melting together in a mutual sigh, a moan of gratitude for something lost, but now found. The kiss was long and ardent, and when their lips parted, it was only to breathe the air more fully.

Rathbone drew back to look at her, at the passion burning in her dark eyes, at the pulse beating wildly in her throat. "Damn," he mumbled, unable to think of another word. Then he kissed her again.

He wanted to go on kissing her forever, tasting her. The dark pleasure of it curled deep within him, warming his blood and hardening his body. She smelled of lavender soap and musky woman. She felt warm and alive, moving beneath his hands, arching to fill them.

He rolled again, and she followed, a willing prisoner of his embrace. Lying atop him now, her hips resting on his thighs, her belly pressing against his erection, Rathbone closed his eyes and felt her hands, which explored his face as if she suspected she was still asleep and dreaming. Her fingertips moved as lightly as a feather, their gentle touch prickling his senses like a sharp knife. The sensation nearly robbed him of his control.

He stroked the fullness of her breasts until she moaned, until the nipples were hard little pearls pushing against the fine muslin of her virginal white nightgown.

Virginal!

One last roll, to put her under him again, to free himself so he could stand, so he could find the door and escape before it was too late. But having regained his senses, he'd run out of bed. They rolled off the mattress and onto the carpet, taking the linens with them, along with the silver bowl of roses that was caught by the corner of the coverlet.

Aroused male and startled female, linens and pillows, silver bowl and red roses all went crashing.

Prudence cried out, certain the world had given way beneath them. Slightly dazed, Rathbone tried to make rhyme or reason out of the situation. Prudence was on top of him again, her hair curtaining his face as she put her knee down, not on the floor, but into the pit of his stomach.

"Damnation, woman, stop wiggling and let me get us out of this thing," he grunted. "And be careful where you put your bloody knee. You'll make a gelding out of me."

"That pleasure will be all mine!"

The venomous threat stopped Rathbone's heart cold. The woman on top of him mumbled her own version of a curse. Slowly, he turned his head toward the now opened door, knowing that this time, Fate was wearing a familiar face.

CHAPTER 8

The Duke of Worley stood in the doorway, his gray hair on end, his robe hastily tied, and his eyes blazing.

Rathbone found his feet and stood up. If ever a man had been caught red-handed, it was he.

"Find a dressing gown," the duke snapped at Prudence. "As for you, sir, I will have an accounting."

Rathbone didn't doubt it.

Before Prudence could move away from the duke, he put an arm around her waist and pulled her to his side. She resisted, but only momentarily.

"I expected better of you," Worley said, looking from her bewildered face to the undaunted expression of the man who had the audacity to enter her room in the middle of the night.

Before Rathbone could come to Prudence's defense, another voice was added to the conversation.

"What's going on here? What's all the yelling about?" It was Lionel, his eyes dazed from sleep, but not to the extent that a quick glance didn't sum up the situation. "Good God, Prudence!"

"I suggest that you save your inquiries for me," Rathbone said. He knew the landscape of indiscretion, having mapped it many times. Society's attitudes toward a wronged virgin were well known.

"If you've harmed her, I'll kill you," Lionel said. His voice softened before he addressed Prudence. "Are you all right?"

"Yes," she said, not totally able to disguise the tremor in her voice. "Nothing harmful happened."

The duke disagreed. "Lionel, stay with Prudence. The viscount and I will settle this downstairs."

"I'd rather do the settling myself. A broken nose should curb his flamboyant ways."

"Who's going to break whose nose?"

Granby poked his head into the room. Unlike the other two men, he was wearing trousers and was buttoning his shirt as he spoke. "Rathbone!"

"I'm going to have your friend's head on a pike," Worley boomed, growing angrier and louder by the moment. "If he thinks to get his hands on the Tamhill fortune, he's badly mistaken."

Rathbone was opening his mouth to object to the duke's last remark when the doorway behind Worley grew even more crowded. Both Ackerman and Sterling had been roused from their beds by the noisy exchange, followed by their wives, each of whom looked beautifully sleepy and thoroughly confused.

"Fitch, what's going on?" Ackerman's wife asked.

"Nothing, sweetheart. Go back to bed. We'll have this all straightened out in no time. Nothing to worry about."

"Nothing a funeral won't take care of," Lionel said. "Sorry, Ackerman, but I'm bloody well going to kill your charming friend."

"Oh, my," Lady Granby said. "It's Rathbone in there, isn't it?"

"Go back to bed," Granby ordered, turning his wife around and giving her a gentle push. "I've got my hands full here."

"Is Prudence all right?"

"She will be," Hilary assured her friends. "Fitch will sort it all out."

"Thank you, madam, for your vote of confidence," Fitch said, pulling her close enough for a quick kiss on the cheek. "However, this time, I fear it will have to be Rathbone doing the sorting. I already have a wife."

"He'll not get her!" Worley vowed. "Bloody scoundrel."

"Over my dead body," Lionel added. His fists were doubled up and waiting for Rathbone to disagree.

"Enough!" Morland demanded from out in the hallway. An instant transformation from chaos to order was established with the sharply spoken word. "Make way here. Ladies, please return to your rooms. Gentlemen, calm yourselves."

It came to Rathbone at that moment that he was calm. Much too calm, considering the consequences he was about to face. In spite of Worley's decree to the contrary, they both knew that marriage was the prescribed remedy for a situation such as this.

He looked down at Prudence, who still stood in the protection of his arms. She was wearing a faintly puzzled expression, as if she were doing her best to wake up from a bad dream.

For the first time since being discovered, Rathbone sincerely wished he had an explanation to offer for his actions, other than the one everyone assumed, of course. It didn't help matters that the real reason was even more abominable.

"Half an hour in the downstairs library," Morland said.

The clear command received no protest. "I trust that will give everyone time to calm their tempers and make themselves presentable."

The duke turned toward the door to discover that not a single one of the ladies had heeded his orders and returned to her room. "Hilary, if you would be so kind as to stay with Miss Tamhill. Catherine, ring for Darling. He'll see that a tray is brought upstairs."

Both Hilary and Rebecca stepped into the room, while Catherine disappeared to summon the butler.

Rathbone checked himself before asking for a moment alone with Prudence. His request was sure to be refused. He lowered his head instead, keeping his voice the lightest of whispers. "Don't worry, sweetheart. Everything will be all right. Trust me."

She looked at him then, her eyes wide, as if she'd only just come fully awake. "Trust you to do what?"

"To handle the situation," he said, adding a smile because she seemed to need it. When she continued to look at him, very much as she'd done that evening by the garden gate, Rathbone kissed her on the forehead. "Don't worry."

"Miss Tamhill." It was Hilary. She was holding out a dressing gown.

Once Prudence was wearing the robe and sitting in a button-back chair near the window, with Hilary hovering to her right and Rebecca standing guard on her left, Rathbone took his leave.

He didn't have to look over his shoulder to know that three of the duke's "lads" were behind him as he made his way down the hall and into his own room.

"What in the bloody hell did you think you were doing?" Granby demanded no sooner than the door had closed behind them. "In Morland's very house, with the Duke of Worley across the hall!"

Rathbone didn't waste his breath answering the charge. Opening the second drawer of a walnut tallboy, he pulled out a clean shirt and tossed it on the bed. He began to dress, gritting his teeth against the humiliation of being forced to propose marriage.

"Prudence Tamhill," Sterling marveled before sinking into a chair near the fireplace. The outcome of the night was a foregone conclusion—marriage. "Your mother will be pleased."

Rathbone still didn't comment. He poured water from a porcelain ewer into a blue china bowl, then, using a square of brown Windsor soap, washed his face and hands. He was taking off one shirt and putting on the other when *the word* was finally spoken aloud by Fitch.

"Marriage. Nothing less will do."

"Except my head on a pike," Rathbone said, repeating the duke's threat. "Where's my bloody jacket?"

"Here." Granby retrieved it from the back of a chair, tossing it his way. "And Fitch is right. Charm won't get you out of this one."

"He did have his pants *on*," Sterling remarked to the room at large.

"At least by the time we got there," mused Fitch.

"On or off, he was caught," Granby declared, a second before he collapsed onto the bed and burst into laughter. "I never thought I'd see the day. We should wake up Waltham. Can't have him sleeping through this one—he'll never forgive us."

"He'll never believe it," Sterling chuckled. "I'll give the chap's door a tap or two. Can't have the last of the 'lads' being called front and center without proper presentation. So, which of us will stand for you?"

"All of us," Granby answered. "One at each of the church exits."

"The devil take you," Rathbone cursed. Having

found his shoes, he sat down on the bed to put them on. "The least you can do is find me a drink. Even a condemned man is granted one last request."

"There'll be coffee and brandy in the library," Fitch assured him. "Or would you prefer hemlock?"

"What I'd prefer doesn't matter now."

"You were in her room," Sterling pointed out. "And it is almost dawn."

"Another hour till dawn," Fitch said. "That makes it closer to the middle of the night. What does a man do in a young lady's room in the middle of the night if he isn't doing what we all know you do best?"

"Looking for a wife, what else?" Granby said, risking another laugh. "Blast me if he doesn't look surprised that he found one."

"What in the bloody hell am I going to do with a wife?" Rathbone's voice didn't change, but his expression was grim. Turn the thing around as he would, he could see no other way.

His friends smiled at him, not in jest this time, but in memory of the past tragedies and triumphs they had shared.

"What every man does," Sterling advised. "Protect and provide for her and the children she'll give you."

"Make her your friend, if you can," Fitch suggested.

"Do you care for her at all?" asked Granby.

"I like her well enough," Rathbone said, unable to discern exactly what his emotions were when applied to Prudence. Each time he tried to give them a name, he failed miserably. "I object to marriage, especially when it's forced down a man's throat, but I don't object to Prudence."

"Then, I'd say you've met your match."

* * *

"Wonderful, Darling brought something to flavor the tea," Catherine said, taking the stopper from a slender bottle and adding a touch of brandy to the steaming cup of tea she'd just poured. "Sip this. It's sure to do the trick."

"I don't need a trick, I need a miracle," Prudence replied woefully. As she took the cup of tea, the ruby ring on her hand caught the light. Her mother's marriage to Archibald Tamhill had been arranged, dictated by her well-intentioned parents. Like so many women, Rachel Tamhill had been reared for the inevitable, to give herself to a man of good social standing, one who could provide a secure future for her and her children. And like so many women, her mother had acquiesced to that predestined future.

But had she been happy? Prudence feared not. A happily married woman didn't take a lover, nor did she write in her diary of "moments of deep regret."

"Do you want to talk about it?" Hilary asked in a subdued voice. "We all know how utterly charming Rathbone can be."

"Nothing happened . . . except a few kisses," Prudence said.

She was still recovering from those kisses, and from the fact that if they hadn't rolled off the bed, Rathbone would have completed his seduction—with her help.

"I know what you're going through," Catherine said, reaching out to touch her shoulder. "My marriage to Norton came about in very much the same way."

Prudence showed her surprise.

"Felicity found me in his room," she went on to explain. "It started out innocently enough. He'd dislocated his shoulder. The details would take some time to explain, but the gist of it is that I felt guilty. Then he kissed me. From there . . . well, suffice it to say, we were discovered in an intimate embrace. I wasn't compromised, not in the true sense of the word, but there was no going back. I swore I wouldn't marry him. But . . ." She paused to smile. "Thank God, he convinced me otherwise."

"Then he loved you," Prudence said, fighting back frustrated tears. Nothing was happening as it should. While she tried to tell herself that a few minutes of rational conversation would set things straight, she felt sick inside. "Rathbone doesn't love me. I don't even know why he came to my room."

"If you didn't invite him, then . . . I'm not doubting your sense of propriety—please don't misunderstand—but knowing Rathbone as I do, it's not his style to force himself on a woman," Hilary said.

"He doesn't have to," Catherine said, expressing her opinion with smile. "They fall at his feet. Disgusting, if you ask me, but then, he does have a way about him."

"I did allow him a kiss," Prudence stated, not daring to confess that she'd allowed a great deal more that night in the gazebo. "But I didn't encourage him to come calling in the middle of the night."

The ladies exchanged glances. Hilary shrugged her shoulders. "As my adorable husband would say, that's water under the bridge. You do realize that they're downstairs right now, setting the date for your wedding?"

Dread swelled up inside Prudence. She left the chair to look out the window. It was nearing dawn. The fading moonlight poured over the front lawn like a spun-out ribbon, leaving shadows among the dark clumps of shrubbery and trees.

Her frame of mind was bleak. Just as her grandparents had constructed her mother's future, hers was being built now, without her consent, without thought to her personal happiness. Would history repeat itself in her own life? Would matrimonial miseries one day force her to seek solace in another man's arms? Or worse, would Rathbone continue the exotic pursuits denied men of lesser means? Would he keep a mistress once the novelty of a wife wore thin?

Before the thought took shape, Prudence rejected it, just as she meant to rebuff a marriage between herself and the viscount.

"I won't marry him," she announced. "I'm almost of age. I can insist on a long engagement, one that will see my next birthday come and gone. No one can force me after that. I'll be my own mistress, with enough money to last me a lifetime. I won't need a husband then. Not unless he's of my own choosing."

"Are you saying you'll refuse Rathbone when he proposes? And mark my words, he will have to *ask* you. I know Morland. The old man will insist on it," Rebecca said, sounding convinced that Prudence's destiny had been set in stone by the night's events.

"It's Worley who matters now," Hilary stated. "I saw the look on his face. He isn't going to be reasonable. Pity, but most men aren't. Especially when it comes to their pride."

Prudence colored slightly, both with shame and anger. What were they thinking, Uncle Horace and Lionel? It was all Rathbone's fault. If only he'd left her alone.

"You should try and get some rest," Catherine advised.

"How can I rest? They're downstairs, cloistered in the library like members of Parliament debating an issue that will have untold impact on people's lives—on *my* life! Rathbone doesn't love me. He isn't ready to commit himself to any woman, let alone to one he barely knows. His reputation is appalling. He thrives on drinking and gambling and—"

"So did Norton, but as Felicity once told me, even the worst scoundrel can be reformed by the right woman," Catherine inserted with conviction. "And I've watched Rathbone watching you. He feels something, I'm sure of it."

"Besides, we all want him to marry. To be happy," Hilary added. "No matter how deplorable his reputation may seem, he's a good person. You should see him with the children. He's their favorite uncle, always bringing them presents and carrying them about on his shoulders. Georgie adores him. Oh, he grumbles under his breath about marriage being a man's downfall, but I don't think he really believes it. His attitude is part of his charm."

Prudence stared at the other two women. They nodded, agreeing with Hilary. "Then find him a wife," she said. "I won't be his salvation, not when he's going to be my demise."

"He's already found himself a wife," Catherine said. "You!"

Prudence shook her head and continued shaking it as Hilary rallied to the cause.

"You're lovely and intelligent and stubborn. It would never do for Rathbone to marry a weak-willed woman. He'd have her cowering before she spoke the wedding vows. No, he needs someone like you, someone who isn't afraid to box his ears from time to time."

"Hilary's right," Rebecca insisted. "Rathbone needs a confident woman, someone who won't stumble into his charming little traps."

"According to my guardian, I've already stumbled," Prudence argued. "And I'm not nearly as confident as you may think."

At the moment, she was feeling anything but confident. Her insides were shaking and her hands were growing cold. She picked up the teacup, cradling it in her palms to borrow some of its warmth.

"But, of course, you are," Catherine said. "Though we've only just become acquainted, I think you and Rathbone are the perfect match."

"It's absurd. Insane," Prudence argued. "Marriage isn't the answer. It will only make matters worse."

"You're tired and upset," Hilary said soothingly. "We'll leave you to get some rest."

Prudence thanked them for their spontaneous friendship, then watched as they quit the room. She couldn't shake off the bewilderment that had arrived with the viscount's unexpected appearance.

What in the devil had driven him to her room? If only she hadn't allowed that first kiss. And she had allowed it. No matter how much of a frenzy she worked herself into, there was no denying she was part and parcel of the problem.

With the first rays of dawn spilling through the window panes, she rang for Fiona. Sooner or later she'd be called downstairs to face her guardian. She needed to get dressed.

"Are you feeling ill?" Fiona asked the moment she appeared. As usual, she was wearing a gray dress and a starched apron, and her hair was already escaping its pins. She looked at the tea tray that hadn't been there when she'd turned down the bed last night. "You'd not normally be up and about this early."

"Something has happened," Prudence said, jerking

at her robe. She suddenly felt as if the garment were suffocating her. "More precisely, everything has gone wrong."

"Whatever are you mumbling about? Here, let me help you. You've got the sash knotted."

"Uncle Horace found the viscount in my room," Prudence confessed. She wiggled the robe down and over her hips, then stepped free of it. "Now he's going to insist that the blasted man marry me."

"What viscount? There's a bloody dozen of them running about the place."

"Rathbone. I woke up and he was here, standing beside my bed."

"The scallywag! In this room, this very room? Last night?"

Prudence nodded, then burst into tears. Fiona was the only one to whom she dare expose her true feelings. The maid rushed to her side, enfolding her in caring arms.

"It's my fault," Prudence stammered, trying to get her rioting emotions under control. "I shouldn't have let him kiss me. I should have screamed my head off."

"Oh, my," Fiona groaned, as though the consequences weighed as heavily on her as they did on her mistress.

"Uncle Horace found us. He's so angry," Prudence said, pulling back to stand alone. "Furious. He's downstairs with Rathbone now, setting the date for our wedding."

"Maybe it's for the best," Fiona said. "And don't be shaking your head at me. He's the one, isn't he? The one who's had you brooding these last weeks."

"Brooding doesn't make a good foundation for marriage," Prudence argued, unable to see any good in the whole mess. "He doesn't love me. And he doesn't want to marry. If he did, there'd be a hundred willing women waiting in line."

"But it wasn't them he kissed," Fiona said consolingly. "It was you. Makes me think there's more to it than the picture you're painting."

Not ready to reveal any more than she already had, Prudence went to the clothespress and withdrew her most severe gown, a day smock of dark dove-gray with black piping around the cuffs. The same black piping outlined the lighter gray panel that ran down the front of the skirt. She had intended to match it with a gray traveling jacket, to be worn on the return trip to North Hill, but the color suited her current mood.

"Please fetch me some hot water," she requested of Fiona, who was still absorbing the shocking news that her mistress would soon be Viscountess Rathbone.

It was a scant half-hour later that a knock sounded on the door. Fiona opened it, not knowing whom to expect.

Lionel stepped into the room. "Prudence, Father wants you to join us in the library."

"What's the verdict?"

"What else can it be but marriage?" he said, his tone more serious than she could ever recall hearing it. "Rathbone has agreed to the match. And with far less arguing than I expected."

"And if I disagree?"

"Then it's to be Freddie. Father said as much, hoping, I think, to give Rathbone a way out. He'd much rather have you wed to one of us, but you already know that."

"I won't be forced into marriage with anyone. Can't Uncle Horace see that? Doesn't he care enough to listen to what I have to say?"

"We both care," Lionel assured her. "Do you think I want you married to that blackguard? The very thought of it makes me furious. I'd much rather take my fists to him."

"Then you would have to take your fists to me, as well," Prudence told him. "It was my room he was found in, not yours."

"Why?" Lionel asked, pursuing the reason. "Surely you're not enamored of him? His reputation is worse than mine."

"No, I am not enamored of him," Prudence replied, hoping she hadn't come so far as to actually fall in the love with the man. "However, I would be lying were I not to admit some fascination."

"And . . ."

"Last night was not the first time he kissed me."

"I knew it. You've been acting strange. I said as much to Father." He moved to where she was standing by the window. Reaching out, he took her by the shoulders, not to shake her, but rather to hold her in place so she couldn't evade his questions. "Just how far has this 'fascination' taken you? Rathbone insists he didn't compromise you, that you're still a virgin. It's the only reason Father suggested Frederick. He'll inherit, but his heir can't come under suspicion."

"Virgin or not, I'm damaged goods, my reputation gone the way of the wind."

"Damnation, but you're stubborn. I warned Rathbone of it. Thought it might scare him off."

"But it didn't."

"He laughed, blast his black soul. Said all women were stubborn in their own way."

"He laughed!"

"Don't set your kettle to boiling," Lionel cautioned her. "It was a bloody inquisition, if you must know.

Father accused him of losing at the tables. Came right out and asked if he needed money. Offered to pay his debts, but Rathbone just smiled. Damned unnerving. Can't say I'd hold up as well if I were under the old man's quizzing glass."

"Rathbone doesn't need my money."

"Doesn't seem to. From what Morland said, he has an alert mind when it comes to business. Makes money hand over fist whenever he dabbles in the Exchange. Actually, the old fox gave him a sterling recommendation. Said he couldn't argue against the match. Thinks it just what Rathbone needs."

"What about *my* needs?"

Lionel took a deep breath, then let it out slowly. There was nothing more to say. The stage was set. "Father's waiting, and I'd think twice before I gainsay his decision. He's primed and ready for a fight, since your viscount didn't give him one. I've already been told to dispatch a message to Freddie. Posthaste. Father wants him home immediately."

A heavy sensation ran through Prudence's nerves, not pain, but something just as acute; like it or not, she was tangled in the threads of fate Rathbone had alluded to the previous evening.

CHAPTER 9

Prudence stepped into the library knowing what to expect but unsure what to do about it. Rathbone was standing near the windows that overlooked the rear gardens, a cup of coffee in hand. He looked at ease.

"Miss Tamhill," the Duke of Morland said, standing up from behind his desk. "Please, come in. I believe an affable agreement has been reached between your guardian and the viscount, but I felt it necessary that you be consulted before the issue is settled."

"How thoughtful of you," Prudence replied, not smiling. She looked at her guardian. "Unfortunately, I don't consider the *issue* settled at all. In fact, there is nothing to be settled."

Worley stood, stiff and starched. "Don't think to get sassy with me, miss. I'll not tolerate it any more than I'll tolerate your recent behavior. A lady knows better than to—"

"With all due respect, Your Grace, may I remind you that the lady is now my fiancée," Rathbone said, just as intently.

The blue of his eyes was lost in the shadows as he moved to stand directly in front of the window, but Prudence knew they had turned dark with anger. Why not? He was being forced into marriage, led to the proverbial slaughter.

She spoke then. "Has it occurred to either of you that I might genuinely wish to remain unmarried?"

When Worley took a step forward, Lionel stepped between them. "You know how stubborn Pru can be, Father." He looked to Rathbone then. "If you think she's going to marry you willingly, think again, old chap."

"Stop talking about me as though I were still upstairs," Prudence demanded. "And there will be no marriage. While the viscount's behavior, and mine, may not be without reproach, there is no earthly reason for us to marry."

"You'll marry the man," Worley insisted. "If not him, then Frederick. I'll not have your name dirtied by scandal. I promised your father that I'd see you properly raised and properly married, and by God, I'll do just that."

"We've already discussed this," Rathbone said, crossing the room to stand beside Prudence. He didn't touch her, but his proximity alerted everyone to the fact that he considered her to be his responsibility. "She won't be marrying Frederick."

"How very gallant of you, my lord," she said, wanting nothing more at that moment than to bash the man over the head with something. Preferably something that would knock some sense into him. "But I don't require your defense. I'm quite capable of speaking for myself."

"Then by all means, rant and rave to your heart's content," he said. "But I warn you, it won't do any good. I've decided to marry you, Miss Tamhill."

"You've decided. *You've* decided!" She was more upset

that she'd been since Worley had walked into her room and found them cocooned in a coverlet. "How dare you presume that your decision takes precedence over mine."

She forgot about her guardian being in the room, forgot about the Duke of Morland and Lionel, and focused all her fury on the viscount. "How dare you assume anything where I am concerned, your lordship. You know nothing of me. Nothing of any value. And I do value myself. I value my future and the people who will be a part of it—people of my own choosing."

"This isn't getting us anywhere," Lionel said. "Pru, you're going to have to marry the man. Father's right, and you know it. There's sure to be gossip, and none of it good."

Gossip.

How it ruled their world, she thought. The all-powerful engine of hearsay had tarnished more than one woman, dooming them to the fringe of Society.

Before pandemonium could ensue, Morland tapped his silver-tipped walking stick against the leg of the desk. "Gentlemen, that will be enough. Miss Tamhill, may I suggest that you think long and hard before you refuse the viscount's proposal. Obviously there is affection between you."

Before Prudence could respond, Rathbone stepped in.

"Perhaps if I were allowed a few minutes alone with the lady."

"Absolutely not," Worley decreed. "You'll not get her alone again, not for so much as a minute."

"I'll go with them," Lionel volunteered, looking tired and ready for a settlement in any arena. "It's light enough to walk in the garden. I won't let them out of my sight."

"If they're to be married, they'll have to learn to talk to one another sooner or later," Morland interjected.

He walked to the French doors that opened onto a small terrace. Opening them, he stepped aside. "A short walk with positive results," he said, directing the words to Rathbone. "The others will be downstairs soon."

"Yes, Your Grace."

Rathbone motioned for Prudence to walk in front of him. A soft wind rose, parting the branches of the nearby trees, so that long shafts of sunlight fell over her as she stepped onto the veranda. It seemed a sign of some sort, a portent that she was about to enter a new and uncertain world.

The brutal facts couldn't be ignored. Society might be treated satirically by those beyond its reach, but the code it demanded was too well established to be rebuffed easily by those who traveled its roads. A woman, especially, could go from respectable to scandalous in less time than it took for the gossips to gather for afternoon tea.

"Would you prefer to walk or sit?" Rathbone asked, indicating a bench near a cluster of dew-kissed lilac bushes.

Opposite the small garden, apple trees were exploding with pink blossoms, spreading a net of color as sunlight began to fill the green cracks and crevices of the garden.

Prudence walked to the bench and sat down. Lionel took himself a discreet distance away.

"I was serious when I said I won't be forced into marriage," she told Rathbone.

Standing next to the bench, he merely looked at her.

"There are options, my lord."

"Those options being?"

"An engagement for form's sake. A lengthy engagement," she said, lifting her chin to emphasize her resolve. "My next birthday will put me beyond Worley's guardianship. I will be independent of anyone's control."

"So we're to be engaged, only to have you leave me standing at the altar in . . . When is your birthday?"

"October."

He shook his head. "Unfortunately, waiting until October isn't an option either one of us is to be allowed. The duke wants you married immediately."

"That's preposterous! Weddings frequently take place a year from the announced engagement."

"I hate to disillusion you, sweetheart, but there's nothing normal about our situation. In case you haven't noticed, you've been compromised."

"You know very well that isn't true."

"Do I? Our interlude in the gazebo went beyond a kiss. In fact, it would have gone much further had I not had a rush of common sense."

The truth was embarrassing, but it was the truth. It had been Rathbone who had walked away that night, not she. Still, Prudence defended her decision. "Common sense should tell you that a marriage between us would be disastrous," she retorted. "We have nothing in common, nothing upon which to base a relationship that will last a lifetime."

"I disagree. Admittedly, some compromise will be required. And although you'd rather choke than admit it, you do like me."

"At the moment, I can't think of anyone I dislike more."

The mischievous glint returned to his eyes. He was remembering the way he'd kissed her, the way she'd kissed him back. As angry as she was, Prudence couldn't help noticing how handsome he looked in the morning light. His hair fell across his forehead in a casual manner that belied the look in his eyes.

Knowing she was doomed to failure if she allowed him to control the conversation, Prudence asked the one question that would put him on the defensive. "Why did you come to my room?"

There was no change in his expression, but she did note a slight stiffening in his posture.

"Why do you think I came to your room?"

"Don't think to dissuade me, my lord. I want an honest answer, if you please."

He considered her for a moment, his eyes bright with energy, as if his mind were racing behind them. "Very well, but first you must promise that you won't become hysterical or slap my face and cause poor Lionel to come running."

"I am not a female who becomes hysterical, my lord. Were that the case, I would have ventured into that state immediately upon seeing my guardian standing in the doorway of my bedroom."

He sat down then, making sure to leave enough space between them to satisfy their chaperone. "I came for the ring."

Prudence lifted her hand away from the arm of the wrought-iron bench. The ruby caught the morning light, sparkling red against the gold that encircled it. "This ring?"

"Yes."

"Why?"

"Are you acquainted with Sir Willard Ramsbury?"

She gave him an inquiring look. "The baronet? I've heard of him, of course. His reputation nearly exceeds your own, but I have no personal knowledge of him.

What has he to do with a ring that belonged to my mother?"

"He wagered I wouldn't be able to get it off your hand." There, he'd done it, confessed all. "I was drunk," he continued in the same vein of sincerity, "not excessively, but I had been drinking and my pride was still suffering from . . . shall we say, several frustrating encounters with a very lovely young woman."

The casualness of his explanation cut like a knife. When Prudence finally spoke, the condemning nature of her words said what her whispered tones couldn't. "So you wagered my reputation? My very future?"

She sat very still, unable to believe that she'd been so gullible as to think that the time she and Rathbone had spent together had actually meant something to the man. She turned away from him to stare across the lawn to where the branches of a weeping willow swept the ground.

Tears threatened, but Prudence forced them back. For a few days, infatuation had blinded her into thinking that the man might actually have feelings for her, real feelings, worthy feelings. To discover that she was no more than a card in a game of chance was far more humiliating than being found on the floor in her nightgown.

"How much?" she finally demanded.

"Five thousand pounds if I produced the ring. Ten thousand to be forfeited if I didn't."

Even confessing what most men would not, Rathbone was able to sit beside her without looking awkward or defeated. But then, why should he appear either way? By marrying her, he'd not only gain the required wife and eventually the necessary heir, but a fortune that would more than compensate for the ten thousand pounds he'd be obliged to hand over to Ramsbury.

"You're despicable. I've been nothing but a pawn in an amusing little game. Have you enjoyed it, my lord? Of course you have. It is what you do best, isn't it? Seducing women into thinking themselves important to you, into thinking that you hold them in some regard."

Nothing that Worley or Morland had said to him in the library—and they'd had plenty to say—carried the sting of Prudence's words. Rathbone flinched under their impact, but all he could say was, "I'm sorry."

"Yes, I suppose you are, having *lost* the wager." She glared at him. "You thought to sneak into my room, to steal from me, and then to traipse back to London and have a good laugh. Pity—had I known that a mere ruby would have sent you from my sight, I would have willingly gifted it."

Rathbone said nothing in answer to the charge except, "I wasn't thinking about the ring when I kissed you."

For a moment, plain facts and a truth that cut with razor sharpness turned Prudence silent. A change came over her, a subtle transformation but a critical one that Rathbone recognized immediately.

"You demanded honesty," he said. "I gave it. But not all of it. I acted foolishly and pridefully, but there is more between us than a wager. Look at me," he demanded in a husky whisper. "Look at me and tell me that you don't feel it too."

Prudence forced herself to meet his gaze. "Go away, my lord. I have no wish to ever set eyes on you again."

"I cannot."

"Cannot or will not? Do you have need of the Tamhill fortune, after all?"

"I have need of nothing but your consent to become my wife." His expression appeared sincere. There was no mocking smile, no mischievous twinkle in his eyes. "If I continue being honest, then I have to say that you intrigue me, Miss Tamhill. I enjoy your company."

"That is hardly a reason for marriage."

"Perhaps not, but in my case, it is a rarity. I am all the things you suspect me of being, but I am not a liar. I think we will do well together, if our passion for one another is any indication."

Prudence wanted to scream, to run from the garden and hide in some abandoned corner of the house where she could cry out her humiliation, but she knew he hadn't spoken the real *truth* to her guardian or to Lionel. If they found out, it would only harden their resolve to see her married as soon as possible, if not to Rathbone, then to Frederick.

Poor Frederick. He had no idea how his own future hung in the balance this fine spring morning. He was the solution to her problem. At least Frederick was truly fond of her—a brother's love, but better than no love at all.

"I know what you're thinking," Rathbone said. "But it isn't going to happen. I was the man found in your room. I'll be the man you marry."

"Why? You have no feelings for me," she retorted, none too politely. "What possible difference can it make to you? You've lost ten thousand pounds. A sizeable sum, I admit, but due recompense for your behavior. Were I to weigh the judgment, it would be ten times that amount."

His expression changed then, hardening as if she had slapped him. "Since you prize honesty so much, shall I return to the library and divulge *all* to His Grace?

Shall I tell him that you melted in my arms the night of Lady Winthrop's ball, that you would have let me do anything to you, that you relented just as easily upstairs? Would Frederick be willing to marry you if I told him exactly what has happened between us? Better yet, shall I accept the challenge that Lionel is itching to issue? Would you like me to fight for you, Miss Tamhill, to bloody my knuckles or set about loading my father's dueling pistols?"

"Don't be ridiculous."

"Then accept that I'm the man you're going to marry."

She knew well what he was thinking: that the possibility of scandal was one she would avoid at all cost, not only for herself but also for the duke and his family; that she'd concede to do the right and honorable thing, just as he had conceded.

"When I marry," she said, using a tone that implied her countless doubts, "it will not be to a man who holds fidelity in light regard. Nor will it be to a gambler or carouser. Marriage requires more than passion, my lord."

"Were I not ready to set certain things behind me, no one could force me to offer you marriage," he replied. "As for fidelity, I'm as capable of it as any man."

"Are you saying that you intend to be a faithful husband?"

"Given the right incentive."

The man was impossible. No matter what she said, his response brought them right back to where they had started—in each other's arms.

Prudence looked toward Lionel, still standing unobtrusively nearby. She saw him with an air of remoteness, as she was seeing everything else around her—through a confusing veil of blurred emotions. She must be mad, but in that madness, she knew she couldn't allow Frederick to be summoned home to salvage her reputation.

"I have one more question," she said, returning her gaze to the viscount.

"Ask it, then."

"This wager—when did it take place?"

He gave her a smile that came close to melting her heart. "After the Winthrop ball. Nearly a full week later."

At least she hadn't been misused from the start. Despite her current anger, Prudence couldn't push away the dismaying memory of his hands on her body, of the way he'd made her feel and continued to make her feel with only a glance of his blue eyes.

Her continued silence became a part of the hush and harmony of early morning.

"If you must know," he said, "the wager had nothing to do with stealing the ring. I was to gain it honorably."

"How?"

"By gaining your trust. It was to be a token of your friendship."

Seconds crawled by as a thousand thoughts raced through Prudence's head. But only one took hold—the very one she was loath to admit. She was falling in love with Rathbone. It was a feeling that could not be born out by any outward evidence. Love, after all, was a product of the unseen heart.

The admission brought both elation and dread. Love was the reason she was fighting against an arranged marriage, a marriage that would give her the man she wanted. She didn't want a lover; she wanted to be loved.

How ironic life could be.

She looked at the ring on her finger. Dare she do what her mother had done, not illicitly, but within the honored bonds of marriage? Dare she love? And in loving, hope that she could bring this man to love her in return? It was a gamble far more challenging than the one Rathbone had accepted from Ramsbury.

When her gaze lifted to dwell on the viscount, all Prudence could feel was love and longing and an aching emptiness that demanded she stop using her head and listen to her heart.

With perceptible reluctance, she gave him her hand.

He smiled, then lifted it to his lips in a show of gallantry and affirmation.

"Prudence?" Lionel said, making sure he wasn't mistaking the significance of what he was witnessing.

"Lionel, please tell Uncle Horace that I have accepted Lord Rathbone's proposal."

"You will not regret your decision," Rathbone vowed. There were no signs of the braggadocio one might expect of a man set on winning a wager so underhandedly.

"I pray not, my lord," Prudence replied, with characteristic candor. For a moment the petulance in her voice was matched by the expression on her face, an expression that was immediately replaced by a beautiful smile. "I can only hope that the wager upon which you have based your proposal isn't one you'll find yourself regretting even more sorrowfully. You are right in saying that I shouldn't marry Freddie. I'm far too fond of him to wish him anything but the greatest of happiness."

"While I, on the other hand, deserve nothing but misery."

"Exactly."

He looked at her then as if he wanted to throttle her, but Prudence refused to be intimidated. She had every right to be angry. The man needed to be taught a lesson, and who better to teach it than the woman who loved him?

"There are details still to be addressed," he said. "My mother would be overjoyed to have the wedding take place at King's Crossing."

"I've heard of your home," she said. "Felicity told me it is beautiful."

"It's near Ledbury in Herefordshire, a monstrosity of a house, full of draughts and inconveniences. It was built by a Saxon ancestor. The chapel has a medieval flair, but I think it suitable for a wedding."

Prudence risked a look into his eyes, knowing how easy it was to get lost in them. "Your mother won't find the presence of a wife intrusive?"

Rathbone's smile broadened into a devilish grin, the curve of his lips full of unconscious invitation. "I assure you, she'll move into the dower house most willingly."

Determined to have the last word, Prudence removed the ruby ring from her finger. "Please accept this as a token of my . . . of *our* new friendship."

Rathbone didn't seem to know what to do with the ring when she placed it in the palm of his hand. It was a small victory, but a victory nevertheless.

"Don't try to reason it out, my lord. There is no modicum of logic to be found in my behavior. You will, of course, donate your misgotten gains to charity. Five thousand pounds should make for a memorable penance. The ring was my mother's, and therefore very precious to me. Please return it as soon as your business with Lord Ramsbury is concluded."

"There's still the little matter of our wedding day," Rathbone said as he tucked her mother's ring into his vest pocket. "Would a month from today give you enough time to acclimate yourself to becoming my wife?"

"A century wouldn't be enough, my lord," she answered, not sparing him the sharp edge of her tongue. "But knowing my guardian as I do, a month should suit his purpose."

"And what of your purpose? Shall I prepare myself to greet a bride when you arrive at King's Crossing—or an enemy?"

Flashing another smile, Prudence replied, "I should say a little of both."

CHAPTER 10

Rathbone tallied the last line in the ledger before closing it. His desk was littered with correspondence, bills from the village shops, and numerous invitations for parties and summer balls from his country neighbors, each wanting to be the first to entertain the new viscountess.

Unfazed by the activities that had servants dashing up and down the stairs of King's Crossing—the wedding was to be at week's end—he laced his hands behind his head and stretched the kinks from his back. The taking of a wife was proving to be more business than pleasure.

After returning to London and claiming his winnings from an astonished and overconfident Ramsbury, he had immediately met with his solicitors. That meeting had been followed by several others, resulting in a stack of documents to be reviewed before the final marriage contract could be signed. The size of Prudence's inheritance was as shocking as the complexity of it.

Tamhill Shipping had thirty-four ships at sea and ten

more currently bobbing on the tide in Thames Harbor. Most were steamers, but there were still clippers used in the Eastern trade. The main ports of call for the Mediterranean fleet were Lisbon, Naples, Cairo, and Constantinople. Atlantic steamers visited the docks of New York, Boston, Charleston, and Savannah, with another segment of ships reserved for the Caribbean Islands. The total cargo tonnage was staggering.

As he rose from his desk, Rathbone smiled. No wonder the duke had accused him of seducing Prudence for her inheritance. It was an impressive dowry. But not as impressive as the lady herself.

Exhilaration caught him as he turned his mind from business to the future. Instead of the expected dread, Rathbone felt only anticipation. Despite the circumstance and his former reluctance to marry, he had to admit that Prudence would make him an excellent wife. She was not a woman given to the glory of her own reflection, a lady consumed by her own wants and wishes, but rather, one who presented herself with assurance and candor.

The more he thought about it, the more he realized the future held its own rewards. When he became a married man, there would be no more brief affairs terminated because boredom reclaimed his attention. No more furtive interludes or drunken follies. Admittedly tired of playing with such fire, he now faced a different sort of challenge—that of being a husband.

When the butler announced that Lord Roebourne, the Duke of Worley's eldest son, had arrived, Rathbone greeted him with a firm handshake. "I've been expecting you."

Frederick Delmont, Lord Roebourne, was the real guardian of the Tamhill fortune, having taken over the responsibility when the demand for travel had taxed his father's health.

It wasn't until the library doors were closed and drinks poured that Frederick spoke his mind. "Blasted inconvenient to be rousted out of one's bed and told to take to the road immediately. I arrived at North Hill thinking Father was on his deathbed, only to be told that Prudence had been discovered on the floor, swathed in bed linens, with you of all people."

"My apologies," Rathbone said. He liked Frederick and always had. "As for being discovered on the floor, it was not my intention to cause the lady embarrassment."

"Knowing you as I do, your intentions need no explanation."

The duke's elder son was a tall man, dark of hair, with eyes that were more hazel than green. His physical features matched his strength of character. His glittering eyes, heavy lidded, missed nothing—or so it seemed to the men who did business with him.

With catlike precision he scanned Rathbone's face, looking for any sign that the viscount had not resigned himself to his fate.

"You want her for yourself," Rathbone said, determined to find out if what the duke had said was true, that Freddie would marry Prudence without hesitation.

"Father's been playing matchmaker between the two of us since Prudence left the schoolroom. Why do you think I keep myself in Portsmouth most of the Season? I adore the girl, but I also remember when she wore pinafores and braids."

"Then you aren't opposed to the marriage."

"No. Of course, that doesn't mean you're going to have an easy time of it. Pru's a stubborn little chit. Not an ounce of give in her when she sets her mind to something."

"She did agree to marry me," Rathbone pointed out.

"That's the surprising part," Freddie told him after lighting a cigar and settling himself into an armchair. "Gave me a talking to before I left North Hill. I'm to put my most gracious foot forward while I'm here and to tend to business. No poking my nose in where it doesn't belong."

"Sound advice."

"However," Freddie said more grimly, "it's universally known that if there is anything worth seeing, an Englishman wants to see it, and if there's anything worth knowing, Society demands full knowledge. That said, may I suggest that you apply yourself to this marriage as fervently as you have applied yourself to folly in the past? While I admit not wanting to marry Prudence, her happiness is important to me."

Rathbone knew the rules as well as anyone. Faithfulness to one's fiancée or even one's wife wasn't required, nor was it expected, as long as caution was used. "Discretion above all things" was the motto of the times. Scandal was to be avoided and the niceties of social behavior preserved to keep one's public face eminently respectable. It was the eleventh commandment behind which many a man shielded himself.

He responded by saying, "From what I can see, managing Tamhill Shipping and taking a wife will monopolize my time."

"The fleet has certainly consumed my life for the last few years," Freddie replied, seemingly satisfied by the response. "I have six managers, all seasoned captains, but I could use six more. As for a wife, better you than me. Though I doubt Father will cease his references to my obligations. Damned tiring to be told that you need to provide an heir before you've even inherited the title."

"His Grace isn't getting any younger," Rathbone said, amazed at his change in attitude. "Then again, you aren't much older than I. Enjoy yourself for a time."

"I fully intend to now that Tamhill is being shifted from my shoulders onto yours."

The balance of the afternoon was spent discussing business. After issuing an invitation for Freddie to stay for dinner, Rathbone took to the stables. The sky was unbelievably blue and there were few things finer than having a good horse and the time to ride for the pure pleasure of it.

He returned in time to change for dinner, only to find his mother waiting. As always, she was smartly dressed, and looking younger than her fifty-four years.

"I understand Lord Roebourne has been shown to one of the guest rooms," she said, turning her head so her son could place a kiss on her cheek.

"Yes."

"Then everything's settled."

"All but saying the vows."

Rathbone followed her into one of the small parlors off the foyer. Once they were seated, she turned toward him. "I know you've received enough lectures on the subject, Benjamin, but I so want to believe that you are looking to this marriage with the right attitude."

"That attitude being?" he asked, knowing exactly what she meant. He was still examining his feelings for Prudence, and while desire was definitely among them, he was having a bit of trouble sorting out the rest.

"I'm certain you'll accommodate yourself to marriage just as your father did."

"Your confidence is appreciated."

She drew back and looked at him, her gaze as sharp as it had been when he was a small boy doing his best to hide an adventure that was certain to gain him a scolding.

"You're your father's son. He was just as daring as you before our marriage, but I know he was faithful to me afterward."

"He adored you."

"He *loved* me. And don't scowl. The word isn't blasphemous."

"I'm not scowling."

"You're looking doubtful."

"Not about Father's devotion to you."

"That's exactly what I'm talking about," his mother scoffed. "You can't even say the word. Your father *loved* me, as I did him."

"I'm glad."

"You're impossible. But I have every faith that Prudence will have you feeling differently before the year is out."

"Perhaps," he conceded.

No matter how often he told himself that he was doing the honorable thing for nobility itself, Rathbone couldn't shake the feeling that ever since Prudence had stepped into his life, right out of the blue, he had changed somehow. As the days ticked on, and spring melted into summer, the feeling remained, forcing him to admit that the change was a permanent one.

When he finished discussing some of the wedding details with his mother, none of which interested him as much as the bride herself, Rathbone resigned himself to counting the hours until Prudence became his lawful wife.

The coming of summer had brought longer days and warmer nights, many of which Prudence had spent thinking of the man she was to marry. The realization that she loved Rathbone had left her thunderstruck, and at the same time filled with a joy she had yet to fully comprehend. But one thing she did know—under no circumstances could she let the viscount know that he had gained the better of her by the taking of her heart. Not until she was sure that she held his heart in return.

She stood at the window, but it wasn't the familiar fields surrounding North Hill that held her gaze. She was at King's Crossing. Tomorrow she would become the new mistress, wife to the Viscount Rathbone.

She had yet to see him, being shown instead to a small suite where she took her supper on a tray while the rest of the guests gathered in the huge formal dining room. To Prudence, the time alone was a blessing.

Instead of becoming her sanctuary, North Hill had become a prison. The duke had insisted that her trousseau be fitted there instead of London, which had prevented her from seeking out the services of the Bow Street Runner she had hoped to employ.

Suddenly feeling as if she had more questions than answers, Prudence concentrated her thought on the huge house that was her new home.

King's Crossing had never seen a battle, but something had inspired its builder to festoon parts of it with turrets and watchtowers. It was an impressive piece of architecture, with arched doorways and massive stone fireplaces. On the front lawn, circled by a graveled drive and bordered by flowerbeds, was a large pond, in the center of which stood a statue that could be any one of a dozen mythological goddesses.

"I hope you like your new home."

Prudence swirled around to find Rathbone standing only a few feet away. She hadn't heard him enter the room, which seemed impossible given his forceful presence now. She could feel it weighing upon her, creating a tangible heat.

She couldn't help but be impressed by his appearance. Her gaze swept over him, taking in the thick waves of golden hair, his broad shoulders, his strong jaw. He even stood beautifully, tall and straight like a soldier.

His eyes glinted, not with amusement, but with sparking interest. They reminded Prudence of a tiger's, or how a tiger's might look when scenting a prey. Since she was that prey, his gaze gave her a moment's pause. When she did speak, it was with a resolute tone.

"It seems, my lord, that you have a bad habit of entering a lady's boudoir without knocking. One would hope the habit doesn't continue after you find yourself a married man."

With a slight shrug that reflected no shame in how he'd lived his life up to now, Rathbone moved toward her. His eyes flashed as he reached out to touch her cheek. "Hello."

The simple word sent a shiver of anticipation through Prudence's body. Never had a man had such power over her.

"I want to kiss you."

Again, the simplicity of his words moved her as no others could. It was dangerous to tease a tiger, but Prudence couldn't resist. "Just one kiss."

He smiled then, that rakish, devil-may-care smile that she had carried in her mind and heart for four long weeks.

Another touch, a long caress of his fingertips against her cheek that did not stop until he reached the corner of her mouth. The sheer catlike comfort of it set her senses to spinning.

When he stepped even closer, Prudence didn't pull away as she should have, but held perfectly still as he lowered his mouth to hers. She knew love was still far away, overshadowed by passion, but she couldn't prevent herself from responding to his kiss. When Rathbone finally released her, she stared into eyes darkened by emotions she desperately wanted to understand.

"I've missed you." His voice held a tenderness she had never heard from him before. He kissed her temple, where a tendril of brown hair curled. "We're to be married tomorrow."

"All the more reason you shouldn't be here," she found the strength to say. "Uncle Horace has only just reconciled himself to our marriage. I hate to think what he might do were he to find you in my room again."

"Engaged couples aren't expected to act like strangers," he said, placing another kiss against the corner of her mouth. "Admit it—you've missed me."

The smugness of his words brought Prudence's wits into play. She pushed herself away from him. "Don't think to ply your charms again, my lord. The circumstances are vastly different now from what they were before."

"We are to be married," he reminded her.

"At your insistence, not mine."

"With your agreement."

She moved a step away from him to gather her composure before he destroyed it with another kiss. She'd spent weeks thinking about him, remembering the way he'd looked, the sound of his voice, the feel of his hands on her body.

She'd warned herself against what she was feeling now, standing in the same room with him, looking into those incredible blue eyes, warned herself against giving in too easily. She'd listened to her heart when she'd agreed to marry him; this time she needed to listen to her head.

"I promised to return this." He reached into the pocket of his vest to produce her mother's ring. "St. Giles Orphanage has a new benefactor."

She held out her hand, but instead of dropping the ring into her open palm, he slipped it on her finger, then raised her hand to his mouth. Prudence flinched as his tongue licked across the bridge of her knuckles.

"I had your wedding ring made to compliment the ruby," he said. "I hope you like it."

"I'm sure I will." She turned away from him to lower her head and smell the light scent of the roses that had been placed on a table near the window.

He was coming perilously close to breaching her defenses. One more step, and she'd be in danger of surrendering again. She refused to look at him for the longest while, feeling oddly naked, and imagining that if she did meet his gaze he would be able to see right through her, down to where her heart thumped heavily in her chest.

Rathbone suddenly realized that his bride-to-be wasn't all that happy to see him. It didn't set well. He'd been living like a monk since that first night in London, a state that didn't suit his natural inclinations at all.

Just how to proceed puzzled him—another rarity since he'd never had trouble keeping a woman in his arms before.

It was a reasonable thing, having a nervous bride. King's Crossing was a massive house, and strange to her, but Rathbone sensed it was more than the new surroundings. He was not so foolish as to think that Prudence would submit easily to his authority, but knowing her passionate nature, he expected more than a cold shoulder after so hot a kiss.

A breeze ruffled the lace curtains behind her. She

looked at him, her gaze as strong as the desire he'd felt while holding her in his arms.

Remembering the day he'd found her in Green Park, he was struck by the fact that he still had no notion why she had gone there. Thinking it over, he admitted more than a small degree of curiosity. But this was not the time to address it. Prudence was taxing his patience as it was, looking lovely and ever so kissable.

"Is there something else you wanted to discuss with me, my lord?"

"You do me an injustice," he said, moving to the bed, where he made himself comfortable on its edge, one hand resting against the poster. "We haven't seen each other for weeks. Haven't you anything to say to me? Not even a word of all that you've suffered since becoming my fiancée?"

"I fear my suffering has only begun," Prudence retorted, knowing he'd chosen to seat himself on the bed as a deliberate reminder of the night they'd been found together. "What of you, my lord—have you suffered from the meeting with the duke's solicitor? The amount of my inheritance has been called burdensome in the past."

His brow knitted in contemplation, then relaxed, as if he'd been mentally tallying her worth and found it satisfactory. "I think my shoulders can bear the weight."

His smugness irritated Prudence almost as much as the gleam in his eye.

He glanced at the small trunk sitting on the floor at the end of the bed. Its size reminded them both that the room in which they were meeting was only a temporary shelter. By this time tomorrow, they would be man and wife. Tomorrow night would find them sharing the same room, the same bed.

Disliking the idea of being patient, but knowing he must, Rathbone stood. "I suppose Mother already gave you a tour of the house."

It was a massive residence with its turrets and towers, its spreading wings and countless bedrooms, its banqueting halls and sprawling kitchens. The size of the house could be measured by the span of the crenellated roof, which amounted to just over three acres in all. Three acres under which a family proud in its heritage had resided for seven generations.

"Some of it," Prudence replied, recalling the sunburst of medieval swords displayed over the arched doorway of the main parlor. "It's lovely."

"I've made some renovations," he said. "But there's plenty of time to see them."

While Rathbone appeared casual, Prudence knew he had plotted each word. "What a wonderful way to frame our future," she replied dryly. "I do own property, my lord. Several properties, in fact. One of them is Tamhill Hall. A rather modest house of forty bedrooms. Ownership of the Hall reverted to me the day our marriage contract was signed. It is not part of Tamhill Shipping."

He left the bed, taking a step toward her.

"Thinking to desert me already," he said, his voice low but meaningful. "If that's the case, sweetheart, then I caution you to think again. While Tamhill Hall may be under your ownership, as my wife, you will be under mine."

"I'm not your wife yet."

"A small formality, since the wedding will take place in less than twenty-four hours."

Her chin went up and her eyes flashed. Instead of backing away from him, she took a step forward.

"A formality with lasting consequences," she replied

in a surprisingly hard voice. "Should you think to avoid those consequences, think again, my lord. I am not a woman willing to be made the fool."

Nothing was said for a long while. The quiet of the room was broken only by the whisper of a summer breeze. Rathbone's first impulse was to continue being patient, thinking things might yet sort themselves out. But his second impulse was stronger—to get Prudence back in his arms where she belonged.

Prudence stared into his steadfast blue eyes, knowing exactly what he was thinking. The man was a natural-born seducer. She was caught between the choice of explicitly asking him to leave the room, a discourtesy which would set a bad example of her tolerance, or risking another kiss. The first choice was out of the question, since she wasn't about to let him think that she was afraid of him, but the second offered no less risk.

"I would think a month sufficient time in which to reconcile yourself to our marriage," he said, while his gaze steadily and methodically stripped away her defenses.

"I agreed to marry you, my lord," she said, recalling the moment she had agreed all too clearly. The authenticity of her reasons made her heart pound even now. She was in love with the insufferable man. "But I did not agree to change, to become what you would have me be rather than who I am."

"I'm content to wed you as you are."

"What you know of me is more assumption than fact."

"I rarely make assumptions," he told her. "As for fact, I know enough to be satisfied that you will make me an amicable wife, once you resign yourself to the position."

"And what position will that be, my lord? While marriage may place me under your lawful authority, I have no intention of submitting my soul to your possession."

His smile was pure deviltry as he moved to close the gap between them. The expression warned her that countless women had tested their skills against him and lost. Her excitement over turning around to find him in the room churned with a new energy. She couldn't move.

"It isn't your soul I'm set on conquering."

His gaze never leaving hers, he slid his fingers into the thickness of her hair and gently, but insistently, drew her toward him until their lips touched.

The kiss was brief but potent.

"Look at me and tell me that you don't want to be my wife."

Of course she wanted to be his wife, but she was afraid. Afraid that loving him would cost more than she could give, afraid that before she found out who she really was, he'd possess so much of her that it wouldn't make a difference.

"Look at me and tell me you don't care for me."

"I—I can't . . ."

Triumph flickered in his eyes as he claimed her mouth again. The intimate exploration of his tongue caused Prudence's head to swim. Every nerve in her body became sensitive to his touch. She was aware of the blood coursing though her veins, of the echo of her heartbeat in her ears, of the heat of his hands as they moved down her back and around to hold her hips firmly against his body. Drawn by a force she had no will to deny, she returned the kiss.

Rathbone clasped her tighter against him; the kiss became more demanding as his role shifted from seducer to lover. He kissed her deeply, more thoroughly than he'd ever kissed her before, awakening desires that had been buried for weeks.

Her response to him was straining the limits of his

self-control. His own heart was hammering. Nothing would satisfy him but possessing her completely. As he trailed his lips down her neck to the starched lace of her collar, he silently cursed the hours that would have to pass before he could make her his wife.

Lifting his mouth, he looked at her, at her flushed face and the rosy fullness of her lips that betrayed how heartily he'd kissed her. What was she thinking behind those soft brown eyes?

Rathbone knew what he was thinking. He was remembering that night in the gazebo—how he'd bared her breasts to his touch, how she'd clung to him afterwards, trembling with desire.

In a vein that suggested he'd found her weakness, he whispered, "Until tomorrow and our wedding night."

Before Prudence could think of a suitable retort, he was gone. She leaned back against the windowsill, feeling the heat of the sun as it joined the sensual fire raging inside her body.

This would never do. She was going to have to find a way to keep her feelings from betraying her. But how was she to manage that when all the blasted man had to do was touch her?

Turning back to the window, she deliberated long and hard on the subject, but no answer came to mind—none but the option of making sure Rathbone didn't touch her again.

With their wedding day on the horizon, that seemed as likely as pigs learning to fly.

CHAPTER 11

Prudence stood at the open window of her new bedchamber. It was a lovely room, the only problem being the set of double doors that connected it to the master suite, behind which her husband was currently being attended to by his valet.

As soon as those attentions were complete, the doors connecting the two room would open and the bride would find herself becoming a wife.

Fiona had unlaced her and helped her prepare for bed, saying before she left that Prudence had only to pull the bell rope beside the fireplace should she need anything more. "It rings straight through to my room, ma'am."

Unfortunately, the one thing Prudence needed was beyond the maid's capability to give.

Leaving the window, she sat down at the vanity table to brush her hair. When uncoiled, her hair reached to her waist, its dark shade vivid against the white of her nightgown.

The bed, covered in blue and white, was clearly visible in the mirror. Prudence looked at the turned-down coverlet and fluffy pillows and felt the knot in her stomach tighten. Even when she was alone, tension filled the air.

She was alternately fearful and excited, her thoughts swinging like a pendulum between hope and the reality that while she was now a married woman, her husband had yet to mention love.

She was still sitting at the vanity table when Rathbone walked in, magnificent in a quilted robe of royal blue satin emblazoned with gold dragons. But Prudence didn't notice how handsome he looked. She was too busy telling herself that the upcoming night was the beginning of a new life, not the end.

Her gaze locked with his, and for a tempting moment, she thought of confessing her true feelings, her hopes and dreams and fears. But logic kept her silent. The man standing before her was a bridegroom come to claim his bride. He had little interest in conversation.

"I wondered how long your hair was," he said, ignoring the flash of panic in her eyes. "It's lovely."

Regardless of her silence, Rathbone knew his bride was a creature of passion. He was determined to make good use of that passion tonight, to put the match to the straw and watch it burn. He would woo her slowly, delaying the inevitable pleasure until she begged him to satisfy them both.

Moving toward the fireplace, he stood with his hands in his robe pockets, giving Prudence time to acclimate herself to the fact that he was her husband, that he was here in her bedroom because he had every right to be.

The silence palpable, Prudence looked about the room, thinking to offer him some refreshment, but there was none in sight.

"Searching for something?" he asked, his voice sounding all too calm against the throbbing echo of her heartbeat.

"I had thought to offer you a glass of champagne, my lord, but it seems there isn't any."

He held out his hand. "Come with me."

Frozen on the edge of indecision, Prudence stared at his outstretched fingers.

"You aren't afraid of me, are you?"

Her hair was loose, her face blushed with light from the gasoliers that framed the fireplace. As he stood looking at her, Rathbone felt the overwhelming need to touch her, to wrap his arms around her, to breathe in the scent of her skin. He'd been patient all day, observing the formalities of a bridegroom, but now he wanted to be a husband, to claim his bride as no other man would ever claim her.

"Come here," he said, wondering if it was fear or something else that had turned her suddenly shy.

She walked to where he was standing, accepting his hand.

Smiling, Rathbone clasped her hand securely in his own, then led her through the double doors. As expected, the adjacent room matched her suite in size and shape, but the ambiance was wholly masculine.

Prudence's gaze was immediately drawn to an elaborately carved tortoiseshell liquor cabinet, its doors inlaid with ebony and ivory. It was a magnificent piece of sixteenth-century craftsmanship. The walls of the room were painted a light brown and decorated with impressive landscapes. A medieval shield bearing the Rathbone coat of arms was displayed over the fireplace.

The gleam of brightly polished brass on the grate fenders added just the right touch of sparkle. The rest of the furniture was just as impressive: a Georgian-style clothespress with brass feet, two armchairs upholstered n wine-colored fabric, a Chippendale lowboy, and a marble-topped washstand.

The bed, a mammoth affair sitting atop a wooden dais, was canopied in dark green velvet. A matching coverlet had been turned down to reveal ivory bed linens.

Rathbone walked to the liquor cabinet and poured her a drink.

"Here, sip this," he said, passing the glass to her.

Prudence raised the glass to her mouth. The rich aroma of aged French cognac filled her nostrils. She sipped the drink, relishing the warming effect it had on her nerves.

She thought of all the times Rathbone had kissed her, of the way he'd touched her that night in the gazebo. She'd felt passion for him then. She felt it now, but tonight was different. This was their wedding night; she could give of herself without worry or regret.

"Don't be shy," he said, coming to stand directly in front of her. "We aren't strangers, after all."

"What are we then?"

"Husband and wife," he said succinctly.

Prudence lifted her gaze to meet his, vaguely aware that her body was turning traitor. She was his wife, and while she wasn't entirely sure how he thought of her, she was determined that her role in his life would take on a dimension he had yet to comprehend.

Taking the glass from her hand, he returned it to the table before drawing her into his arms. He kissed her lightly, repeatedly, creating a soft stirring deep within her.

Prudence tried to hold onto to her thoughts, to the resolve that had supported her throughout the day, but it vanished under his tender attack.

"Please," she finally whispered, unsure what she meant the word to express.

Lifting her in his arms, Rathbone walked toward the bed, his mind and body alert with a new consciousness. Marriage vows bound him to this woman in a way he'd never imagined possible. The simple, glimmering awareness stirred his blood.

He'd had lovers, had known passion. But what he was feeling tonight wasn't to be compared to past experiences. Prudence was his wife. The word formed images in his mind, but none that matched the look on his bride's face as her head came to rest against the pillow.

She reminded him of a newly awakened flower, soft and sweet and fragile. He smiled, then reached out to trace the curve of her lower lip. A living fire seemed to spark from his fingertips, and she flinched.

Not wanting to rush her, he chose a more coaxing game. He sat on the bed next to her, his hip pressing against the line of her upper thigh. He reached out and placed a hand upon her breast, brushing the nipple underneath the fine fabric of her gown with the back of his knuckle.

"Do you know how many times I've imagined you this in bed? How many nights I've thought of nothing but seeing every sweet inch of you?"

Prudence lay quietly under his gaze. Then his fingertips followed a path from the valley of her breasts to the slight rise of her lower stomach. Dear God, but this was torture. To lay so still when what she really wanted was to touch him in return.

His robe had parted over his chest, revealing crisp blond hair and bronzed skin over tight muscle. His eyes had grown dark, his gaze more concentrated.

"Do you like my touch?" he asked, gently squeezing her hip.

She swallowed hard, unable to form a coherent word. Lowering her gaze, she watched as his hand continued to caress her, his fingertips tracing the swell of her breasts, circling nipples that had grown hard.

"I think you do," he answered for her. "I think you like it very much. There's no shame in admitting it."

Unable to tolerate his touch without reciprocating, Prudence placed her hand over his, stilling its movements. "A husband doesn't need to seduce his wife, my lord. I'm prepared to do my duty."

"Duty be damned."

He left the bed. A moment later his robe was tossed to the floor. He stood in front of her, splendidly naked.

If he thought to intimidate her, he was wrong. She looked at him, at all of him, and although she found his attitude patronizing, like that of a benevolent schoolmaster, she couldn't help but be delighted that one of her fantasies was finally coming true.

Daring all, Prudence left the bed. Standing in front of him, she slowly undid the ribbons and buttons at the neckline of her gown. Then, with unpracticed seductiveness, she caught the hem of the gown and raised it up and over her head. Finally free of it, she dropped it on the floor.

Rathbone stared at her for the longest time, his gaze moving upward from her knees to pause at the dark triangle of curls between her legs, then higher to where her breasts were flushed and her nipples hardened by arousal. Her skin glowed, every luscious curve of her as perfectly formed as the petals of a flower.

Standing in front of him with her hair in disarray, her long legs bare and her dark eyes wide with an erotic blend of defiance and excitement, she was the most enchanting female he'd ever seen.

"Turn around," he said. "I want to see all of you."

Prudence did as he asked, shocked by her own wantonness. But then, passion was shocking. She could feel the heat rising beneath her skin, feel the anticipation pounding in perfect time with her heart. When she was facing him again, Rathbone smiled.

"You enjoy my boldness, my lord?"

"I enjoy a woman who isn't afraid to be bold," he replied candidly. "But I should have known your fondness for honesty would affect other parts of your personality."

"My personality has many facets."

"I look forward to discovering all of them," he said, his mouth curving into a faint smile. "Would you like the windows opened or closed?"

"Open," she said, desperately needing the cooling effects of the night's easterly breeze.

He turned down the lights, then drew back the draperies and opened the window. The merest sliver of moonlight spilled onto the carpeted floor.

Prudence prayed the darkness would last, needing the balm of its soft blackness to hide her nervousness, but it wasn't to be.

Rathbone walked to the table, his naked body a sleek shadow in the moonlight. The sound of a match being struck broke the silence, and soon two candles were burning.

Prudence climbed into bed and under the coverlet, lying absolutely still, her eyes closed, her arms resting at her sides.

A moment later, her husband joined her.

"I refuse to believe you to be shy," he said. "Open those beautiful brown eyes and look at me."

When she did, he touched one of her nipples, tentatively at first, then more insistently, until her body grew heavy with a need that ran all the way to her toes.

"You like being touched," he said, as his hand moved from her breast to the indentation of her navel. He paused there to circle it several times. When Prudence flexed her stomach muscles, he laughed. "You are a delight," he told her. "A delight I intend to enjoy inch by inch."

He began to stroke her, his hands brushing up and down her thighs, over her hips, then around to draw random circles on the soft skin of her belly. She heard the rustle of sheets as he moved, reaching down to repeat the pattern but starting at her knees this time, and then down again to her ankles. He was a versatile lover, using infinite care to arouse her.

When he finally placed a kiss on her stomach, Prudence clenched her hands in the bed linens. It was torture, this slow loving, this endless intoxication of the senses.

He kissed her navel, then higher and higher, his lips scorching her skin as they made their way to each breast to feast on a nipple, then higher still until he settled on her mouth. When he did, Prudence purred with pleasure.

It was all so beautiful. She was glowing deep inside, her body humming with arousal, her mind as weightless as a rainbow.

The kisses went on and on, first light and teasing, then deep and demanding. Kisses that fulfilled every want and need she'd ever imagined. Suddenly, her husband shifted his position, moving her tightly against him, rolling them both so she was lying on top of him, his erection pressed intimately against the junction of her thighs.

She touched him then, sliding her hands over his chest, delighting in the tautness of his muscles. Finding her breath, she whispered, "Do you like being touched, my lord?"

With a deep groan that was all the answer Prudence needed, his hands went into the dark cloud of her hair.

He tilted her head back, capturing her lips, kissing her hungrily. Then his touch was everywhere, on her breasts, her hips, her thighs, and in-between. He stroked her with a gentle persistence that made her bones melt and her limbs go weak.

While his fingers plied their magic, his teeth nipped at her breasts, biting the hardened crowns ever so gently, until the desire shimmering inside her became a full-fledged fire.

Unaware of anything but the earthy scent of the night and the musky perfume of their own bodies, Prudence matched the movement of her hips to the expert stroke of her husband's fingers.

"That's it," he whispered. "Ride my hand. Ride it, sweetheart. Let me please you."

And please her he did. Prudence twisted her hips, wanting more of his touch, demanding it as his fingers dipped and teased, probing then withdrawing, stroking that special place that made her feel as if she'd been struck by lightning.

Rathbone caught his breath at the urgency of desire that shot through him. Prudence was wet and ready, whispering his name, writhing against him—wanting him. Giving her no reprieve, his fingers continued to tease. He kissed her, tasting her mouth, her skin, slowly but surely bringing her passion to a boil.

"Good God, you're beautiful," he whispered against the silky softness of her throat.

Dipping deeper into her sweet well, he rubbed the inside of her channel with two fingers, then withdrew to circle the swollen nub. She went stiff for a moment, then trembled, the tiny shivers intensifying as he held her on the summit until the pleasure forced the air from her lungs and she went limp against his chest.

"There's more," he whispered, biting at her lips.

"Impossible," she murmured.

He rolled her onto her back and pushed his hands under her, lifting her hips as he nudged her legs apart with his knee. He placed himself at the entrance of her body, then slowly pressed forward.

"No, don't tighten your muscles. Relax and let me inside. It's going to be good, sweetheart. So damn good."

Brown eyes looked into blue as he joined their bodies.

For Prudence, the invasion of her husband's flesh was a feeling that stretched and filled and renewed her love.

For Rathbone, the slick complicity of their union was passion itself. He entered her slowly, as tense as a predator, stalking her heat, reading the pleasure in her eyes, smiling at the soft moan that escaped her as he pushed even deeper.

"Lift your hips," he told her. "Move with me, take me inside and hold me there for as long as you can."

"How?" she asked breathlessly.

He showed her with his hands, lifting her hips as he withdrew, pushing them down into the mattress as he thrust forward, moving with slow deliberation, forcing the pleasure to last while he taught her how to please him.

Together they found the perfect rhythm, urgent yet unhurried, their movements culminating in a pleasure so intense it brought tears to Prudence's eyes.

"That's it, sweetheart," he breathed heavily against her throat as the pleasure took hold too tightly for him to control it. "You're mine now. Give yourself to me."

Prudence thought of all that had happened between them, all that was happening this very instant and of their joined bodies and the pleasure that came from being male and female, husband and wife. When she looked into his eyes, she saw more than passion on the brink of exploding; she saw her life and the man who would shape it from this night until the day she died.

"Give yourself to me," she demanded before closing her eyes. Only then did she permit the whole of her love to be released in a shimmering miracle of body and soul.

Rathbone managed a smile just before the power of passion overcame him. His body went tense as he pushed deep one last time, his senses spiraling to a blinding climax that left him luxuriously weak.

In the silent moments that followed their lovemaking, Prudence impulsively lifted her left hand. The wedding ring, encrusted with diamonds and rubies, was paired perfectly with her mother's smaller ruby.

A bittersweet smile came to her face. She had never felt so happy or so sad. She couldn't bear the thought of slowly dissolving into a life that repeated the one her mother had lived, of existing within the bounds of matrimony but never feeling truly married.

She lay perfectly still, alone with her doubts, wishing she could look into her husband's mind and heart and know what he felt, what he was thinking. Could a man make love to a woman as passionately as he had made love to her and not *feel* something?

Of course he could. Rathbone's reputation spoke for itself. He was a passionate man accustomed to having a woman in his bed.

Suddenly afraid that she'd made the biggest mistake of her life, Prudence turned to look at the man she had married. His eyes were closed, his breathing even now, his chest rising and falling with the oblivion of sleep. A small smile played at the corners of his mouth, a mouth that could evoke such feelings, such desires.

She was sitting up, about to put her feet on the floor, when an arm encircled her waist.

"Where do you think you're going?" he asked, pulling her back into bed. He kissed the side of her neck, his breath warm against her skin.

Jostled from her inner thoughts, Prudence searched her mind for something to say, but the words needed to describe her decision could only betray her heart.

"I'd like to return to my room," she said, her voice taking on an edge of discontentment.

He moved, pinning her beneath him. "You belong in this room. With me."

"Do I?" she whispered, determined not to show her vulnerability. He'd satisfied all the longings and hungers of her life in one glorious, breathtaking night of love-making. But what she was feeling inside was so much more than that.

For a moment, Prudence almost choked on the very honor that bound Rathbone to her, when what she wanted was for him to love her as gluttonously as she did him. His eyes held her, and after a moment he smiled.

"You belong to me," he repeated. "In this room. In this bed."

"I've fulfilled my duty," she said, forcing the words out, knowing they'd cut into his pride. But if he didn't care for her, what difference did it make?

"Duty!"

Prudence untangled herself and left the bed, not looking at him until her nightgown had been found and pulled over her head.

"What the blazes are you talking about?" He pushed

the hair from his eyes and sat up. "You wanted it as much as I did."

Not denying the charge, Prudence walked to the doorway separating their rooms before turning to face him. Despite the passion he'd aroused in her earlier, she was cold on the inside. "You felt obliged to offer me marriage, my lord, and I felt obliged to accept."

His jaw tightened. Tossing the coverlet aside, he rose from the bed, magnificently naked and unquestionably aroused. His eyes glittered with fury, sparking like blue fire. "Obligation doesn't make a man hard, sweetheart, and it sure as hell doesn't make a woman wet."

The crudeness of his words cut to the bone. But before Prudence could walk out of the room, slamming the door behind her, she was swept up and into her husband's arms.

"I don't know what kind of game you're playing, but I won't be dangled from any woman's string and set to dancing."

That said, Prudence found herself being carried into her own room and tossed onto the bed. He stared down at her for a long moment, his expression set in stone.

"Don't touch me," she said, glaring back at him.

He laughed, a cold sarcastic laugh that pierced her heart. "Don't worry, sweetheart. I have no intention of *touching* you again tonight. Or any other night. When you're ready to be a real wife, you can bloody well knock on the door and say so."

CHAPTER 12

Rathbone sat in his study, his elbows propped on the desk and his fingers pressed to his temples, trying to massage away the weariness that had been with him since sunrise. It had been four days since he'd dumped his lovely wife onto her own mattress and spent the balance of his wedding night with a bottle of Irish whiskey.

He fixed his gaze across the room, the patterns in the carpet and furniture blurring as he concentrated on what he was seeing inside himself. Things he wasn't comfortable seeing or feeling. Things that he'd told himself weren't necessary for a man to be happy. But regardless of his intent, the memory of what it had been like to hold Prudence in his arms refused to be dislodged. Dark eyes that had shone with fear and passion. The taste of cognac when he'd kissed her. The sensation of her body accepting his.

Jostled out of his inner thoughts by the sound of servants in the hallway, Rathbone forced his attention back to the present. A pile of correspondence lay in front of him, an inventory report from the London warehouse of Tamhill Shipping. He'd tried to read it four times, but couldn't get beyond the second sentence. A set of ledgers and invoices were stacked on the corner of his desk. His steward would expect them reviewed and ready for a reply when they met later in the day.

A gust of summer wind blew through an open window, rustling the papers and caressing his face. Rathbone shuddered as though the warmth of the day was mocking him. Outside, beyond the stone walls of King's Crossing, the gardens were laden with roses showing their colorful faces to a bright, warm sun.

Inside, the master of the house was miserable.

"With good reason," he grumbled aloud. "I'm a married man with no wife in my bed."

The irony of it was enough to curl one side of his mouth. The reality of it was enough to make him furious. Three nights spent tossing side to side, with only brief intervals of sleep, added to his bad humor.

He knew he was being selfish in wanting Prudence back in his bed without regard to her own feelings, but he hadn't anticipated marriage turning him into a eunuch.

Determined to outlast his wife's stubbornness, he applied his attention to the work on his desk. He was halfway through the invoices when a knock on the door interrupted him.

"Yes, what is it?"

A footman opened the door, then replied. "A visitor, milord. From London."

The footman handed Rathbone a card that read, *Mr. John Fenstermaker.*

"What does he want?"

"Came all the way from London to see Lady Rathbone."

"Lady Rathbone. Which one? My mother or my wife?"

"The new viscountess, milord. Asked for her specifically, he did."

Having no idea how Prudence spent her time when she wasn't sleeping behind closed doors, Rathbone was forced to ask, "Where is my wife?"

"In the morning room, milord, meeting with cook and Mrs. Cutler."

Mrs. Cutler was the housekeeper, a tall woman who wore steel-rimmed spectacles that emphasized the darkness of her eyes. The glasses gave her an air of severity, but she was good-natured and, quite admirably, kept King's Crossing running like a well-oiled clock.

"Very well. Show Mr. Fenstermaker into the main parlor, then ask my wife to join us." The footman was halfway to the door when Rathbone altered his original instructions. "On second thought, give me a few minutes alone with the gentleman before informing Lady Rathbone that we have a visitor."

"Yes, milord."

The main parlor where Mr. Fenstermaker was waiting was a lavish but comfortable room that faced the front lawn. The chairs were covered in crimson velvet to match the Belter sofa. An armless chaise longue with a gold lap rug draped over the back caught the sunlight that streamed through a row of tall, arched windows. A fresh bowl of white and yellow chrysanthemums sat on a neighboring drum table.

Rathbone took a moment to study his guest. Mr. Fenstermaker was a gaunt man, standing rigid and erect in front of the fireplace. He was elderly, but nothing about his features gave the impression of infirmity. His face was as sharp as a hatchet, his eyes a steely gray.

His clothes were fashionably cut, a black frock coat worn with pin-striped trousers. Long thin fingers remained hooked behind his back as he turned to faced Rathbone.

"My lord," he said, bowing a balding head. "Please forgive the intrusion."

Rathbone looked at the card the footman had handed him. "Are you a man of business, Mr. Fenstermaker?"

"In a manner of speaking."

Rathbone's gaze grew more earnest. "Are you employed by Tamhill Shipping?"

"No."

"You are aware that I have only recently married, that Lady Rathbone has been my viscountess for less than a week."

"Yes, milord. Your marriage is the reason for my visit."

"In what way?"

A maid delivering a tray of tea and cakes delayed Mr. Fenstermaker's answer. Once the proprieties had been observed, Rathbone rephrased the question.

"What business have you to conduct at King's Crossing, sir?"

"The business is a small matter, nothing that will take an inordinate amount of time once Lady Rathbone joins us," Mr. Fenstermaker replied diplomatically. "I do apologize for interrupting your honeymoon, my lord, but my instructions were specific."

"And who gave these instructions?"

The older man, who looked for a moment as though he was going to say something, stirred his tea instead. When he finally replied to the question, it was with the same deliberate vagueness he had employed since his arrival. "I ask for your patience, my lord. I am an old man who will find the saying far easier if I have only to recite it once."

Rathbone hesitated. There was little use in insisting that as Prudence's husband, he had every right to know what kind of "business" Mr. Fenstermaker had traveled all the way from London to discuss. It was clear the old codger wasn't going to tell him anything until Prudence showed herself.

They sat silently as Mr. Fenstermaker stirred his tea with an odd air of distraction, as if he were used to waiting.

Fortunately, they waited only a few minutes before Prudence joined them. She looked slightly tired, as though she'd been sleeping as sparsely as her husband, but she was still eye-catching in a dress of deep peacock blue.

She walked regally into the room, casting only the most cursory of glances toward her husband before moving to where he was now standing, ready to present her to their guest.

"My dear," he said, slipping an arm casually about her waist as a silent reminder that while she might be able to avoid him in such a large house, there was no denying her status as his wife. "May I present Mr. John Fenstermaker, recently of London."

"Lady Rathbone, may I offer my congratulations on your marriage."

"Thank you."

"Mr. Fenstermaker has business to discuss," Rathbone said. He guided Prudence to the sofa. He smiled ruefully and sat down opposite her. "It seems that the business is with you."

"Me?" She looked toward their guest, the gaze of her dark eyes perfectly steady. "Does it involve my father's estate? If so, I will defer you to my husband. Lord Rathbone is now managing affairs for Tamhill Shipping."

"My business has no association with Tamhill Shipping," Mr. Fenstermaker told her. "I am here on a matter of property."

"What sort of property?"

"A small estate in Kent, on the coast between Dover and Folkestone."

"I know of no such property," Prudence said. Her voice altered slightly, but Rathbone couldn't gauge the reason, beyond that of being surprised by Mr. Fenstermaker's visit.

"The estate has been deeded in your name. The house hasn't been occupied for a number of years, but a staff of servants has been engaged to see it opened. The housekeeper's name is Mrs. Blaine, a woman of excellent reference. The grounds are small compared to King's Crossing, a mere sixty acres, but well situated, and the house is in good repair."

"Whatever are you talking about?" Prudence asked, looking toward Rathbone as if he might be able to explain. Shrugging his shoulders, he settled back in his chair, as curious now as his wife.

"The property is unencumbered," Mr. Fenstermaker told her, "the deed properly registered by me on the tenth of this month. Should you care to visit, I will inform Mrs. Blaine so that all is ready upon your arrival."

"Deeded to me by whom?"

Rathbone noticed that when she spoke, Prudence reached down to slowly turn her wedding ring. It was an unconscious gesture, but he couldn't help but wonder if she found wearing it a discomfort.

"The property is yours to do with as you may," Mr. Fenstermaker continued. "It is a very nice square of land, and the house well built. I'm sure it would take little effort to find a buyer should you wish to dispose of it."

"Sell it? I didn't even know it existed until today," Prudence replied somewhat tartly. "I'm sorry, I don't mean to be rude, but it does come as a surprise that someone, whose name I have yet to discern, has given me an estate in Kent."

Rathbone decided it was time to intervene. "My wife's surprise is understandable. One does not simply gift another person an estate, large or small, without motivation or explanation."

"The reason is not mine to say," Mr. Fenstermaker replied, bestowing a placid smile upon them. "My services were retained to see to the transfer of the property and to the hiring of a suitable housekeeper and staff."

"Retained by whom?" Rathbone inquired.

"I'm not at liberty to say."

"This is ridiculous," Prudence announced. "Who would want to give me an estate when it's common knowledge that I've recently inherited a small fortune?"

Mr. Fenstermaker reached down for the small leather case he had brought with him. "As I said, the deed is unencumbered." He pulled out several sheaves of papers, sorting them into a presentable order before passing them to Prudence.

She studied them, then, to Rathbone's surprise, passed them to him. "This shows the previous owner of the property as yourself, Mr. Fenstermaker."

"I have held the property in trust for several years."

"How many years, and why?" Prudence asked.

The man from London remained mute.

Prudence stood up and started pacing. It was impossible not to notice the spark of intense interest in her eyes, as if she were about to explode with questions. It was masked a moment later, but not before she inquired, "Does this have anything to do with my mother?"

"Not to my knowledge," Mr. Fenstermaker said succinctly. "I apologize if my answers aren't satisfactory, Lady Rathbone, but I assure you, they are as truthful as I can make them."

"Why the secrecy?" Rathbone asked. "I have to agree with my wife. None of this makes any sense."

"I do not question the reasoning of my clients, my lord; I simply carry out their instructions. It is the wish of this particular party to remain anonymous. Therefore, I am obliged to withhold the name." The leather case was closed. "The property is Lady Rathbone's to deal with as she pleases."

"And that's that," Prudence remarked.

"And that is that," Mr. Fenstermaker replied. He came to his feet and prepared to take his leave.

"Will you not stay for supper?" Prudence asked.

"I would not think to impose on a couple so newly married, Your Ladyship, but I thank you for the invitation."

"I'll see you to the door," Rathbone said.

"That isn't necessary, my lord. I can make my own way out."

Prudence moved to the window, leaving her husband to see Mr. Fenstermaker to the parlor door, where a footman was ready to fetch the man's hat and gloves. She looked through the mullioned panes to the wooded area that surrounded the lawn. The oldest of the ancient trees were gnarled by the years, with forked trunks tarred over where branches had been lopped off by conscientious gardeners.

Today the lush grass beneath the trees was starred with white and yellow wildflowers. A wild hare was poised under the shelter of a sprawling oak, seemingly content to remain still and watch the fleecy pyramids of cloud pass overhead, their shadows swarming across the green lawn like the wings of an enormous bird.

"A most unusual man, our Mr. Fenstermaker," her husband remarked, interrupting her private thoughts. "Bearing a most unusual wedding present."

Prudence turned away from the window, her mind and body alert to the fact that she and Rathbone were once again alone behind a closed door.

The last few days had been endless, but no weight of circumstances could entirely interrupt life at King's Crossing. The huge house was like a great heart that went on beating inexhaustibly. There were meals to be prepared and served, beds to be freshened, linens to be washed, floors to be scrubbed, furniture to be polished, clocks to be wound, and duties to be performed.

The most difficult of those duties was appearing, for appearance's sake, to be getting along blissfully with the man she had married. She ached from smiling when what she wanted to do was scream with frustration.

"I take it you were as surprised by his announcement as I," Rathbone said.

"Bewildered," she admitted. She looked into his eyes and felt a sudden, strange relief that she hadn't received the news alone. "I can't imagine why anyone would want to give me property in Kent."

"Can't you?" He returned her gaze for moment. "I'm beginning to think you a complete mystery, madam."

"There's nothing mysterious about me," she said, certain he could see through the falsehood.

Her life had begun with a mystery—a father still waiting unidentified. And now she had a nameless benefactor. Dare she hope that they were one and the same, that the man who had once loved her mother might be, in his own way, reaching out to her now? All she could do was hope.

"As I recall, our first meeting was under rather mysterious circumstances," her husband said. He was observing her closely, like a hunter watching his quarry, intent and a bit quizzical, slyly measuring his effect on her. "You have yet to tell me what you were doing in Green Park."

Suddenly impatient with pretense, Prudence recalled the look in her husband's eyes when she'd stood naked in front of him on their wedding night. There had been no slyness then, no steely gaze. His eyes had warmed with desire. His embrace had been tender, his lovemaking an experience she would never forget.

Regardless of the rift between them now, a gap she had created herself, she was still his wife, and a married woman was no longer a singular individual, but part of a pair. With that thought in mind, she met his gaze.

"I was in Green Park to meet a man, a jeweler," she said, wondering what her husband would think of the truth when it was finally presented to him.

"One normally meets with a jeweler in his shop."

"Yes, well, that is where I met him the first time."

"A young, handsome shopkeeper then."

Prudence gave him a slow, lazy smile. "An elderly craftsman who fashioned the ring you showed such an interest in before we were married."

Her husband received the remark with a shrug, appearing only mildly chagrined. "Why a meeting in Green Park?"

Prudence looked at him, then at the large painting over the fireplace, a bold depiction of the Battle of Trafalgar in a gilt frame. In her mind, she tried to see Rathbone as the man who had marched across the street and hauled her back to his carriage—a rakish, overconfident womanizer whose charm could sway the most determined heart. It couldn't be done. All she could see was the man who had kissed her so tenderly as they stood by the garden gate.

"Is there something you want to tell me?" he asked, closing the distance between them. "I am your husband."

"Yes, you are that." She smiled fleetingly before turning her gaze away from the painting, then to the window, then finally back to him. "While you had possession of my mother's ring, did you by chance notice the date engraved inside the band?"

"Yes. The eighth day of October. Your birthday."

"The first time I saw the ring, I thought it a present from my father to my mother. A gift to celebrate my birth."

He watched her closely, saying nothing.

She hesitated, then volunteered: "It was a gift, but not from Sir Archibald Tamhill."

He stepped close enough to touch her, though he made no move to do so. "Some things are best said without excess thought."

Prudence took a quick breath, then followed his advice. "Archibald Tamhill was *not* my father."

She waited, searching his face for a reaction that never materialized. Instead of appearing shocked, he simply asked, "Then who is?"

"I don't know."

Prudence's eyes followed him as he walked to a corner cabinet, selected a bottle of brandy, and added a small helping to her unfinished tea.

"Try this," he said in a solicitous tone, handing her the cup.

She took it, sipping delicately before looking at him. "Thank you."

"For what? Showing husbandly concern, or not being shocked out of my knickers because your family tree has a crooked branch?"

"Both."

"Why don't you sit down and tell me about it?"

When she did as he asked, he sat next to her. Prudence glanced at him out of the corner of her eye. He was being his usual charming self, not at all what she'd expected. But then, she was rarely able to predict how he was going to react.

"What makes you think that Tamhill wasn't your father? Did your mother tell you, or did he?"

"Neither. I found my mother's diary in one of her old trunks and read it. She refers to a man, a man who made her feel cherished and truly loved."

"And you think this man was your real father?"

"It explains a lot of things."

"What things?"

She moistened her lips with the tip of her tongue. It was all Rathbone could do not to pull her into his arms then and there and let her know that he didn't give a damn who her father might or might not be.

He was a passionate man whose desires had been repressed, and passion too long pent-up could be hard to control. Knowing his wife's ardor would be sufficient for his needs, he had imagined their relationship being vastly different. On the other hand, he was a husband now, and that role carried certain responsibilities. Seeing to his wife's welfare was one of them.

"Did Tamhill mistreat you?" he asked.

Prudence let out a shaky breath. She sat waiting for her heart to stop pounding. When it didn't, she realized that the only way to cure her nervousness was to finish what she'd started.

"I wasn't abused—merely neglected," she finally said.

"I was educated and treated in the same way any other child with a wealthy father would have been educated and treated. He was never irritable with me. If anything, he was boorish and silent. When he died, I tried to mourn him as I had mourned my mother, but I never could. We were strangers."

Rathbone thought of his own father, of the last day they had spent together. The scene played out in his mind, bringing the man vividly back to life.

It had been raining, the mist rolling down from the hills to spread across the meadows like a mantle of gray lace. The library had been toasty warm, a fire blazing cheerfully on the hearth, while they sat talking. Over drinks, his father had inquired into his studies and asked his opinion of the spring planting. Then, without a moment's warning, he had started violently in his chair, with a gasp for air. His eyes had grown alive, suddenly intensely blue. The moment passed, his father waving it aside as nothing more than a twinge of discomfort.

He had died later the same night.

But unlike Prudence, Rathbone had mourned his father's passing. George Ashworth Exeter had been a vibrant man, gregarious and witty, intelligent and intense, strong and caring. He had been a good father and husband.

Rathbone felt a sudden sense of urgency, though he couldn't put his finger on its exact cause. He wanted to reach across the gulf between them and say something, but what?

Wordlessly, he pulled Prudence into his arms and held her.

Like ripples in a pond disturbing the water, things had changed between them. A confidence shared, a step taken.

He tipped up her chin, then offered her a smile, the rakish one that had been one of the reasons she'd fallen in love with him. Only now it was more than a reason; it was comforting and just the reassurance Prudence needed to go on talking.

"I was only eight when Mother died," she said, "but I still remember her clearly. She was beautiful and fun-loving. We used to take long walks. In the winter she'd bundle me up in mittens and a cap and a red woolen scarf and we'd walk in the snow. But none of those memories include my father. It was always just Mother and me. For a long time, I thought it was because I wasn't a boy. Then I realized my sex didn't make any difference. My parents weren't happy with one another. The only time they spent together was in public."

He tightened his hold on her, a silent reassurance that he was listening, that he cared.

Her spirits warmed for a moment . . . but only for an instant. Then the doubts came flooding back. Looking into her husband's eyes, Prudence wondered if she'd ever feel as her mother had felt, truly cherished and unquestionably loved.

The thought caused something inside her to break, and her fingers knotted in the lapels of his jacket.

What came next scared the hell out of Rathbone. Prudence burst into tears, clutching at him, crying in deep, awkward sobs that shook her whole body.

Acting instinctively, he lifted her onto his lap, her skirts billowing out around them as he rocked her as gently as a child. He stroked her hair, pushing his hand underneath the cluster of curls to massage her neck.

"Your mother made no mention of the man's name in her diary, nothing you can use to identify him?"

"No," she whispered. "She referred to him as if he were a shadow, seen but never meant to have a name."

"Perhaps he didn't," Rathbone suggested. "If she was unhappy, then the man in her diary might have been a fantasy, the lover she would have liked to have had. Some women enjoy fantasizing. It gives them a freedom they aren't allowed in real life."

The tears stopped. "My mother wasn't like that. She was kind and generous and she loved to laugh. She wasn't secretive or evasive."

"You were a child. Children don't always see things the way they should be seen."

She left his lap, her eyes brightened by more than tears as she smoothed the wrinkles from her skirt. "Why should any woman be happy if her lot in life is marriage to a man who's more concerned with business than family, a man who spends more hours tallying ledgers and counting his money than he does conversing with the people who live under his roof?"

"I'm not defending your father."

"He wasn't my father. I felt it years before I discovered my mother's diary in the old trunk. Sometimes I think he left it there, under her wedding dress, so I'd be sure to find it, so I'd know that I was the product of an illicit affair, and not truly a Tamhill."

"That explains the clandestine meeting in the park with a jeweler. You want to find your real father."

"Yes, if he's still alive. I thought about hiring a Bow Street Runner to find the old servants. One of them might remember seeing or hearing something. A name, a face—anything that could point me in the right direction."

Rathbone tried to rationalize the situation. "If Tamhill had any doubts about you being his child, he could have left you with a small allowance and assigned the bulk of his estate to someone else. It is a sizeable fortune."

"He was too proud of the Tamhill name to allow it to be tarnished by gossip or speculation. The few times he actually spoke to me, there was always a reminder of who and what I was that was added to the conversation. I had a responsibility, he'd say. The Tamhills might not be part of the aristocracy, but they were just as influential. I was to grow up a respectable young lady and marry well. I think that was primary reason he chose Worley to be my guardian. He knew that being the ward of a duke would guarantee me a place in Society."

"Are you sure there's no hint of the man's name in your mother's diary?"

"Nothing," Prudence assured him. "I've read it a dozen times."

"What if you discover his name? Then what? Do you mean to approach him?"

"I'm not sure. I suppose it will depend on the man. But even if he isn't alive, I need to know *who* he was." A stitch of anxiety knotted in her stomach. "I think Mr. Fenstermaker knows his name."

Rathbone had to agree. "The anonymous benefactor of a property in Kent."

"Who else could it be? Mr. Sauer, the jeweler, told me that the man who bought this ring for my mother was a well-dressed gentleman, a man of means. Maybe the same man wants me to have the property in Kent because he never had another child. Maybe the strange gift is his way of saying, 'I know you exist and I'm sorry I couldn't be a part of your life before now.' Maybe it's nothing more than compensation for his conscience."

"Anything is possible," Rathbone said, knowing that most men didn't hold themselves accountable for fathering a child when the child's mother was married to another man.

Prudence held her breath for a moment, wishing she

could make sense of it all—the past, the present, her marriage, an emptiness that pierced through all the layers of her life. She took a deep breath, desperately trying not to build too many hopes on the news that had arrived with Mr. Fenstermaker—the hope that her real father was reaching out to her.

"I want to know who I am."

Rathbone's expression turned serious. "It doesn't matter who your father was or is," he said. "All we take from our parents is our name. A person's true identity is dependent upon themself."

"Sometimes I feel like a nobody."

He pulled her into his arms. "I won't have you thinking that. You're my wife."

His lips pressed against her hair, and for an instant Prudence wanted to melt into him. Here, in his arms, without thought or sense, was all the security she needed, the answer to the poignant confusion she had felt for years. And yet, she couldn't escape the truth. She didn't want to escape it.

"I *need* to know," she told him. "I can't be anything until I know who I am."

Rathbone understood her meaning immediately. While he didn't like ultimatums, he could understand how his wife was feeling. In retrospect, how would he feel if he didn't know his true parents? Who would he be if he wasn't his father's son?

"We'll leave tomorrow."

"You'll take me there? To Kent?"

"To Kent."

"You don't think I'm chasing ghosts?"

"Whatever or whomever you're chasing isn't important. I would have you content. With yourself, and with our marriage."

His gaze settled on her face, and for a heart-stopping

moment Prudence felt as if he'd just told her that he loved her.

She groped for a way to thank him, a way to tell him how very much his agreeing to take her to Kent meant to her, but words were inadequate to express what she was feeling.

When he lowered his head to kiss her, it seemed the most natural thing in the world to kiss him back.

Striving for nonchalance, Rathbone held on to his control and ended the kiss before he lost the ground he'd only just gained. Until his marriage, the only thing that had interested him was the challenge, the chase, the game. But marriage was no game. If he wanted to make Prudence happy, he knew he was going to have to look beyond the bedroom door.

Holding to his resolve, he placed a second kiss on his wife's upturned nose before reminding her that if they were to leave for Kent in the morning, there was much to be done.

One of those things was a visit to his mother. He called on her that afternoon. She was taking afternoon tea in the garden behind the dower house.

"Extraordinary," Lady Augusta remarked, as she rose to greet him with an affectionate kiss. "Quite extraordinary."

"Whatever are you talking about?"

"You don't look a bit different," she said. "I thought that perhaps after waking up and finding yourself a married man, you might have turned gray overnight, or lost weight, or taken to drink. I'm delighted to see that you look as healthy after the wedding as before."

"Really, Mother, you can be most tedious at times. I came to tell you that Prudence and I are leaving in the morning. A short trip to Kent."

"Kent? Whatever for? Surely my residence here in the dower house isn't causing her embarrassment. I thought her much too practical for that sort of thing."

"She is practical, and our trip has nothing to do with your taking up a rightful residence here. King's Crossing is your home. It always will be. The reason is simply that Prudence inherited a small estate in Kent, one she has never seen. I promised her a few days there. We should be back by the end of the month."

His mother looked at him, seeing what only a mother could see. "Is something wrong, Benjamin? Don't tell me that you and Prudence are quarreling already."

"I wouldn't call it a quarrel."

"It isn't my place to pry, but . . ."

"But a disagreement of any sort after only four days of marriage doesn't bode well for a blissful future, I know. I'm confident things will sort themselves out. By the time we return from Kent, Prudence will have settled into the role of viscountess and I into the role of husband. Who knows—you may even have a grandchild by this time next year."

She gave him a wistful smile. "I so look forward to the day when King's Crossing has more than servants and hunting hounds running about the place."

"Marriage normally results in children." He shook his head and smiled. "I know it sounds rather strange coming from me, but I have to admit that I am looking forward to installing my heir in the nursery."

"Oh, Benjamin," she said, reaching for his hand and giving it a tight squeeze. "You are happy with Prudence, aren't you? I had hoped the marriage was more than it appeared to be at first."

"Actually, Mother, I'm beginning to believe less and less in appearances. I do know that Prudence is a fine woman, and that I'm lucky to have taken her to wife. As for children, I imagine I'll manage as well as Granby or Sterling."

They talked a while longer, discussing the normal affairs of an estate the size of King's Crossing, before Rathbone said his goodbyes and returned to the main house to prepare for what he hoped would be the resurrection of his honeymoon.

CHAPTER 13

Done in the Tudor style, the Kent house consisted of four stories covered by sloping shingled roofs, from which protruded tall, multiple chimneys. The roofs ended in gables that overhung the windows, shielding them from direct sunlight. A railed veranda banded the front and sides of the ground floor. The heady scent of roses perfumed the air, and large shade trees, at least a century old, spread their elegant branches like great feathered wings over the path that led to the garden.

A long sward lay behind the house, perfect for archery or croquet. Tall trees and masses of rhododendron and wild roses graced the rest of the property. A dovecote and an ample stable were the only other buildings.

Prudence thought the house perfect, gift-wrapped in summer green: the lawns, the shrubs, and the tree-covered hills climbing behind it and swooping protectively around it. And to the east, in a dip between the hills, a glimpse of the English Channel.

As they drew up in front of the main entrance, Prudence marveled how a house that had been so obviously designed to impress could look so cheery. Wide marble steps led up to a double front door flanked by gas lamps. It was a rustic country home, free of pretension and fussiness, appearing comfortable and cozy.

A maid answered the pull at the bell. The young girl's russet complexion, fat cheeks, and bright button eyes revealed a country lass of not more than fifteen or sixteen.

"Oh, my," she stammered, stepping back so fast Prudence feared she might end up on her backside. "It's you . . . I mean to say, it's your lordship and . . . Oh, my!"

"Is there a butler about?" Rathbone asked, barely able to contain his laughter. "If not, Mrs. Blaine will do."

"Yes, milord. I'll fetch her right off."

The maid disappeared, leaving the lord and lady who had so surprised her standing in the foyer.

Unable to contain her curiosity, Prudence walked to an open door and looked inside. The parlor windows were draped in moss-green velvet. The furnishings included a Chippendale desk and a battery of comfortable arm chairs. An elegant Sheraton console, inlaid with exotic fruitwoods, stood against one wall underneath a gilt Georgian mirror. There were fresh yellow roses in a blue porcelain vase and a profusion of crystal figurines on the mantelpiece.

"I beg your forgiveness, Lady Rathbone; I was not expecting you until tomorrow."

Prudence turned around to find a middle-aged woman dressed in housekeeper black, with a ring of keys dangling from her belt. "Mrs. Blaine."

"At your service, milady," the housekeeper replied, revealing a slight brogue. "Welcome to Summer House."

"Summer House. What an enchanting name."

Two footmen appeared, both looking eager to please. While one relieved her husband of his hat and gloves, another scurried outside to see to the unloading of luggage and to direct the second traveling coach that had brought Fiona and the valet around to the side entrance.

"The name does suit the place," Mrs. Blaine agreed. "Would you like to be shown upstairs to your rooms, or would a spot of tea be more to your liking?"

"Tea, if you please," Prudence said.

"This way, then."

They followed Mrs. Blaine down the hall and into another parlor, this one even more cozy than the first. The room had blue damask walls and silk draperies. The delicately colored Aubusson rugs and pastel brocade chairs and sofa were a perfect setting for the sunlight that streamed in through windows that had been washed and polished until they sparkled. A silver tea service already sat atop a low walnut table.

"Would his lordship be wanting something more substantial than tea?" Mrs. Blaine asked as she walked to a black walnut sideboard. The top was covered with a marble slab, on which stood crystal decanters of sherry, port, claret, and brandy.

"A glass of port would be appreciated," Rathbone said. "Our driver took advantage of the dry weather and longer summer days to get us here ahead of schedule."

"You'll not be inconveniencing anyone here, milord. The house had been scrubbed and waiting for you to pay it a visit for more than a month now."

Prudence cast her husband a quick glance. "How long have you been employed here?"

"Six weeks or so," the housekeeper answered. "A week longer than the rest of the staff."

Trying not to show her disappointment, Prudence made herself comfortable in a chair near the window. The breeze fluttering the draperies carried the scent of the sea. "Is everyone on the staff new, then?"

"Aye. All of us. The house was shut up for years. But with the Channel being just over the ridge and the wind blowing nigh on every minute of every day, it didn't take long to get the mustiness out of things. It's a lovely old house. All it needed was a little spit and polish. Beggin' your pardon, milady."

Prudence smiled. "That's perfectly all right, Mrs. Blaine. May I commend you and the staff on your hard work."

The housekeeper beamed. "I'll be passin' the compliment on to them. Especially poor Sally, she was surprised out of her wits, openin' the door to find you and his lordship standing there. I hope she didn't offend. She's a mite young, but she's a good lass."

"I assume most of the servants are from one of the nearby villages?" Prudence asked casually. She was convinced that Summer House held the answer to her father's identity. It had to be more than a coincidence that the house had been opened at the same time that her engagement to Rathbone had appeared in the London papers.

"Nary a one," she was told. "Most worked in London."

"None?" Rathbone asked. "That's unusual. Did you interview them yourself, or was the hiring done by Mr. Fenstermaker?"

"Mr. Fenstermaker handles everything connected to Summer House. Staffed it from attic to wine cellar without any help from me."

After informing them that supper would be served at eight o'clock, Mrs. Blaine went about her business in another part of the house.

Prudence waited until the door closed behind the housekeeper before putting down her teacup and addressing her husband. "Doesn't it seem strange that Mr. Fenstermaker hired the staff himself?"

"It is a bit unusual," Rathbone agreed. "Then again, everything about our Mr. Fenstermaker is a bit odd. Folkestone is the closest village. The local merchants should be able to supply a few answers."

"Thank you," Prudence said, grateful that he didn't think her quest fanciful. "I'm not sure how I would be reacting were I alone. I've dreamed of finding my father for years, but now that I'm on the trail, so to speak, I'm not entirely sure where to look for clues."

"That's the challenge of any puzzle."

"And the risk," Prudence added.

He smiled, saying nothing for the time being. They had done quite a bit of talking in the coach—three days of travel had given them ample time to discuss a dozen different subjects, but not their marriage. He was biding his time and minding his manners. He'd even rented separate rooms at the inns along the way, determined to hold true to his word. The next time Prudence shared his bed, he wanted duty to be the last thing on her mind.

Unfortunately, biding his time was taking its toll. He wasn't accustomed to abstinence, especially when temptation was within reach. But at times likes these, when Prudence was looking at him with those big, dark eyes, he felt more than a physical need to hold her in his arms. He didn't want her withdrawing into some corner of her mind that he couldn't enter.

During the trip from King's Crossing, she had stared out the carriage window, her eyes fixed on a place or a thought far beyond the carriage in which they had been riding, as if she were looking for someone.

Selfishly, Rathbone wanted that someone to be him.

It was a bewildering truism, but true nevertheless.

"You must be tired," he said, setting aside his drink. "I for one could use a hot bath." Leaving his chair, he pulled the service cord.

A maid, not Sally this time, but an older girl with copper-colored hair and freckles dashed across her nose, arrived within moments to escort Prudence to her room. Fiona was already there unpacking.

Prudence smiled as she entered the large upstairs room. The furnishings reflected the mood set by the exterior of the house: tables with delicately carved legs and tiny clawed feet, a pale gold brocade chaise longue with petit-point pillows, Irish lace curtains, and several vases of brightly mixed garden flowers. The lace canopy on the four-poster bed touched the ceiling.

Quickly shedding her traveling clothes for a dressing gown, Prudence made herself comfortable on the chaise longue before telling Fiona what she'd learned from Mrs. Blaine.

"Be discreet, but ask as many questions as you can," she instructed the maid. "There are sure to be deliveries made to the kitchen. The staff may not be locals, but the merchants use local men to carry their goods. Surely someone knows the name of the family who lived here before the house was closed."

"And what will you be doing while I'm flirting with tradesmen?"

"Asking questions in the village, and calling on the vicar or anyone else who can tell me about Summer House."

"It ain't my place to be saying, but it seems to me you'd profit more by paying a call on your husband."

A scowling expression froze on Prudence's face. "You're correct. It isn't your place."

Fiona accepted the reprimand but, true to character, she didn't let it keep her from finishing what she'd started. "It ain't right for a wife to be keeping her husband on a leash."

"I am not keeping Rathbone on a leash."

"What would you call it—saying goodnight in the hallway, then tucking yourself into bed like you was a nun instead of a married woman? That's a right handsome man you've gotten yourself. One used to being a man, if my guess is right."

"Please see that the green dress is pressed by dinnertime," Prudence said, refusing to discuss her husband's virility. She didn't need Fiona to remind her that Rathbone was handsome, and she certainly didn't need anyone pointing out the closed door between their bedrooms. "And tell Cook that I'd like an early breakfast. I want to do some exploring in the morning."

The maid nodded, but her expression said Prudence was being foolish. Foolish and stubborn.

The large dining table had been covered with a white linen tablecloth, with another of lace on top of it. Directly under the gaslight chandelier was the centerpiece, a raised silver bowl that contained a bed of apples and sweet pears.

Seated at opposite ends of the table, the newlyweds were first served oysters in lemon sauce. The second course, snapper soup, was followed by roast lamb and steaming vegetables—potatoes and turnips and carrots—and a silver basket of oven-warm rolls. Dessert was a cake flavored with rum and dusted with sugar. It was an excellent meal. Lord Rathbone sent his compliments to the cook.

After dinner, Prudence surprised her husband by asking if he'd like to walk with her. "The evening air is warm, and the moon full enough to light our way."

"Feeling restless?" Rathbone asked as he refilled his wineglass. Before lifting it to his mouth, his gaze poured over her, making her acutely aware that they were alone in the room.

"Adventurous," Prudence replied before realizing that he might take the answer the wrong way. Trying to right the wrong, she quickly added, "Three days in a coach is enough to make anyone want a long walk and some fresh air."

His gaze lingered on her, his eyes a warm blue, accented by a smile that made her heart beat faster.

Neither husband nor wife spoke as they walked, each engrossed in private thoughts. When they reached the end of the garden path, Prudence turned to look back the way they had come. The windows of Summer House were aglow with soft amber light, the French doors of the terrace open and inviting. "It is a lovely house, isn't it?"

"Yes." He was looking at her as if to read her thoughts. His expression changed, his eyes unfathomable in the moonlight. "You seem disappointed."

"I suppose I am," Prudence admitted, letting out a small sigh. "I had hoped that someone might be able to tell me something, some small clue that would set me in the right direction. But everyone's as much of a stranger here as I am. It's all so very confusing."

"We've only just arrived." He reached out and tucked a windswept strand of hair behind her ear. "Be patient."

"I've been patient for five years. I don't have to read my mother's diary anymore. I can recite it line by line, entry by entry."

"Was she really that unhappy?"

"Not at first," Prudence told him, recalling the notations that had detailed the balls and parties the young

Tamhill couple had attended. Then the entries changed, or rather, the tone in which they were written had changed. "One can be content with the circumstances of one's life and still be unhappy at heart. You of all people should know that. Your name has been linked to several married women."

"Gossips often made free of my name," he said, disliking the direction of the conversation.

He didn't want Prudence thinking about past affairs, his or anyone else's. He wanted her thinking about him, about their marriage, about becoming the wife she had vowed to become, forsaking all others. Admittedly, it was selfish, but he was on his honeymoon and he wanted his wife with him, both in bed and out of it.

He fixed his gaze on her and knew his patience was close to running out. The time spent with Prudence was heaven and hell. It had taken them three days to travel from King's Crossing to Summer House, three days of sitting across from her, three days of listening to her voice, of watching her, of thinking how much he wanted to kiss her and touch her.

If a man could go insane from sexual frustration, he was close to it.

Walking on, they found a little path tunneling through the rhododendrons. They followed it and soon heard the murmur of the surf. After a moment, moonlight glimmered and flashed through the screen of leaves. Prudence couldn't see the Channel, but she could hear it and smell it. With the aid of her husband's hand, she went a few yards farther, until the path dipped down and the foliage gave way to rock that stopped abruptly, falling away to the sea.

The water was as pale as the moon. The waves rose and fell, rolling onto the rocks and foaming up into

white crests before drawing back and blending into the
Channel again, like dreams, one into the other. Nothing
but sky and water, high tide and low, the sea eternal.

The night turned unusually quiet as they stood there,
side by side, holding hands. The darkness was soothing,
with that mysterious stillness that often falls on a place
shrouded once the sun had set.

"It's beautiful," Prudence whispered.

Rathbone squeezed her hand, saying nothing, and in
that moment, all Prudence's attitudes and defenses, the
bulwarks she'd fashioned about her life with the indus-
try of a bee, vanished.

Sensing the change in her mood, Rathbone brushed
a kiss across her hair, and even the crashing of the waves
against the rocks at the bottom of the cliff couldn't
drown out the sound of her heartbeat as it quickened.

Since the moment she had looked up to see Rathbone
marching across the street to haul her out of Green
Park and into his waiting carriage, she'd been assaulted
by emotions. The few times she'd tried to fight those
emotions, her victories had been temporary. Even on
their wedding night, she'd tried to deny them, telling
herself that passion wasn't enough. It still wasn't enough.
But if it was all he could give for the time being, was she
wrong to accept it?

A shiver of lightning illuminated the horizon where
the water of the Channel molded to the contours of the
earth. The wind smelled of saltwater and things unseen,
of possibilities and passion.

Daring a look at the man standing by her side,
Prudence wondered how many women had uninten-
tionally fallen in love with Benjamin Exeter. She'd tried
very hard not to be one of them. But she'd failed.
Before that evening in London, she had rarely thought
of any man, but since that night, when the pressure of

Rathbone's mouth had awakened her body and his slow, roguish smile had warmed her heart, she'd dreamed of a man that had a name, and a face, and a touch that couldn't be forgotten. And miraculously, as if fate had a hand in dosing out miracles, that man was now her husband.

"It's going to rain," Rathbone said, looking toward the approaching squall line. "We'd better get back to the house."

"Yes, I suppose we'd better," Prudence said, her tone belying the turmoil inside her.

He continued holding her hand until the soft grass of the lawn cushioned their steps. When he released it, Prudence turned her face into the wind and blinked back the tears in her eyes.

It was nearing midnight when Prudence admitted to herself that she was facing more than another lonely night in a lonely bed. She was facing a lonely future. She should have known, from their first tender encounter that night by the garden gate to the explosive passion of their wedding night, that what she felt for Rathbone couldn't be denied by simply closing a door.

Unable to sleep, she gazed out at the broad, dark heavens and found a star that gleamed with an unwavering light—a celestial beacon set to guide a wayward soul.

Fiona was right. She had put Rathbone on a leash. And herself. While her husband might not entertain the same feeling for her that she felt for him, he was still her husband. The past few days had proven that he could be more than physically attentive. He had listened to her when she spoke of wanting to find her real father and had immediately agreed to bring her here to Summer House. During the journey he'd shown her every consideration, and how had she reacted? By saying good night in the hallway.

As she stood gazing out the window at the stars, her sober thoughts seemed to reach up to the heavens and down again.

Life was filled with avoidance of risk. The human heart naturally drifted toward self-preservation, and yet it also reached out to others. No one, man or woman, succeeded in love unless they were willing to climb out on a limb. If she wanted Rathbone to love her, she was going to have to entice him to join her on that limb—to take a risk.

Turning, Prudence looked at the door that separated her room from that of her husband. A sliver of light made its way under the door. He was still awake.

Not daring to hesitate for fear her mind would change, she walked to the door and delivered a firm tap to the inlaid upper panel. When the door opened, she found the courage to say, "You said I had only to knock."

Her husband's blue eyes narrowed as he examined her alertly, the novel in his hand forgotten. "May I say, madam, that you have the most unpredictable nature of any female I have ever encountered."

"And may I say, my lord, that you are not without your own set of faults."

"Is that why you interrupted my reading? To list my faults?"

"No." The spoken truth cast a spell between them, like the arcane words of a magician. "I knocked on the door because I don't want to spend my honeymoon alone."

His mouth curved into a sensual smile as he pushed the door wide, then moved aside so she could step across the threshold and into his private lair.

Prudence couldn't look away from him—from the blaze of heat that suddenly lit his gaze, the tiny scar on his chin, the rakish way his hair curled over his forehead. She suddenly felt feverish. Cold one moment, hot the next.

Then strong fingers reached out to remove the restricting pins that secured her hair atop her head, and the profusion of curls came tumbling down. The feel of it on her neck and shoulders had a direct effect on the rest of her body. Her muscles felt soft and languid.

He kissed her as if he had been longing for her, not for mere days, but all his life.

Prudence closed her eyes so he wouldn't see how much she wanted him. And, oh God, the wicked heat between her legs. The fever had turned to pure fire. It was as if her senses were waking up after a long, deep sleep.

The tip of his tongue kindled a new fire, making Prudence shiver and her toes curl. The touch of his hand, sliding around to rest at the base of her neck, was scorching.

He was tender at first, but there was nothing tentative about his desire. She could feel his muscles go taut, his chest tightening as he pressed her closer, close enough to feel his heart beating in unison with her own.

Filled with need, she leaned into him and heard him expel a deep velvety groan. It dawned on Prudence that he liked it when she kissed him back. She tugged at his clothing and worked her hands inside until she could feel warm skin over hard muscle and bone.

The pressure of his hands, one on her neck, the other resting on her hip, prevented her from moving away. The even lighter pressure of his mouth as it moved up and down her throat was as elemental as a summer wind. She was imprisoned by his touch, wrapped in sensations too sweet to describe.

"Ask me to make love to you," he whispered into her ear just before his tongue darted out, sending a wild, wicked shiver down her spine. "Tell me you want this as much as I do."

She couldn't stop kissing him long enough to answer, but then, she didn't need to actually say the words. Her body was screaming yes. Yes. Yes. Yes!

She had never imagined that a man could turn kissing into an art, but her husband did. Each stroke of his tongue was more devastating than the last. Oh, dear God, how had she thought to do without these feelings?

He continued to adore her, telling her with his hands and his kisses, summoning up all the passion she had buried for a long, lonely, prideful week.

He lifted her and carried her to the bed, talking softly between kisses, and sliding off her wispy nightgown. Then he turned down the lamp, allowing pale beams of moonlight to wash through the room.

They lay naked in the dark like blind lovers, discovering each other only with their fingertips—the line of her neck, the slope of his back, the softness of her breasts, the hard muscles of his thighs. She wanted him to prolong the voyage of discovery; he seemed to know that and touched her lightly, slowly, intimately, seducing her with words she'd never heard before. Words that carried a blatant, earthy description of what he wanted to do to her, with her.

The slow, luxurious ritual went on and on, and her thoughts followed as he cradled her breasts in the palms of his hands, lovingly exploring them with his tongue, kissing her belly, then moving down between her legs . . . The pad of his thumb brushed lightly across her swollen center, sending a bolt of excitement into her belly. Then his mouth opened and he was tasting her, licking her like a stick of sweet candy.

Prudence strained against him, catching her breath, then releasing it in a gasp of pleasure. He raised up and over her, finding her mouth, filling it with his tongue and the taste of her own essence. It was wicked. Wonderfully wicked.

"I'm going to eat you up," he whispered against her parted lips. "Then I'm going to take you, again and again, until you're too weak to move. Until I've had my fill of you."

It was Prudence who took his mouth this time, her restraint completely gone. She'd never been so flooded with feelings, so on fire, inside and out, wanting and needing and aching all at the same time.

He swore softly as he broke the kiss and returned to torment her, cupping her with his open hand, then gently separating and teasing her flesh with the tip of his tongue before plunging deeper. She was seized by the most shocking sensations as he claimed her in the most intimate way.

He kept her there, on the edge of paradise, for several exhilarating seconds, his tongue inside her, caressing her with his fingertips, forcing her to feel, taking his revenge.

"Please," she moaned, convinced she was going to die if he didn't do something to end the fiery fury, the endless building pressure that had her ready to explode.

Then he mounted her, pushing into her with one smooth, deep stroke. Prudence moaned with delight.

"Oh, you like that, do you?" he teased, nipping at her lower lip. "I want you to like it. I want you to need it more than you need to breathe, to hear, to speak."

With an urgency unlike anything he'd ever felt before, Rathbone pushed hard between her legs and felt her quicken almost against her will, every muscle contracting, as if part of her was resisting him.

He looked down at her, at her eyes abrim with the invitation of a lover. He buried his hands in her hair and kissed the mouth he had kissed a thousand times in his dreams. He wanted her as he'd wanted no other woman. A hypnotic haze descended over him as he surrendered to that need and became captured in a dream that was all too real.

Her nails dug into the skin of his back. Beads of sweat formed on his forehead. He moved inside her, deep thrusts followed by slow gliding strokes, until she was hovering on the edge again.

"Give it to me," he urged. "Everything. I want it all."

Prudence couldn't deny him, couldn't hold back or control what was happening. She strained against him while he kissed her, catching her lower lip between his teeth, biting gently at the same time her body coiled as if she'd been struck by a whip of fire. He drove into her again with a deep thrust that tore a harsh cry from her throat.

Then the sultry voice came again, teasing her back to consciousness, telling her he wasn't done with her yet.

She clung to him, trying not to cry, but crying anyway from the beauty of it all, the blissful, weightless beauty that made her think of stars and butterflies and white puffy clouds.

A breeze blowing through the open window caused the draperies to undulate, sending delicate slivers of moonlight and shadow rippling over their naked bodies. Prudence lay quietly under him, soaking up the delicious sensation of having him still inside her, still moving slowly, erotically.

She gasped as he plunged deep again and again, causing the muscles in her abdomen to contract as if she were in pain. But it wasn't pain. It was pleasure. She rocked up against him, encouraging him, wanting him to find the same heavenly oblivion.

Rathbone held on to her hips as he pounded into her again and again. His body had been starved for too long. She had stubbornly defied him, and he had stubbornly denied the urge to open the door himself. Now he was consumed, controlled by the need to mate, taking her, claiming her. He pushed deep and felt everything within him being torn away. With a soul-wrenching shudder, he collapsed upon her, his weight celebrated as she wrapped her arms around him and held him tight.

"I'm glad you knocked on the door."

It had started to rain sometime during their lovemaking. The slanting downpour changed to veils of water that rose and fell like delicate curtains before hissing against the dark panes of the windows her husband had closed only seconds before the storm struck.

He was standing near the window now, his body outlined by a flash of lightning that was as sharp as the edge of a knife. Just looking at his lithe body aroused a new surge of desire in his wife.

Prudence drew back the coverlet, silently bidding him to come back to bed. "You mean, you're glad I came to my senses."

He laughed as he joined her. Once she had been returned to the warm circle of his arms, he kissed her on the cheek before asking, "What changed your mind?"

"A lot of things," she said noncommittally.

He touched her, letting his fingers luxuriate in the

softness of dark hair that was spread across the pillows. "No more separate beds," he said.

"No more separate beds."

They shared a passionate kiss as his hands moved from the tangled disarray of her hair to the curves of her body. He cupped her derrière, positioning her against him. Moments later, he rolled to his back.

Prudence wasn't sure what to do at first, but he told her how to please him.

Taking him inside, she did as he asked, fulfilling the fantasy that had kept him awake a good portion of the previous night. He was still amazed that someone so outwardly calm and imperturbable, so mature in outlook and appearance, could create such a need in him.

He caressed her breasts, giving special attention to their rosy crowns. When she arched her back with pleasure, he touched her where they were joined and Prudence went up in flames.

When they finally slept, Prudence dreamed. She was walking along a narrow road, through a landscape so barren it was blank, as if the road itself had no verge, but melted into the outreaching land. But the bleakness didn't bother her; she was walking toward a horizon of such breathtaking loveliness, a crest of rainbow lights, pale colors melting into one another, and a light so glorious that it was less seen than felt. Even buried in the dream, her rational mind wondered if she'd died in her sleep and was now seeing her first glimpse of Heaven.

Except that as far and as long as she walked, she didn't get any closer to the horizon. The colored light didn't dim, didn't recede; the distance never shortened. Her destination was *out there,* but she couldn't reach it.

As the dream continued, the euphoria was replaced by panic. Would she never find what she sought?

Unaware that she was moaning her frustration, she tossed and turned until Rathbone awoke.

"What's wrong, sweetheart?"

His arms came around her to find that she was drenched in sweat, as if she'd been dropped off the cliff and into the Channel. Her heart was pounding and she was gasping for breath.

"Shhh, it's all right now. It was only a dream. Nothing more. You're safe with me."

Even though she was awake, the trauma of the dream stayed with Prudence. Emotions engulfed her in the dark, the sound of the fading storm echoing through the air just as the memory of the unreachable light echoed in her mind.

"Prudence, open your eyes and look at me."

The concern in his voice was Prudence's undoing. Tears burst through the dam the moment she opened her eyes and looked at her husband.

"Shhh, now. Stop crying and talk to me."

She only hiccupped and snuggled closer.

"Talk to me."

Prudence nestled even closer, her tears dampening his skin. Finally, she described the dream, how it had started out so lovely and peaceful, then turned into a nightmare.

He raised her left hand, the hand where her mother's ruby ring and her wedding band encircled her finger, and kissed it. "Your father is part of your life, but he isn't your entire life. You've been hoping for days that this house would give you a clue. Maybe it will, but no matter what we find out, or don't find out, you're not alone."

He continued to hold her, rocking her back and forth like a child. When she finally stopped crying and looked at him, he smiled. "At least it wasn't my love-making. For a moment, I was worried that I'd lost my touch."

"Never that, my lord."

Their lips met in a brief kiss, an exchange of breath. But soon that wasn't enough. "Make love to me again," she whispered.

While the lightning flickered through the windows, growing dimmer and dimmer as the storm moved on, Rathbone did as she asked, taking her more gently, more tenderly than he'd ever taken a woman before.

Prudence cried because it was even more beautiful than the heavenly horizon she'd seen in her dream. But this time, she reached her destination. It was a place both torrid and tranquil, where nothing existed but herself and the man she loved, a timeless place where she wanted to stay forever.

CHAPTER 14

The late breakfast that was served on a tray in the master's bedroom caused Prudence no embarrassment. She was too content to be concerned about proprieties, and they were, after all, on their honeymoon.

"Do you think we can find our way to the beach this morning?" she asked as she spread a thick layer of jam over a wedge of toasted bread. She was amazed at how hungry she was this morning.

"I should think that a bright sun and a set of directions from one of the gardeners would set our feet on the right path," her husband replied.

She missed the satisfied smile on his face as he stirred cream into his coffee. Although he was more than pleased that Prudence had finally reached the conclusion that one bed served them better than two, he knew his wife's main occupation still centered around her father.

Rathbone had no problem helping her discover the man's name, but he was concerned how she might react if that name proved less than admirable.

It was apparent that she held her father in high regard without knowing the slightest thing about him, viewing him in the loving light in which her mother had painted him. Rathbone's own life experiences made him doubtful. —

He had been pursued by too many married women to think them saints, the very reason he meant to make sure Prudence didn't follow in her mother's footsteps. Having accepted the role as her husband, he would now devote himself to it with the same enthusiasm he had once applied to his former endeavors.

It was nearing noon when the lord and lady left the house. A walk to the stables produced two delighted smiles as they discovered Summer House was as well stocked with horseflesh as it was with capable servants and good food.

"My wife wishes to ride on the beach," Rathbone informed the stablemaster, a man in his later years with a thick Irish brogue that left no doubt he knew what he was about when it came to horses.

"Take the south lane. There's a bridle path that leads down to the water."

They rode without speaking, each taking in the wonder of a new day. Glancing at Prudence, Rathbone thought she looked lovely with the sunlight gleaming on her dark hair. She was smiling, and he secretly hoped he was partially responsible for the expression. While he had a long way to go in understanding her, he was making progress.

There was still a part of her he had yet to learn, the inner part that defined her true nature—the part that was still the child who had lost her mother at eight and her presumed father at twelve, and who had been shut-

tled into the house of a duke. The vulnerable part that
made her a prisoner of the poignant past.

As they neared the bridle path, he took the lead.
Prudence followed, her mare seemingly content to follow the chestnut hunter Rathbone had selected for
himself.

As they made their way down the path, twisting and
turning between limestone boulders and tufts of beach
grass, the sound and smell of the open water rose to
meet them. Gradually the path gave way from dirt to
sand, ending in a damp beach, littered by dark sea grass
at low tide.

To the north lay the towering white cliffs of Dover; to
the south, an endless stretch of beach broken only by
an occasional outcropping of rock.

Rathbone dismounted and turned to lift Prudence
from her saddle, but the expression on her face stopped
him. She was staring at the Channel as if she were waiting for a ship to show itself on the horizon, her gaze so
focused he knew she had no idea that he was standing
beside the mare.

"What do you see?" he asked.

She blinked, then shook her head. "It's not so much
what I see as what I feel."

He helped her to dismount, then gathered the reins
of both mounts in one hand. They walked south toward
a point where the waves crested on an outcropping of
rock that would be underwater at high tide.

"What is it you feel?" Rathbone asked.

She bit down on her lower lip, then shook her head.
"Not yet."

They walked on, their riding boots sinking into the
damp sand, their footprints scuffed as the horses followed.

"That rock," Prudence said, pointing. "If we go beyond it, there's a cave."

"How could you possibly know that?"

She stopped, her expression similar to the one he'd seen come over her face a dozen times during their trip from King's Crossing.

"Because I've been here before."

She no sooner got the words out of her mouth than she was running, kicking up clumps of wet sand as she dashed down the beach.

Wondering how she expected to get beyond the outcropping without treading waist-high in water, and afraid that she'd hurt herself in the attempt, Rathbone dropped the reins and ran after her. Catching her by the upper arm, he pulled her to a halt.

"Let me go," she demanded. "I know the cave's there. I know!" She turned to him, her eyes misty with tears. "Don't you understand? I've been here before! When I was a little girl. Oh, Benjamin, I remember! My . . . my father lifted me high over his head, then sat me on his shoulders. We walked around the rocks, through the water. I remember! He called me Poppin. I can hear him saying it."

She was crying full-force now. "Please."

Rathbone had no intention of letting her go. Not in her present state. Instead of releasing her, he pulled her into his arms. She fought him at first, as if he was keeping her from discovering the man himself.

"Calm yourself," he said soothingly. "If the cave is there, it isn't going to disappear in the time it will take for us to approach it cautiously."

"It *is* there," she said, twisting her head so she could look down the length of beach to where waves foamed and crested around the limestone rock that was as tall as a two-story house. "Just on the other side. I know it."

She slumped against him as suddenly as she'd begun to fight, still crying, still shaken by the memory that had been buried in her mind all these years.

"What else do you remember?"

Looking up at him, her eyes wet with tears, she sniffed, then shook her head. "I'm not sure . . . a day like today. Bright and warm. The water. Voices . . . my mother laughing."

Convinced she wasn't going to sprint away from him, Rathbone loosened his hold and watched as she closed her eyes, concentrating on the image that had formed in her mind.

"She was with us. Mother was here, too. All three of us were together!"

"Then your father knew he had a child. She didn't keep it from him. How old were you?"

Another shake of her head brought her hair out of its pins. The wind caught it, fanning it around her face. "I'm not sure."

"You said the man lifted you high in the air before he put you on his shoulders. You couldn't have been very old."

"It wasn't a *man*. It was my father."

"How can you be sure? Maybe your mother was here with Tamhill."

She glared at him, anger gleaming in her still damp eyes. "In the twelve years I lived with Archibald Tamhill, I cannot remember him touching me. Not once. Not so much as a kiss on the cheek before I went to bed."

"I'm sorry." He tried to hold her, but she pulled away.

Prudence's heart was pounding so hard she felt lightheaded. She continued to look at him, her glare softening to one of acquiescence. "I want to see the cave. Please, Benjamin. Maybe it will help me remember something else."

"Not until I know it's safe."

"It's low tide."

He tugged her back up the beach to where the horses stood, their reins in the sand. "I'll go first. You will remain with the horses."

"But—"

"There is no 'but' to the matter, madam. You will remain here until I have judged the way safe, is that understood?"

Taken back by the haughtiness of his tone, Prudence's chin went up a notch. "I don't like being told what to do."

"You will like it this time."

Prudence was torn between anger at being held back from the very thing she'd come to Kent to discover and joy at her husband's concern for her safety. She relented, smiling as Rathbone shed his jacket, draping it over the hunter's saddle before sitting down on a dry patch of sand to tug at his boots.

"Had I known I would be taking a dip in the Channel, I would have chosen an older pair of riding breeches."

"You could take them off," Prudence suggested shamelessly.

"Were I to remove them, sweetheart, your cave would be forced to wait until the next low tide."

Prudence laughed, feeling lighthearted at last. Summer House was a gift—a wedding present from her father.

Her father!

"Hurry," she said impatiently.

"I will have a kiss before I go," he said, his feet now bare.

"And one when you find the cave, and one when you take me to it, and one—"

Laughing, he pulled her into his arms to claim the first kiss, but it was several kisses later before he released her.

"I will have your promise that you will not move from this spot while I'm gone."

"I promise. Now hurry."

He walked into the water, where an incoming wave immediately drenched him to the shoulders. Rathbone cursed under his breath.

Prudence watched as he waded through the surf that was bombarding the jutting rocks. A dozen questions and conflicting emotions assailed her, leaving her motionless and without words. An anxious expression joined the turmoil as she stared at the rocks.

Benjamin was right. She couldn't have been more than three or four when she was last here, on this isolated stretch of beach with her parents. What were her earliest memories? The nursery at Tamhill Hall; Miss Hunnicutt's voice insisting that it was time to put away her toys before taking an afternoon walk with her mother; the smell of the kitchen when the cook was baking her favorite treats.

Why had she remembered being here when the house had stirred no recollection? More importantly, why hadn't she remembered before today?

The question went unanswered as her husband showed himself again, wet but smiling.

"You found it," Prudence called out, her excitement showing in every line of her face. The wind snatched her laughter and tossed it out across the waves.

Rathbone chose to wait until a shout wasn't necessary before telling her what he'd discovered. Dripping from head to toe, he smoothed back his wet hair with both hands. "It isn't much of a cave, but it's there."

Prudence clapped her hands. "I want to see it."

Knowing there was no point in arguing, Rathbone watched as Prudence stripped off her shoes and stockings. The jacket of her riding habit joined her husband's, draped over the hunter's saddle.

"You will hold tightly to my hand," he cautioned. "The current isn't strong, but the waves will force you into the rocks if you aren't prepared for them."

Prudence took his hand. "I won't let go."

The water was colder than Prudence expected, sending a rash of goosebumps over her flesh, but the thought of another memory being shaken loose from her mind kept her going. The first wave soaked her through to the skin. The second caused her to stumble, but true to her word, she didn't let go of her husband's hand.

When Rathbone finally led her out of the bubbling surf, it was to stand on a small expanse of coarse sand, littered with driftwood and sea grass. Cliffs rose like white sentinels on three sides of them, blocking out the rest of the world. The cave was a deep hole in the base of one cliff, an opening cut by the ceaseless rush of water that rolled and tumbled against the limestone rock at high tide.

Prudence stared at the cave, but despite her best efforts, no new memories sprang to life. The tiny beach was a haven, an isolated piece of earth that brought contentment regardless of her inability to recall anything new.

Walking toward the deep indentation in the rock, Prudence couldn't help but think of pirates and stolen loot, but the cave was too shallow. While tall and wide, it lacked the depth pirates required to hide their misgotten gains. The sand was still damp from the previous high tide, and once out of the sunlight, she could feel the dampness that issued from the rock walls.

Her husband's inquiring expression was all the question she needed. Prudence shook her head. "I don't remember anything else."

"Maybe later," he said, putting his arm around her and pressing his lips to her temple. "Take one piece of the puzzle at a time. Eventually, you'll be able to see the whole picture."

"Do you think so?" she asked anxiously, refusing to let the current disappointment stamp out her gleam of hope. Nor would she allow herself to believe that all was truly lost where her heart was concerned. With time and the proper incentive, things might yet be brought to a happy resolution.

"I'm sure of it," Rathbone said, smiling at the natural optimism that was so much a part of his wife's personality.

In the short time he had known her, Prudence had presented the ability to deal with difficult situations in ways that no other woman he had ever met could duplicate. In that regard, everything about her was more fact than metaphor. Her spirit, as much as her sensuality, had captivated him from the start.

Prudence turned into her husband's waiting embrace. An instant later, his lips found the hollow where her shoulder joined her neck. His mouth was warm against her skin, taking away the wet chill of the water.

"Take off your clothes," he said.

Prudence looked at him as if he'd just asked her to swim across the Channel to fetch him a bottle of Napoleon brandy, but her husband was too busy taking off his own clothes to notice.

"You can't mean to—"

"Make love to you under a clear blue sky," he said,

shaking out his shirt and draping it over a piece of drift-wood to dry. Reaching for the buttons on his trousers, he added, "We are soaked to the skin, madam, and the sun is warm. Before I go splashing about in the surf again, I intend to make good use of the afternoon."

"We're only going to get wet again," she pointed out.

"Passion isn't practical," he said, as he stripped down to his bare skin.

Prudence cast a quick glance over shoulder, search-ing the blue-green Channel for any sign of life. None was to be seen, which was very good, because a second later she was picked up and carried to a patch of sugar-white sand and stood back on her feet.

She stood quietly for a while, just looking at her now-naked husband. He was infinitely more handsome in the flesh than any daydream might make him out to be. Her eyes lingered on the hollows of his face, the outline of his mouth.

She looked at his hands, wondering how he would touch her. Gently, as he had last night after her dream, or with the fury she saw burning in his eyes?

Splendidly naked, his pale wet hair gleaming in the sunlight, he tugged at the boyish cravat she was wear-ing, tossing it to where his trousers lay before starting on the buttons at the front of her blouse. Her riding skirt followed, and then his hands were beneath her undergarments, his fingertips brushing across her taut nipples, circling her navel, making her smooth flesh tingle.

He stood back, letting his gaze travel expectantly up and down her body. She slept by his side now, her right-ful place, but he couldn't wait to sink into her again, tantalized by her scent, entangled in those slender arms and legs.

Prudence closed her eyes and let the glory of the day wash over her, the breeze caressing her skin, the sun warming her, accompanied by the smell of salt air, the texture of the sand beneath her feet, and her husband, the man she loved, making love to her.

When his firm body was finally pressed against hers, Prudence stopped thinking altogether. She could feel the strength and firmness of his muscles, the crisp golden hair on his chest, and the throbbing of his penis at it rested against her bare belly.

He kissed her lips and stroked the sides of her breasts, and she moaned approvingly. He pulled her down on top of him and kissed her strongly, his hands holding her head lightly but firmly as his mouth explored her cheeks, the underside of her chin, and her mouth. She could hardly breathe for the pleasure.

Small, puffy clouds scudded across the blue sky above the cliffs, but she didn't see them. Birds sang as they floated on the wind, but she didn't hear them. All she could see, hear, or feel was Benjamin. Her mind filled with his name. She was the sea, the air, the sunlight, lost to a wave of joy that gained its force from deep within her.

"You're beautiful," he whispered as he stroked her from shoulder to thigh. "My wife. Whoever would have thought?"

Prudence held his gaze for a moment, then closed her eyes and turned into his body, pressing her naked breasts against his bare, damp chest. When he was with her like this, his touch gentle, his expression serene, she could almost believe that he truly cared for her.

He could come to love her, she was sure of it. The possibility was in the way his body moved, the sound of pleasure in his voice when he touched her. Could any man take a woman with just delight, or so enjoy the taking of her, unless he felt with his heart as well as his body?

He entered her erotically, reverently, and Prudence shuddered with pleasure as he touched a delicate spot.

"Slowly," he whispered, his mouth near her ear, his breath as warm as the sun on her skin. "I would have this last a very long time. You feel so good, so damn good. All hot and sleek and creamy around me. I could come right now, but I'm not going to."

Prudence didn't want to go slow. She moved provocatively, arching her back and raising her hips, forcing him deeper inside her. He laughed, giving her more of what she wanted, burying himself to the hilt before pulling back, almost freeing himself, then pushing deep again.

The rhythm went on and on, his patience testing hers, until Prudence thought she would scream.

"Now," he demanded. "I will have you now. And you me."

Spreading her legs wide, he increased the pace, rolling his hips as he drove into her until Prudence yielded to the sensation, to the pure sensual pleasure of their joining. She let herself go and her hips circled rhythmically, matching his movements until she erupted with him and he lay panting for breath.

They lay there, covered with a blanket of summer sunlight. She brought her gaze down, away from the castles she had been building in the clouds, and looked at him.

"I feel like Eve," she said, stretching so the warmth of the sun touched every inch of her. "Is that wicked?"

"No," Rathbone said, turning over onto his back. "There's nothing wicked about a husband and wife giving each other pleasure. In fact, I doubt there's anything more glorious in the world."

He dozed then, but Prudence remained awake, thinking about the pain of life's cruel disappointments and misfortune, and about hope, more potent than all the ills found in that terrible box of Pandora's. Hope was love's handmaiden, for where there was love, there hope must also abide.

She had come to Kent with the hope of finding the path that would lead to her father. She had married Rathbone with a similar hope—that one day he might love her in return.

Looking at him now, she thought about what it was truly like to love someone, to love with every fiber of one's being—the way her mother had loved only one man, the way she now loved the Viscount Rathbone.

How rare that was. Love was a gift God gave to mortals—but not to every mortal. It wasn't always permitted to everyone to share in that glory—to give his or her heart away and in return receive another's for safekeeping.

Prudence smiled to herself. For years she'd thought her mother had died unhappy, but now she realized that no matter the circumstances, her mother had died knowing love, both in the giving and the receiving, and in that, Rachel Tamhill had been blessed.

CHAPTER 15

It was mid-afternoon when Fiona entered the parlor. Prudence, working on her embroidery, rested her needle as she looked up, waiting to hear what the maid had to say.

"There's someone in the kitchen you should talk to," Fiona said. "His name is Samuel Huebner."

Prudence set her embroidery aside and came to her feet. Her husband had gone into Folkestone to ask questions about the former residents of Summer House. It had been four days since their arrival. The vicar had called the previous day but, like the servants, he was new to the village. He had been assigned from the seminary in Knole after the death of Reverend Howard, who had served the parish for over forty years. The visit had been pleasant, but uninformative.

In the course of the last three days, Prudence had spoken to most of the servants, introducing herself and casually asking about their former employment. Most had come from London, hired through an agency that specialized in domestics. Having met with Mr. Fenstermaker's discriminating approval, they had been given a week's wages in advance, plus a traveling stipend to get them to Kent. None of them knew anything more than the duties they had been hired to perform.

"Who is Samuel Huebner?" Prudence asked Fiona.

"He drives an old pony cart. Delivers the fish from the market in Dover. When I asked him, he said he'd lived hereabouts all his life." The maid flashed a satisfied smile. "He looks as old as Methuselah."

"Ask him to come into the parlor."

Fiona turned to go back the way she had come. Prudence walked to the open window, allowing the sunshine to warm her face. Her eyes swept the horizon. Everything looked as it should, the lawn rich and green, the sky a brilliant summer blue, the trees swaying gently in the relentless breeze that blew in from the Channel.

She smiled as she thought of the last three days—and nights. There had been several heartening occasions when she had felt closer to her husband than she'd ever felt to another human being. Not just physically, but emotionally.

Sometimes he would turn to her with a look of such frank and simple affection she felt as if she could reach out and capture all the wonder of love in the palm of her hand. Though he never mentioned his feelings, they spoke freely, all inhibitions gone. At the end of the day, they sat silently on the veranda, watching the dusky twilight turn to darkness.

Yesterday the sky had changed in the blink of an eye, going from palest blue to mother-of-pearl, from calm sunset to a windswept squall that had sent them inside. They had escaped the weather, coming into this very room. Her husband had locked the door, then made love to her on the floor. Afterwards, they had lain in each other's arms, listening to the rain.

A light tap on the door drew Prudence's attention back to the present. Fiona opened it, then stepped aside so a stoop-shouldered, parchment-faced old man could shuffle into the room. Dressed in a faded brown frock coat with missing buttons and a threadbare waistcoat, he looked about suspiciously. Tradesmen weren't invited into the parlor.

"Please sit down," Prudence said, motioning toward a chair. "Would you like some tea?"

"No thank yer." He held his cap in blue-veined hands with fingers twisted by years of hard work on the Dover docks.

"Mrs. Digby does a fine buttered rum," Fiona suggested.

The old man's eyes brightened.

"Then a buttered rum it is," Prudence said, sensing that Samuel Huebner had a lifetime of stories to tell to anyone willing to listen.

Once she was seated, sipping tea while her unexpected guest enjoyed a tall cup of rum, Prudence inquired into the history of Summer House.

"My husband and I have only just gained the property," she said. "It's such a lovely house. I'm curious as to who built it."

"Well, now," he began kindly. "That's easy enough to tell. Parish Galloway built it back before the war with the French."

"Galloway," Prudence said, disguising her soaring hopes with a curious smile. "Did the family live here for long?"

"Three generations of them that I can count. 'Course, there wasn't much family to speak of after the war. Parish had three sons. Captain Nate was the only one to come home. His wife died. That left him and his daughter, Madeline." He paused to scratch the thinning hair on the side of his head. "Odd female, Madeline was. Always as prim and proper as a church social, nary a hair out of place or a smile on 'er face. Walked on the beach every morning. Had two dogs. Those big spotted ones."

"Dalmatians."

"Aye, those be the ones. Sat next to her in the cart she used to drive into Folkestone every Friday as sure as the ticking of a clock. Looked like two spotted cushions, they did, wedged up next to her on the seat."

"Did she live here alone?"

"Never saw no one about the place that didn't belong—servants and such, I mean. She died . . ." he scratched his head again. "Don't recall the exact year."

"That's when the house was closed?"

He shook head. "Not right off. Staff stayed on for a while. Captain Nate had a sister, can't tell yer the lady's name. The house passed on to her after Miss Madeline died."

"Did she ever come here?" Prudence did her best to phrase the question as casually as possible, but it was difficult. She had a name, a family that had more than one branch. If she followed the trail Mr. Huebner was laying out . . .

When he emptied his cup, Prudence offered a second.

"You were telling me about the Captain's sister. Did she visit often?"

"Once, I think, can't say fer sure. It was a long time ago. I did see a man once."

Prudence had to bite her tongue to keep from interrupting the old man's storytelling.

"I was out checking my nets. It was early morning and there was some fog, but I saw him clear enough. Tall. Well-dressed, in fancy riding boots and a fine white shirt. In the prime of his life by the way he walked, head high and shoulders straight."

"When was that?"

"My old mind can't recall things as well as it used to," he said apologetically. "Twenty years, maybe more. I wasn't sailing the frigates no more, just fishing in the Channel and selling what I caught. Can't even do that now. Too old to stay afloat if the dinghy gets caught in a squall and I'm heaved into the water."

"Tell me about the Galloways," she urged, wondering if there had been a prodigal son among them.

"They were sailors," he said with pride. "Old Nate had a clipper. As sleek and fast as any lady to take to the sea, she was. Sailed her around the Horn of Africa once and came back to tell the tale. Brought Madeline a fancy Chinese fan with an ivory handle."

Prudence wondered if Samuel Huebner had once been enamored of the odd Miss Madeline. His pale old eyes were gleaming, but she couldn't be sure if the reason was Mrs. Digby's buttered rum or the man's own youthful memories. Still, he seemed more relaxed as he continued talking, telling her about the party Captain Nathaniel Galloway had hosted after his return from Madagascar.

"The wine flowed that night, I'll tell yer. The captain invited the whole village and half of Dover. First and only time I ever saw Miss Madeline dance. She waltzed with her father."

Mr. Huebner took his leave an hour later. While he hadn't been able to tell Prudence anything more of the man who had once visited Summer House and strolled along the beach, she was no less excited about the information she had gleaned from the old fisherman. She waited for her husband to return, pacing the parlor floor until she couldn't stand the waiting any longer, then took to the garden, where she had a view of the road and any approaching rider.

The moment Rathbone came into view, Prudence waved. He waved back, smiling as she hastened across the lawn toward him, the skirts of her yellow muslin day dress billowing out around her like the petals of a daisy.

Dismounting, he tossed the reins to a waiting stable boy before scooping up his smiling bride and swirling her around. Laughing, Prudence admonished him for his manners, but she didn't release his hand once they were walking back toward the house.

She stopped short of the entry steps and looked up at the tall chimneys. Only one, the stack belonging to the kitchen fire, was belching smoke. "This house was built by a Mr. Parish Galloway," she announced gleefully. "He was followed by three sons. Two lost their lives in the Peninsular War. One, a Captain Nate Galloway, returned to England. He had a daughter—"

"Named Madeline Galloway," Rathbone finished for her. "She never married. The house was bequeathed to the next of kin, a distant cousin of the grandfather, Parish Galloway. A Miss Mary Elizabeth Galloway, who later married, becoming Lady Mary Elizabeth Montague."

"Who have you been talking to?" Prudence asked, unable to hide her excitement.

"The proprietor of the Gull and Anchor. He was more than willing to share the local lineage with me once I put a few coins on the table. Who have you been talking to?"

"An old fisherman by the name of Samuel Huebner. He couldn't remember the name of the woman who inherited Summer House after Madeline died, but he did tell me that he saw a man here once. A young gentleman who enjoyed morning strolls on the beach."

"When was this?" His arm wrapped around her waist

as they made their way up the front steps and into the foyer, with its gleaming mirrors and tall vases of fresh-cut flowers.

"He wasn't entirely sure. More than twenty years ago."

Leaving his hat and gloves in the hands of a footman, Rathbone followed Prudence into the parlor, where she'd sat talking with Samuel Huebner a good portion of the afternoon. After pouring himself a drink, he sank into an armchair, taking his wife by surprise when he tugged her down and onto his lap.

Before Prudence could bombard him with a dozen questions, he kissed her. It was several heated kisses later, when she was resting in his arms, her face flushed with color, that he told her what else he had learned in Folkestone.

"Mary Elizabeth Galloway married an earl from Cromwell, thus becoming Lady Montague. After talking to Mr. Pennyward, the proprietor of the Gull and Anchor, I paid a call on the local magistrate, a sour-faced man by the name of Edward Sheffield. According to the records, Summer House was deeded to Lady Montague twenty-three years ago, then promptly sold within a fortnight to our enigmatic friend, Mr. John Fenstermaker."

"That doesn't make any sense. Why would Lady Montague, whom I have never heard of before today, give me property?"

"I'm not entirely sure she did. The house and grounds were deeded to Mr. Fenstermaker before you were born. We'll need to excavate a little deeper into the legacy of Summer House before we can be sure of anything."

"But where do we start? If no one around here knows anything about the Montagues or Mr. Fenstermaker, who do we ask?"

"The logical place to start is London. I think it's time I paid a call on Mr. Fenstermaker."

"You." She squirmed in his lap until she could look him straight in the face. "We will both pay a call on Mr. Fenstermaker, my lord. I won't be shut out of this. It's *my* father we're seeking."

"I know whose name we're after," he said, giving her a scowl. "What I want to know is what you're going to do with the information once you've uncovered it. Will knowing the man's name be enough?"

Prudence frowned. "I'm not sure. I think it will depend on the name. And the man."

"And if he's still alive?"

She shook her head. She looked toward the mantelpiece where an old carriage clock ticked out the time. It seemed to her that there was a very special significance to that ticking now.

"I'm not sure what I'll do with the name if I ever discover it. All I know is that I can't think about the future until I've cleared up the past."

"Very well," he said, with quiet understanding. "We will languish here at Summer House for another few days, then make our way to London."

"Languish," she said, raising one perfectly arched dark brow. "Are you in distress, my lord?"

"Since the moment I sat you on my lap."

She wiggled, feeling him rock-hard beneath her, and smiled. "Shall I lock the parlor door and see to your relief?"

He was reaching for the buttons on her gown when he said, "An excellent idea."

CHAPTER 16

It was a bright Tuesday afternoon when Lord and Lady Rathbone boarded a carriage to take them from Belgrave Square to a meeting with a man Prudence hoped would be able to further her investigation.

They were quiet for the first few minutes, lost in their own diverse thoughts. Rathbone used the time to study his wife. As usual, her silence was deep, like the shadows that gathered in the corner of a room just before sunset. He knew what she was thinking, what she was always thinking about when he wasn't diverting her attention with lovemaking: her father.

Only one clear point had emerged from what they had learned so far—the fact that Prudence was absorbed in her quest to discover her father. At the same time, Rathbone didn't relish the prospect of identifying the man if, once known, his name would bring displeasure to his wife.

But regardless of the outcome, he had promised his help, and he would do whatever he could to see Rachel Tamhill's lover revealed. A few conversations at the clubs with friends who lived in London year-round, using invitations to country lawn parties to break the routine of the city, had turned up nothing unusual associated with the name Montague.

Deciding Mr. Fenstermaker would remain as close-mouthed during a second visit as he had been when calling upon Prudence at King's Crossing, Rathbone had decided to hire a man of inquiry. The recommendation had come from, of all people, the baronet Ramsbury.

"Do you really think this Mr. Covertly will be able to find the servants in the ledger?" Prudence asked, unconsciously stroking the leather book on her lap as if it were a genie's lamp.

"Ramsbury said Covertly is capable of finding anyone, given an adequate fee."

"I don't care how much it costs. Are you still angry with me for refusing to be left behind?"

"I explained the reason most thoroughly," Rathbone replied, wishing she had listened to him. "Ramsbury arranged the meeting with Mr. Covertly thinking I would speak to the man alone."

"And you think a meeting in the Horse and Hound too unsavory for a lady to attend?"

Rathbone remained silent, not wishing to repeat what he had already said several times since making the mistake of telling his wife of his decision to hire an investigator.

While Southwark was a fairly respectable portion of the city, certain quarters of the community had a raffish reputation. Many of the houses were occupied by mistresses of the rich and were discreetly disguised as family homes. Nothing, however, was kept more private than the illicit affairs of the upper class. That, along with a dozen other problems, was the difficulty they would encounter trying to uncover the affair Rachel Tamhill had had over twenty years ago.

Only scandals were openly discussed. Discreet love affairs weren't remembered by anyone but the people having them.

"I would speak with the man directly," Prudence said, repeating what she'd said that morning at breakfast. "It is my father we seek. I will not be—"

"—left out of things," Rathbone sighed. "Very well, but you will do as I say when we reach the tavern."

"Of course, my lord."

It was as much the way she said the words as the words themselves that made Rathbone rumble with laughter. "You, madam, are an imp."

"And you, my lord, are a charming rascal. But your charm will not work this time. I will see this through to the end."

"I have no doubt," he replied.

Having stated her resolve for the third time since rising that morning, Prudence turned her attention to the neighborhood of Southwark. There was little to see that reinforced her husband's reluctance in bringing her along. The houses were what she would have expected to see in most London neighborhoods. Tall, mostly three stories, they stood side by side, like a regiment of stone soldiers awaiting inspection.

Thaddeus halted the horses near a narrow gate in a stucco wall. Rathbone stepped down from the carriage, handing Prudence down to join him. A small sign swung from the gate, indicating that the Horse and Hound could be found at the end of the alley.

The tavern itself was small and built in the rustic style of an earlier time, with a stout outer porch and a long wooden bench beneath a bay window.

Much to her husband's relief, it wasn't the tavern itself they sought, but the rooms above it. Turning into a smaller brick-paved alley, Rathbone gave Prudence his hand as they mounted a set of wooden steps. Arriving at the landing that fronted a weather-blistered door, Rathbone used his gold-tipped walking stick to announce their arrival.

The door opened to reveal a tall, slender man in his late forties, with thick, wavy brown hair and a ruddy face.

"You be the man Ramsbury told me about?" he said.

"I'm Lord Rathbone. This is my wife."

The door was opened wider, allowing them to step into a room with long windows, now barred with wooden blinds against the harsh afternoon sun. The ceiling fixture, a rusty gasolier suspended by even rustier chains, cast bands of yellowish light across the unpolished floor.

The room itself was sparsely decorated, furnished with two faded armchairs and a military traveling desk which, if it ever had to be transported, would need an elephant to carry it. The walls were painted a bland white and unadorned except for a portrait, of medium size and some quality, of a young woman who bore a distinct resemblance to Queen Victoria.

"Have a seat," Covertly said. He was halfway into a closet, the door of which was painted the same color as the rest of the room, and his voice was faintly muffled. He emerged backwards carrying a dusty bottle and a corkscrew. "I can't offer the lady anything, but if his lordship likes brandy, this is as old as it gets." He poured two glasses, raising one to his nose to savor the aroma. "Stole it meself, back when I was working for Her Majesty."

"You worked for the Queen?" Prudence asked with undisguised surprise.

"Aye, for more years than I care to remember," Micah

Covertly announced as he passed a second glass to the well-dressed gentleman who had come to hire his services. "Worked the docks mostly, alerting the coppers to any ship smuggling goods. Paid myself a bit extra by taking this here bottle of brandy. Keep it for sharing with my *gentleman* clients."

Rathbone accepted the glass. He raised it in a salute and received a wide grin from Micah Covertly. It proved to be excellent brandy, very smooth and dark. He took a second sip while his wife seated herself in a manner that made the ugly armchair appear as rich as a throne.

Admiring her ability to adapt to the circumstances, Rathbone took the other chair. He was beginning to admire a lot of things about his wife. First and foremost was her persistence. The lady had the tenacity of a bulldog when it came to getting what she wanted.

His prediction, for better or worse, was that she would eventually identify the man who had sired her. While he understood her reasons, it often made him feel extraneous, excluded from the energies of her life. And that he didn't like.

"You may find it hard to credit," Covertly said as he sat down behind the enormous desk, "but I wasn't always what I appear to be now. That said, how may I be of service to you, milord?"

"We're looking for someone. A man."

"My father," Prudence said without hesitation.

"Lost him, have you?"

Prudence frowned. In contrast to what she had expected a man of inquiry to look like, Mr. Covertly appeared unrestrained in both manner and speech, and he was suitably matched to the shabby comfort of his office. Had he looked and acted in the same manner while working for the Queen, she could well imagine why his pension had not been set to provide him better accommodations. In fact, this person—whoever he was—had absolutely nothing to recommend him. No manners, no anything. She was beginning to think Willard Ramsbury had played another of his ill-fated jokes on her husband.

Rathbone, having mixed with all sorts and conditions of men, moved to take over the conversation. "My wife's true father is unknown to her, Mr. Covertly. We have very little information to give you. His current age is estimated between forty and sixty. We know that in his younger years he was tall, with dark hair. A well-dressed, educated gentleman."

"That's all yer know? Egads, you've just described half the men in London, not counting the rest of the bloody Empire."

"We had hoped that you might be able to locate some of the servants in this ledger." Prudence handed over the leather-bound book, sliding it across the scarred desktop and into Micah Covertly's waiting hand. "I'm hoping one of them can give you the details we are unable to provide."

While Covertly was inspecting the ledger, a cat appeared from the nowhere only cats seemed to inhabit.

"Well now, Sorcerer, I was wondering where you'd hidden yourself," Covertly said, giving the feline a good petting that brought about a deep, satisfied purr.

Lean and sleek, the black cat wove a path across the desk, before curling up on the corner closest to Prudence. It blinked once, then tucked its tail around its nose and went to sleep.

Thinking cats the most discriminating of all creatures, Prudence decided Mr. Covertly might have one saving grace after all.

"You know who I am?" Prudence inquired after the ledger was closed.

"Aye, can't work the docks and not know the name Tamhill. I read about your marriage to Lord Rathbone."

"Then you realize that discretion is necessary. For my husband's sake, more than mine. All I'm interested in is finding my real father."

"No one will ever know about you or your father should I be lucky enough to find him. It ain't going to be easy. Not much to go on unless one of the servants has a mouthful of gossip he's willing to spill."

"There is something else," Rathbone supplied. It took half an hour to give Mr. Covertly the details of what Mr. Fenstermaker had told them, along with what they had learned in Kent. "Granted, it isn't much, but if you're as discerning an investigator as Ramsbury led me to believe, I'm confident you'll be able to discover something."

"I'll need to do some traveling. Sure as the Queen wears black, the folks in this ledger are scattered after so many years."

"Whatever expenses you incur will be reimbursed, along with a hefty bonus should you provide the name I seek," Prudence assured him. "I'm prepared to pay you a reasonable retainer, followed by periodic payments as the information is supplied."

"I can't promise you any results."

"All I'm asking for is your best effort."

"Very well. I'll start poking my nose into things, discreet-like, of course."

The meeting with Mr. Covertly proved to be both climax and deathblow to Prudence. Later that week, she couldn't stop thinking there ought to be more she could do. While her husband nursed a brandy, she stood gazing out the library window, her cup of lemon tea untouched on the table near the chair she had just vacated.

The windows were closed to keep out the rain that had come in from across the Channel, offering relief from the summer heat and freshness to the sour-smelling Thames. Despite the closed windows and the splattering of raindrops on roofs and windows, Prudence could hear the street noises.

In the years she'd resided in London, she had learned to distinguish between the different city sounds. The milkman had only one horse, the iceman a team of four. The vegetable and fish vendors had strange calls that echoed up and down the streets, and the junkman's horse usually wore a cowbell that made a horrid jangle whenever its owner stopped to collect rags left on the curb. The sound she heard tonight was that of a hansom cab, its one horse slowly clopping its way over the wet streets. When it stopped, she supposed one of the neighbors had returned home after a busy day.

"Don't brood," Rathbone said. "We've done all we can for the time being."

"Have we?" She turned to face him. Her hands were locked together in front of her, her expression strained. "There are the London offices of Tamhill Shipping. As its new owner and manager, you could pay a visit. Ask a few questions. There are men there who worked under my father; perhaps they—"

"There wasn't anything to hear, sweetheart. Tamhill wasn't a man to let a breath of his wife's indiscretion go beyond the walls of his own home. You've described him too vividly for me to suspect otherwise."

"No," Prudence sighed. "There was no scandal. Whether the doing was Tamhill's or my mother's, I can't say. It's just that I feel so bloody useless."

Rathbone was on the verge of suggesting how his wife might prove herself useful should they retire early when a tap on the door interrupted him. A footman entered to announce a visitor.

"Who is it?" Rathbone asked.

"A Mr. Covertly, milord. Said to tell you he regrets the late hour, but that it's important."

Rathbone didn't have to look at his wife to know that her anxiety over feeling useless had turned to anxiety over the news Mr. Covertly had come to deliver.

"Show him in," he said, moving to the sideboard to renew his drink and to pour a fresh one for their guest.

When Mr. Covertly was shown into the room, he surprised both Rathbone and his wife by being as immaculately dressed as any gentlemen set on spending an evening about the city. He gave a slight bow to Prudence before smiling and accepting the drink Rathbone had at the ready.

"I apologize for calling at such a late hour," he said. "But I thought her ladyship might like some good news."

"Good news?" Prudence asked eagerly. "What have you found out?"

"Not what you're hoping to hear, but news nevertheless."

Prudence realized almost immediately that his voice lacked the uncultured tones she had heard that day in Southwark, and wondered if there was more to the investigator than met the eye. His recent use of a barber was also apparent. His hair, though still thick and wavy, had been cut to just above the collar.

"Please sit down," she said, remembering her manners. "Whatever news you have is welcome."

Prudence shut her mind to failure as she took a seat beside her husband, needing his closeness to ward off the fit of nerves that had her hands suddenly chilled and her pulse beating double-time.

"The first item of news is Mr. Fenstermaker," Covertly began after taking an appreciative sip of the claret his host had poured. "The address in London that he gave you to contact him is a small office that employs one clerk. Mr. Fenstermaker doesn't keep hours there. Never has. The clerk collects the mail and delivers it to the old gent's home. Not your normal man of business by any means. Caters to a very high clientele."

"How high?" Rathbone asked.

"I'd ventured a guess that his name is mentioned from time to time at Buckingham Palace."

Prudence wasn't sure what to make of the remark, so she looked at her husband. Rathbone seemed impressed but cautious.

"Lives in Regent Park, just off Albany Street." He passed Rathbone a card with the address. "Never married. No family. Staffs his house with a minimal number of servants. His name isn't listed on any of the club rosters. A very private gentleman."

"You said he has a respectable clientele. Just what does he do for them?" Again, the question came from Rathbone. Prudence was still trying to imagine John Fenstermaker paying a call at Buckingham Palace.

"Whatever they want done. His highest recommendation is his discretion."

"The same could be said of any solicitor," Rathbone remarked.

"Not in the way it's said of your Mr. Fenstermaker. And his clients don't chose him. He does the choosing. Won't handle anything with the least bit of tarnish on it. Very uppity, this one."

"What about Lady Montague?" Prudence inquired,

joining the conversation. "There must be a link between her and Mr. Fenstermaker. The property she inherited was sold to him."

"That's the part I'm still working on. I plan to take a train ride to Cornwall tomorrow morning. Ask a few questions, maybe even speak to the lady herself, if she's still alive."

Neither Prudence nor her husband asked how Micah Covertly intended to gain an interview with the wife of an earl. It was enough that he'd found the elusive Mr. Fenstermaker, whose name didn't appear in any of the legal listings.

"What about the ledger? Have you been able to trace any of the servants who were employed at Tamhill Hall?"

"Aye, that's the good part. I found your governess, Miss Hunnicutt. She's right here in London."

Prudence all but clapped her hands. "Miss Hunnicutt's here in London? Where?"

Another card was passed, this one displaying an address in Finsbury. "Her brother is a clock maker. She lives with him above his shop on Roseberry Avenue."

Prudence thought of the soft-spoken, wren-like woman who had been with her from as far back as she could remember to the day she had left Tamhill Hall in the Duke of Worley's coach as an orphan. There had been teachers at North Hill, but none of them had possessed Miss Hunnicutt's benevolent nature and caring smile. It would be good to see her again.

"I should be back from Cornwall in a week's time, maybe less. I'll be in touch as soon as I return."

"Thank you," Prudence said as Mr. Covertly prepared to leave. "I appreciate your time and effort."

"It's what you're paying me for," he replied matter-of-factly. "Good evening."

"I'll walk you to the door," Rathbone said.

The two men left the room. As Covertly regained his hat and gloves from the butler, Rathbone asked for a moment of private conversation.

"When you return from Cornwall, I will meet with you alone," the investigator was told. "While I share my wife's enthusiasm for finding her father, I will be the first to hear whatever information you have to report."

Covertly nodded. Both men knew that while it might be the name of Prudence's father they were seeking, it was the viscount who had employed him, and the viscount to whom he would answer should the information cause Lady Rathbone any distress.

"I'll get word to you," Covertly said, drawing on his gloves. "Not to worry. I know my business. There'll be no damage done to her ladyship by anything I say or do."

"Excellent," Rathbone replied. "As for Mr. Fenstermaker, I will pay the gentleman a call myself."

Again Covertly agreed.

Rathbone waited until the man had climbed into the waiting hansom before returning to the library and his wife.

Prudence paced the room, telling herself to take what satisfaction she could from Mr. Covertly's visit. He had gained some valuable information, or at least information that could lend itself to valuable answers. However, she still felt that she should be playing a more active role in things.

"I assume you want to call on Miss Hunnicutt," Rathbone said.

"Yes. I shall pen a note before going upstairs," Prudence told him, "asking if it is convenient for me to call tomorrow afternoon."

"I would prefer that you wait until the day after tomorrow before going to Finsbury. Being in the city, I had arranged to handle some business tomorrow. If Miss Hunnicutt can receive you the following day, I will accompany you."

"I'm quite capable of taking myself to Finsbury and back, my lord."

"That isn't the point. I do not want you upset should she have unpleasant news."

"There is nothing new about the fact that my mother had an affair. As for the interview turning unpleasant, what could Miss Hunnicutt tell me beyond the name of the man I am doing my best to discover?"

He stared at her, obviously disliking her stubbornness. "I am not questioning your capability to traverse London, madam. I am requesting that you contain your impatience and schedule your call when I can accompany you."

"Why? Are you afraid that discovering the man's name will send me into a senseless tizzy? I assure you, it will not."

While Rathbone was growing more content with his marriage, he had yet to accommodate himself to his wife's independent nature. "I am simply asking that you wait."

Prudence considered the matter for a moment, unsure why it was important to him, then relented. "Very well, my lord. I will ask if a call the day after tomorrow will be convenient."

"Thank you."

He opened his arms and she walked into them, resting her cheek against the starched pleats of his shirt. "I'm sure he's a good man," she said. "My mother wouldn't have loved him otherwise."

Rathbone didn't comment. His philosophy had always been to avoid the complications of love. It was apparent his wife held an opposing view.

But the real question was, did she love him?

While he wasn't sure what his own feelings entailed, other than an unwaning passion, he found himself wanting Prudence to feel as strongly for him as her mother had felt for an unnamed gentleman years ago. It would certainly do no harm for a wife to love her husband, and it could prevent a repeat of past actions, for he could think of nothing he disliked more than the idea of Prudence turning to another man in the years to come.

Filled with an overwhelming need to make sure that this would never happen, Rathbone applied his natural talent to diverting his wife's attention away from the past and onto the present.

CHAPTER 17

The rain had stopped by the time Prudence came downstairs, having slept late due to her husband's amorous attentions the previous night. By noon, patches of blue had begun to blossom in the sky, and she was feeling restless.

Taking herself into the morning room, she sat down at the small rolltop desk and penned a note to Miss Hunnicutt, then gave instructions to a footman that it be delivered immediately.

That done, she picked up her embroidery.

When the tall clock in the front entrance struck the hour, the suddenness of it seemed to absorb all other sounds in the house. Prudence realized her hands had been idle; not a single stitch had been added to the work.

Discarding the linen square, she walked to the corner of the room and pulled the bell cord. A few moments later, the butler appeared in the doorway.

"Have a carriage made ready for me," she instructed him. "I am going into the city."

Palrey hesitated, his expression saying he wasn't entirely sure his lordship would be pleased. A moment passed before he submitted to Prudence's stubborn glare and ordered a lingering footman to the mews with the order that a carriage be readied immediately.

Prudence left the house a short time later, wearing a royal blue walking dress that draped itself gracefully as she moved. It was cut fashionably and flowed over a small bustle in the back. She carried a parasol trimmed in black lace.

Armed with Mr. Fenstermaker's address—she had noted the number of his residence when her husband had put the card on the table before escorting Mr. Covertly to the door—Prudence was of a mind to confront the man and learn something of his business connection to her father. It went without saying that he must have one, for there was no other reason that could explain Summer House coming to her in such a mysterious manner.

The trip from Belgrave Square to Regent's Park was a pleasant one despite the growing summer heat. While she preferred the country, the city never ceased to fascinate her. London was a world unto itself, threaded by alleys, cobblestone avenues, shops, and stylish homes. Circled by factories and warehouses, it existed as if the open realm of forest and field and stream had yet to be discovered.

Its people were even more diverse. Set off and apart by privilege and poverty, the garish, sprawling girth of the city encompassed the citizenry with an odd equality. While the circumstances of her life had presented her with a sophisticated environment, Prudence was not immune to the hardships of others, and had encouraged her husband to increase the charitable donations from her inheritance. Rathbone had agreed, mostly to please her, but he was not unconscious of the need himself.

In fact, her husband was proving to be a very generous man. Theirs was a precarious relationship at best, but he had set aside his duties at King's Crossing to take her to Kent. While she appreciated his generosity, it also puzzled her. The charming viscount, whose reputation had once gone hand in hand with scandalous gossip, now appeared the devoted husband.

But for how long? Until his passion for his new wife faded and he once again sought the excitement of the London night with its gambling halls and brothels? Prudence knew she could not bear to be the wife of such a man, and yet, she had married Rathbone more willingly than anyone supposed.

Because she loved him, yes. And because she was convinced that she could bring his heart to love her faithfully in return. The thing she must now face was the possibility that it had been a conceited dream, blurred by romantic fantasies. Although his passion seemed focused solely on her, he had yet to speak a single word of true affection.

Before she could reason out what it would take to get him to voice his feelings, the carriage stopped in front of No. 12 Albany Street, an inconspicuous residence with a waist-high iron gate separating its cleanly swept walk from the street.

The driver had jumped down to open the door for her when Prudence eyed an all too familiar carriage parked across the street. It seemed she was late. Her husband had already arrived, was inside even now, and without so much as a whisper to her of his intentions.

Doing the only thing she could under the circumstances, Prudence exchanged one carriage for the other, giving her own driver a brisk order that he could return to Belgrave Square.

Thaddeus, sitting atop her husband's carriage, looked at her with slight surprise before climbing down from his perch and opening the door. Once she was seated, Prudence began formulating how she was going to make her husband regret his arrogance.

Her temper was boiling by the time Rathbone showed himself, leaving Mr. Fenstermaker's house and making his way across the street. His only show of surprise at finding his wife waiting inside the carriage was a slight hesitation as his foot reached the step. Once he'd pulled himself inside, and after a firm tap on the roof to let Thaddeus know it was time to set the horses in motion, he presented Prudence with a frown that had absolutely no effect on the tongue-lashing she had prepared for him.

"I was not so sleepy when I left this morning as to forget that I had a passenger," he said, as if she was the one to be held accountable and not he.

Prudence studied him for a long while, her response so long in the coming that her husband found the wait onerous. "Do not think to put me on the defensive, my lord, for I will not allow it. Nor will your charm, notably irresistible on most occasions, prevent me from demanding an explanation."

"And what explanation would that be, madam?" he asked levelly. "It's apparent what business I've been about and with whom."

"It is the *why* of it I wish explained. What right have you to come here without telling me? It is *my* father—"

"The right is mine as your husband," Rathbone said, cutting off her protest. "A right that was handed to me the day I took responsibility for you."

"Responsibility!" The word spilled over Prudence like a deadly acid. "May I remind you, sir, that I never asked to become your responsibility. In fact, I questioned the advisability of our marriage. A question that presents itself again, this very moment. You said nothing to me of coming to see Mr. Fenstermaker, made no indication that your business was anything more than it would normally be in London. You intentionally deceived me."

"That's ludicrous. I have every right to protect you."

"Protect me from what? If you think to shield me from discovering that my father may not be the man I hope him to be, that his actions now and in the past were not made with noble intentions, then you are wasting your time, my lord. I am not so foolish as to think him a saint."

"While your words sound eminently sensible, they do not describe the emotion you are capable of, my dear. I know you far better than you think. You are obsessed with finding the man. So much so, I fear you may do something impulsive when his name is finally presented. It is for that reason that I am trying to act as an intermediary. I will not see you hurt or your good standing diminished because of something your mother did."

Prudence tightened her grip on the reticule laying in her lap. "Do not use a mask of concern to hide your real intentions, my lord. You are trying to control me. You think me incapable of handling my emotions, just as Uncle Horace thought me incapable of handling my own affairs. It is an insult. One that seriously offends me."

"And what offense will take place should you discover that your father is alive? What if he is married? What if his wife is a respectable woman who has no idea of her husband's previous dalliances? What if he has other children? Do you plan to present yourself to them as a long-lost sister? I do not begrudge you the need to find your father, but there may well be more than the two of you involved, should the time for disclosure arrive. Have you thought of that?"

Prudence found she couldn't speak. In all the years and months and days that she had longed for a fateful glimpse of her father, her thoughts had brought her only to that moment of discovery—never beyond it.

Her temper cooled as she leaned back against the velvet cushions, her shoulders slightly slumped by the enormous weight her husband had just rested upon them. If she discovered her father's identity, would that in itself be enough? Could she finally recognize him for who and what he was and not interfere in his life? Not covet a place by his side?

Rathbone regarded her silently, knowing he had achieved his goal, but disliking the guilt he felt because of it.

"You are right," she said flatly. "I don't know what I shall do if I find him. I only know that I must."

"I would spare you hurt, if I can," he said, his voice softening to match the mood. "There was no deceit in my calling upon Mr. Fenstermaker today. I sought only what he might tell me, either intentionally or accidentally."

"What did you discover?" Prudence asked, putting their argument aside for the moment.

"Nothing," Rathbone replied with total honesty and obvious frustration. "Absolutely nothing. I doubt the man could be persuaded to divulge his secrets were he handed over to a Spanish Inquisitor. As much as it tests my patience, his loyalty cannot be slighted."

Loyalty and gentlemanly honor were the unwritten

laws of the day. They were not to be broken lightly or without consequence, especially if one expected to be looked upon with any degree of respect. Her husband had been born under those laws, reared with them, thus understanding what few men assumed a female mind could comprehend.

But Prudence did understand. If her father was alive, it was natural to assume that he would show reluctance to accept now what he had not been able to acknowledge at her birth—that he had had an affair with a married woman and created a child.

Under those conditions, Summer House could well be a balm for his conscience, not the clue she hoped it to be. If that was the case, then why gift it to her? The house and the memories that had come into focus after visiting it fed her obsession more than the words in her mother's diary.

Rathbone wasn't sure what was going on inside his wife's lovely head. The anger that had consumed her when he'd climbed into the carriage had been replaced with a mood of inner reflection.

Telling himself he had every right to be as angry as she, Rathbone couldn't help but feel like an unnecessary appendage.

"Mr. Fenstermaker was not the only call I made today," he said, forcing her attention away from the window and onto him. "I visited the offices of Tamhill Shipping before having lunch at my club. I accepted an invitation for tonight, a reception to celebrate Lord Thornton's appointment as Secretary to the Foreign Ministry."

"I had read he was being considered for the post," Prudence replied. The admission might have been accepted strangely by some men. Ladies were not supposed to read more than the social pages or fashion columns, and only then with their husband's consent. But Rathbone showed no such disapproval.

Instead, thinking their argument over, he smiled. "The city offers few diversions this time of year. I thought a little outside company might suit."

"Are you growing tired of your confinement, my lord?"

The remark was so desperately predictable that Rathbone had to smile. Prudence was worried that their honeymoon had lost its appeal. "On the contrary, madam, I find myself eager to get home. While a carriage offers certain possibilities, I prefer the comfort of our bedroom."

"Our bedroom will not be shared until later tonight, my lord."

"You're still angry?"

"Very much so."

Her husband didn't look amused. "I should have known."

"Yes, my lord. You should. While I may relent and say that your explanation for calling upon Mr. Fenstermaker is a valid one, your lack of confidence in me is most upsetting."

"I have every confidence in you."

"If that is the case, then why didn't you tell me of your plans to visit him?"

There was a glimmer of a smile in his eyes when he replied by asking the same of her. "I heard no mention of you taking to town today, madam. You would not be sitting in this carriage now had you not entertained the same thought. Have you no confidence in me?"

Prudence took a breath as if to speak, then changed her mind. She wondered if her husband had any idea just how strongly she felt about him. There were times when she felt transparent, her emotions as readable as the bold print of the *London Times*. And other times, like now, she wondered if he cared to know how she felt, other than to hear her admit that as his wife she was subject to his authority.

All in all, there seemed little point in pursuing the matter of feelings, either on her part or on her husband's. His actions today spoke as clearly as any words. He'd proposed marriage because there had been no alternative. What he thought of her when they were in bed was just as easy to ascertain. She was his lover, a woman to give him pleasure. That concluded, she had come full circle in her thinking. While she enjoyed the role of lover, she would much rather be loved.

When Prudence descended the staircase that evening, it was to meet her husband's approving eyes. The gown she had selected was of gold silk with sheer lace sleeves, decorated with a delicate beading at the neck and shoulders that did alchemistical things to her eyes. The bustle was narrow and elegantly draped, caught up in a silver bow that provided a sharp contrast while adding a touch of elegance. She wore a necklace of blood-red rubies and large, perfectly matched pearls. The effect made Rathbone want to carry her back upstairs and to hell with Lord Thornton's reception.

Upon entering Lady Newsome's Mayfair residence, Lord and Lady Rathbone were immediately recognizable under the blazing light of the twin chandeliers, and Prudence realized it was the first time since their wedding day that Society would view her and Rathbone as a married couple.

Conscious of her role as a viscountess, she stood patiently on her husband's arm while the majordomo introduced them. The announcement, made in a resonant voice, drew every eye in the room.

Used to social events of any magnitude, Prudence smiled as she descended the three steps that would take her into the room. Their hostess, Lady Newsome, was the first to greet them. A uniquely striking woman, tall and slender, with rich auburn hair and a fortune inherited from her husband, she was all smiles.

"How very wonderful that you were in the city and could attend," she said. "And please accept my congratulations upon your wedding. I must say you make a handsome couple."

The amenities concluded, they spent the next fifteen minutes drifting from one small group to another, receiving belated congratulations and engaging in the superficial pleasantries that went hand in hand with political receptions.

"Oh, look, it's Hattie," Prudence said, relieved to see someone she knew. "And Mr. Counce is escorting her."

"Your matchmaking seems to have worked," Rathbone said, guiding her in the direction of the young couple, who was standing near one of the many open windows. It was an excessively warm night.

"How very wonderful," Hattie exclaimed at seeing her best friend again. "I didn't know you were in the city."

"Only for a few days," Prudence told her. "Benjamin had some business which required his attention. But I'm just as surprised to see you."

Hattie, normally shy and rarely vocal above a whisper, smiled from ear to ear. "I am engaged."

Titus cleared his throat, as if Prudence might not realize to whom. While he was being congratulated by Rathbone, something that would have been inconceivable three months ago, Prudence hugged her friend. "How wonderful. Oh, Hattie, how absolutely wonderful!"

"I can't believe it," she said, smiling all the more when Titus returned to her side. "Papa agreed that we need not wait for months. You will come to the wedding, won't you? I'll never be able to manage without you. There's so very much to do. We're going to honeymoon in Greece!"

Prudence couldn't resist giving her friend another hug. "It sounds very romantic," she whispered.

True to character, Hattie blushed a deep red.

It was an hour later, after enjoying a light supper of cold meats, pastries, and an assortment of sherbets, before Prudence could find a moment of privacy in which to speak with Hattie again. Rathbone was standing across the room, talking to a stout looking man with a garnish of medals on his chest.

"Finally, a private corner," Prudence said, motioning Hattie into a small room off the reception hall. They sat down on a brocade tête-à-tête. "I'm so very happy for you."

"And you, are you happy?" her friend asked in reply. "You look happy, and so very beautiful when you came walking in on Lord Rathbone's arm. I never told you, but the day you were married, I couldn't help but think that I've never seen two people so well matched. He's so very handsome."

"Yes, he is," Prudence said, replying to the latter without answering the real question. "Will you be wearing your mother's wedding gown? I recall you saying it was always what you wanted."

"Yes. Mademoiselle Dupree is altering it for me. That's why I'm in the city."

They spoke about the wedding and the trip to Greece,

before Hattie turned serious. "Oh, Pru, I must admit I have reservations. Titus is so very well-versed in traveling. Did you know he speaks six languages? He wants to continue making his way as a scholar, going to the most exotic places, most of which I can barely pronounce."

"Do you love him?"

"Yes."

"Then do not allow yourself to be left behind," Prudence insisted. "Go with him. To the ends of the earth, if his interest is drawn there."

"But what shall I do? I dislike meeting new people, even if I can put on a brave face for a short while."

"You can write about it. Keep a journal. There has never been any shyness in the correspondence we've exchanged. When you return to England, you can have your notes published. Many women are doing just that. And more. Some of them are exploring on their own."

"Without the benefit of a husband?"

"Why not? Women have two legs, just like men. They are as mobile in body as they are in mind, regardless of what some would have us believe."

Prudence glimpsed Lady Wallingcroft, Hattie's future in-law, across the room, looking quite forlorn in a gown of dark gray satin that did nothing to complement either her hair or her complexion. "Enjoy your life, Hattie. Travel, and be thankful that Titus sees you as an equal."

Hattie followed her friend's line of vision. "I do not wish to become like Lady Wallingcroft. She is not a happy woman."

"Then do not be like her. Titus is not like his uncle. He is intelligent, not pompous; generous, not conceited. And you have the kindest heart I have ever known. Be happy."

"Excellent advice," Rathbone said, walking up behind them. "Ladies," he added, slipping effortlessly into the charming role he had played for so many years. "I do not reprimand you for finding a quiet corner in which to talk. Wretchedly boring conversation going about the rest of the room. Politics and more politics. I, for one, would rather stroll about the garden with a lovely woman on my arm."

Offering his arm, he silently bade his wife accept it.

As always, Prudence felt an immediate rush of excitement. Rathbone was gazing upon her with such intensity that it was impossible not to know what he planned once they passed into the shadows of the garden.

"I should find Titus," Hattie said. "He dislikes politics, but he felt obliged to accept Lady Newsome's invitation when she extended it."

"As did most of the people here," Prudence replied with her usual candor. "Do come by tomorrow afternoon for tea."

"I will," Hattie promised before hurrying off to find her fiancé.

They were midway through the room, walking toward the terrace doors, when Prudence saw a man glancing about the room, his eyes wandering from person to person as if he were seeking one in particular. He seemed vaguely familiar, but Prudence couldn't place where she might have seen him before, though it was very likely he had been at one of the hundreds of balls and parties she had attended with the Duke of Worley or Lionel.

When the man's eyes came to rest on her, his expression took on a purpose. He began to walk toward her, his tall frame moving lithely through the crowd. As he drew closer, his face appeared more interesting than handsome: his nose too long, his mouth a little too full beneath a well-groomed mustache. Silver had taken over most of his dark hair. His presence was commanding, and his intelligence apparent in the dark gleam of his eyes.

He stopped just in front of them, gracefully blocking their path. "Lady Rathbone," he said, his voice deep and smooth. "I knew your mother years ago. You look like her. May I take this opportunity to congratulate both you and Lord Rathbone on your marriage."

Prudence's heart did a quick somersault inside her chest. The man had known her mother. The slight tightening of her husband's arm around her waist told her Rathbone knew what she was thinking.

"And you are, sir?"

"Daniel Bartlett. Captain Bartlett. I once commanded a Tamhill ship. It was a long time ago."

Had it not been for her husband's arm, Prudence would have found it impossible to stand. Although the man claimed to have captained a Tamhill ship, it was her mother he had mentioned, not the man who would have been his employer.

"And what occupation do you carry now?" Rathbone asked.

"The sea will always be my home," Bartlett replied with mild amusement. "I captain my own ship now. The *Providence.*"

"You said you knew my mother." Prudence studied his face, imagining what he would have looked like twenty years ago.

"Yes," he acknowledged. His gaze lingered on her; then—deliberately, she felt—he changed the way he was looking at her, his expression becoming more casual. "Before she married your father. As I said, it was a long time ago."

Prudence's heart skipped another beat. Was Daniel

Bartlett her father? Had he once been in love with her mother? And she with him? Had they renewed their relationship after her mother's marriage?

"Have we met before?" Prudence asked, schooling her features.

"Once. But you were too small to remember." He smiled again, only the barest shadow showing behind the memory. "Your parents were attending a party at the house of Lord Thornton, the very man we are honoring tonight. It was summer and you were playing in the garden. You asked me if I knew any pirates."

"Did I?" Prudence replied, smiling. "Do you? Know any pirates, that is?"

"A few. Piracy isn't an uncommon thing in the Eastern seas."

"And that is where you sail? In the Orient?"

"Yes."

"I was just taking my wife outside for a breath of fresh air," Rathbone said, his tone of voice implying that Captain Bartlett was welcome to join them.

The captain extended his arm to Prudence, adding his escort to that of her husband.

"Tell me of your travels in the Orient," Prudence asked once they reached the stone balustrade that rimmed the terrace. She was grateful for her husband's nearness.

"The Orient isn't easily described. It's a culture unlike any known to Europe. Savage at times, sentimental at others. Civilized, but not in the way an Englishman would think of civilization."

"Yet it draws you," she said, hearing the warmth and admiration in his words.

"Yes," he answered quickly. "I've never seen anything as blue as the South China Sea, or anything as grand as the Great Wall of China."

"Have you met Titus Counce?" Rathbone rejoined. "He's only recently returned from China."

"On my ship," Bartlett said, his full mouth touched with humor. "An enthusiastic young man, and an extremely intelligent one."

"He's engaged to Lady Corry," Prudence told him. "Henrietta and I have been friends most of our lives."

"Titus introduced me to her," Bartlett said. "I think she will suit him well."

Prudence nodded, unable to keep a smile from her face. She rested a gloved hand on the balustrade, and Rathbone gently covered it with his own. It was a small gesture, but one Prudence took to heart.

"May I ask how you knew my mother, Captain? Are you perhaps from East Sussex?"

"I was born in Liverpool. My father was a sailor, just as his father before him. My sister, Deborah, introduced me to your mother. They attended the same finishing school." His expression changed again, becoming melancholy as he looked down at her. "We were friends, your mother and I. I've never met a woman who enjoyed laughter as much as Rachel. She was always laughing. Always smiling. Forever optimistic."

"We have something in common, Captain. I often think of my mother's laughter."

"Then you have the best possible memories."

Prudence waited, trying to keep her own optimism from showing. Still by her side, she looked at her husband. His smile was tender, but she could read the caution in his eyes. He didn't want her jumping to conclusions.

"My husband and I will be in London for a few more days," she said, acting upon her feelings. "We would be honored to have you join us for dinner."

"I'm honored by the invitation."

"And please bring Mrs. Bartlett with you," she added,

her words casual while her heart hammered away inside her chest.

"There is no Mrs. Bartlett. A life at sea rarely mixes well with a wife on land. I have never married."

"Tomorrow night then," she said. "We make our home in Belgrave Square." She gave him the number, asking if eight o'clock would be convenient.

There was a sadness that was close to tears in her eyes as Prudence watched the captain return to the crowd that filled the reception hall. Torn between elation and doubt, she turned to Rathbone. She didn't have to say a word. Her hopes were written on her face.

"Captain Bartlett does present a possibility," Rathbone said. "But tread carefully, sweetheart. An introduction, while both unexpected and timely, does not mean he knew your mother as more than a friend."

"You must admit the pieces fit," she said, mixing logic with excitement. "If Titus sailed home on Captain Bartlett's ship, then he's been in London since late spring. He could have read of our engagement in the newspaper and arranged for Mr. Fenstermaker to deed the property. He's of the right age, and he's tall. And his hair. It had a generous touch of gray in it now, but it is dark. And being here tonight . . . approaching me, mentioning my mother. It can't all be a coincidence. And he does look familiar."

"How familiar? Do you see him as the man who carried you on his shoulders that day on the beach? There are thousands of tall, dark-haired men in London. And hundreds that you could have met in any manner of ways."

"You're right. It's wishful thinking." A frustrated sigh escaped her. "If only I could remember more about the time I spent at Summer House."

He put a consoling arm around her waist and drew

her close. "It will come back to you. Summer House jiggled loose one memory. Another is sure to follow."

Prudence took a deep breath and tried to relax. So much had happened of late. Meeting Rathbone, having him invade her bedroom, then her entire life. Falling a little more in love with him every day. All piled on top of the wish to find her father. A wish that was beginning to look as if it might become a reality. No wonder her customary energy was waning. So many thoughts, so many feelings. It was enough to make one weary.

"You have invited him to dinner, and he has accepted," Rathbone said compassionately. "If Bartlett is reaching out to you, then you must be patient and allow him to do so in his own way. In the meantime, we will call on Miss Hunnicutt."

"Patience is not proving to be one of my virtues," she told him. "I've dreamed so long of finding him. Of regaining my family."

"We will make our own family."

The remark, so unlike any she'd heard or expected to hear, brought Prudence's head up and around.

"Don't look so surprised," Rathbone said. "Considering our compatibility in the bedroom, it's inevitable."

Unsure if her husband regarded family as just the required heir or in the truer sense of the word, Prudence was just as unsure of a response. Rathbone rescued her by lowering his head to place a not-so-chaste kiss on her mouth, then further shocked her by saying, "While I require a son, I find myself thinking of a little girl with big brown eyes, forever in mischief."

"I think any child of yours would be forever in mischief, my lord."

"True enough, but with you as their mother, I've no worry that they'll grow up uncontrollable hellions."

"Just charming scoundrels," she said teasingly.

"Only the lads. My daughters will be every bit as lovely, and stubborn, as their mother."

The compliment was reaffirmed by an appreciative gleam in his eyes and a smile so endearing that it caused Prudence's heart to swell. If Rathbone could talk about children in such a way as to make her think he did indeed desire a real family, then perhaps she'd made more progress with his heart than first imagined. God knew, he certainly owned hers.

When they returned to the ballroom, Prudence scanned the crowd for another glimpse of Captain Bartlett, but he was nowhere to be seen. Her disappointment lessened as she saw Hattie and Titus engaged in conversation with their hostess, Lady Newsome. She'd never seen her friend looking happier.

"I should pay my respects to Lord Thornton," Rathbone remarked, upon seeing the man unoccupied for the moment. He had been surrounded by a circle of political cronies most of the evening. "Then, if you have had enough public activity, we will take ourselves home to more private entertainment."

The warmth of his smile gave Prudence the courage to counter his suggestive remark with one of her own. "It's rather late for parlor games."

He lowered his head and whispered, "I wasn't thinking of the parlor, madam, but now that you've mentioned it, there is a particular chair that might serve the purpose. The large one near the fireplace."

Prudence managed not to laugh, but she couldn't keep a smile of anticipation from coming to her face. "It does look comfortable."

Upon arriving home, it was not the parlor chair Rathbone chose but the armless chaise in the study. After locking the door, he led Prudence by the hand, and with each step her anticipation grew. With his most charming smile, he drew her into his arms and kissed her, and the anticipation turned into a thrill of desire so keen that Prudence immediately reached for his cravat.

"Impatient, are we?"

"If I am, it is entirely your fault, my lord."

Before her husband could reply, Prudence reached up and drew his lips to hers.

It was a good hour later, when she was resting quite comfortably atop her husband, that Prudence suggested the addition of a chaise to their bedroom at King's Crossing.

CHAPTER 18

Prudence drew a steadying breath as, hands clenched, she waited for the carriage to make its way north along the Strand to Finsbury and the clockmaker's shop.

"When was the last time you saw Miss Hunnicutt?" Rathbone asked.

"The day after Sir Archibald's funeral. The maids had packed my things and I was waiting in the withdrawing room for the Duke of Worley. Miss Hunnicutt came in to say goodbye to me before I left Tamhill Hall for North Hill. She told me not to worry, that all would be well."

"And it was."

Prudence smiled with the memory. "The first time I saw Uncle Horace, he was standing beside my father's grave, dressed in black and looking very severe. Later that evening, I was called downstairs to the library. The duke told me that he was to be my guardian. I handled the news well enough, until he mentioned that he was a widower with two sons. The thought of having brothers scared the wits out of me. I envisioned them as miniature tyrants who'd put spiders in my bed."

"I can't imagine such upstanding men as Frederick and Lionel doing any such thing," he said teasingly.

"They didn't. At least, not at first, but I was terribly frightened of them. Frederick was nearly as tall as the duke, and just as forbidding. If it hadn't been for Lionel, I think I would have taken to my room and stayed there."

"They both regard you as a sister," he said, recalling the way Lionel had threatened to punch his face in the night he'd been discovered in Prudence's bedroom.

"They still frightened me the first time I saw them," Prudence confessed.

Her husband laughed, and it eased some of the tension she had felt since getting dressed and coming downstairs. This morning's call upon Selene Hunnicutt would be the first time she'd seen anyone connected with Tamhill Hall since the day she'd ridden away from the estate in the duke's traveling coach.

In that sense, the morning call would be a home-coming—one Prudence hoped would finally put the ghosts of her childhood to rest.

Edward Hunnicutt's shop looked very much like any other business establishment to be found outside the expensive perimeters of Bond and Oxford Streets. Two large windows framed by reddish-brown brick displayed a variety of timepieces.

Upon entering the shop at precisely eleven, Prudence and her husband found themselves surrounded by chiming clocks: bracket clocks with ormolu mounts and enamel cartouches, musical clocks with figurines that turned in time to the music, brass tabernacle clocks with swaying pendulums, porcelain mantel clocks with gilt trim, and sturdy table regulators, one with *Tempus fugit*—"time flies"—painted on the dial.

The corners of the shop were just as crowded, each displaying a longcase clock, some with brass-capped columns, others with ornately carved finials.

While her husband waited for the chiming to cease so he could ring the brass bell on the glass counter and summon either the clerk or Miss Hunnicutt's brother, Prudence admired a finely made tallcase clock with a swan's neck pediment and gilt finials. The entire case was painted with flowers, trophies, and strapwork, and the dial with Arabic numerals. The delicate craftsmanship reminded Prudence of Summer House. She decided to purchase it before leaving.

When the chiming stopped, Edward Hunnicutt appeared, wearing a leather apron over dark trousers and a blue shirt.

"My lord?" he asked, apparently unsure if the couple standing in his shop were his sister's expected guests or potential customers.

"My wife, Lady Rathbone, has come to call upon your sister."

"I trust Miss Hunnicutt is in good health," Prudence inquired, stepping forward.

"Aye, Your Ladyship, she's getting along fine," her brother replied with a light nod of his head. He was a man of medium height with no extravagance to his features. "This way, if you please," he said, coming from around the counter to guide them through a door at the rear of the shop, then up a flight of dark narrow stairs that led to the second floor.

He gave the door a light tap before opening it.

Prudence entered a small front parlor with a threadbare Oriental carpet. The room would have been as dark as the hall except for the shaded gasolier above a gilt-framed mirror in need of resilvering, overly ornate for such a simple room and very probably purchased from a junkman's cart. Upon seeing her former governess, Prudence immediately forgot the state of her surroundings and smiled.

Selene Hunnicutt, wearing a blue merino shawl over her shoulders, stood before the upstairs window overlooking Roseberry Avenue. While she was older and not as well dressed as she had once been, her welcoming smile brought back a flood of memories. The one thing Prudence didn't recognize was the cane in her right hand.

"Are you ill?" she asked immediately, rushing forward to give Selene a hug. "Here, let me help you sit down."

She guided Selene to a nearby chair, one as threadbare as the carpet. "I wouldn't have come if you had told me you weren't up to receiving callers."

"It's not an illness, but an old injury," Selene said. Looking up from the chair, she smiled, shaking her head slightly, as if unable to believe that Prudence was standing in front of her. "Look at you, my lady. As pretty as your mother, and married to this fine lord. It does my heart good to see you again."

"My heart feels remarkably good at the sight of you," Prudence replied. "Now, tell me how you were injured."

"First, some tea," Selene said, looking toward her brother. He left the room, parting a set of curtains over an open doorway and disappearing. "Excuse my manners, my lord." She looked to Rathbone. "Please sit down."

To Prudence's pride, her husband stepped forward, lifted Selene's hand, and bowed over it as if he were meeting the most aristocratic of ladies. "It's a pleasure to make your acquaintance, Miss Hunnicutt. My wife speaks of you with great affection."

Further conversation was delayed as Edward Hunnicutt returned with the tea tray. He declined his sister's offer to join them, insisting he had work downstairs. As Selene poured tea, Prudence made a second inquiry about her health.

"It was a silly accident. One of those things that catches a body off guard and unprepared. I caught the heel of my shoe as I was coming upstairs. Tumbled back down the steps, head over heels. I broke my hip. The bone didn't knit well. But, no worry on your part, my lady. I'm getting along just fine."

It was apparent to Prudence that Selene was not "getting along just fine," but she kept the matter to herself for the time being.

"Now that I'm here, I'm not sure how to go about the matter that brought me," Prudence said. "It concerns my mother."

Miss Hunnicutt nodded, her eyes never leaving Prudence's face.

"It's a delicate matter. One that you may not feel comfortable discussing, but one which is extremely important to me."

"I know you well enough to have come to that conclusion already," Prudence was told. "What is it?"

Rathbone sipped his tea, which was quite good, while he listened to Prudence voice her suspicions. If Miss Hunnicutt was shocked, it didn't show.

When his wife was finished, her former governess stared at her levelly for several seconds, her hand tightening over the handle of her cane, as if to fortify herself for the response she was about to make.

"It's of no news to you that Sir Archibald and your mother didn't have the best of marriages, my lady, so I'll not pretend they did. There were too many arguments overheard by the staff and by you to voice an opinion to the contrary. As for your mother . . . I can't be sure if there *was* another man. What I can tell you is that shortly after I was employed, one of the parlor maids warned me to be careful. She said Mrs. Tamhill's lady's maid had been discharged by Sir Archibald. According to the gossip, it was out of turn. Seems she knew too much about something she had no business knowing."

"I don't recall my mother having any maid except Frances."

"There was another before Frances came. Her name was Helen Barnaby. I never met her; she had already left Tamhill Hall when I arrived."

"If she came to Tamhill Hall with my mother, then she must have been employed by the Gundersons before my mother married Sir Archibald."

"I can't say for certain," Miss Hunnicutt replied. "What I can say is that I never heard or saw your mother being anything she shouldn't. She loved you very much."

"And I loved her." Prudence smiled as she returned her teacup to the tray on the table. While Selene hadn't given her the name of the man, she had provided another piece of the puzzle. Helen Barnaby. The reason for the maid's discharge could very well have been her knowledge of Rachel Tamhill's indiscretion.

"Sir Archibald wasn't the easiest man to please," Selene said. "If your mother . . . What I mean to say is that if she did find consolation with another man, I'd not blame her. Nor judge her. And it would explain why Sir Archibald showed so little interest in you."

Rathbone hid his irritation at the remark. Not because Miss Hunnicutt had been indelicate enough to say it—Prudence had urged her to tell the truth—but because he'd very much like to get his hands around the throat of the man who had caused his wife to feel inadequate. Though not an expert on children, he did have the common sense to know they needed love and encouragement.

"I neither blame nor judge my mother," Prudence said. "I loved her with all my heart. My only concern now is finding the man or at least discovering who he was. Are you sure you never heard any gossip? Anything out of the ordinary?"

"Not taking my meals in the kitchen with the rest of the staff, I wasn't privy to the talk that went around the table. I did make friends with the scullery maid, Sarah. She was a nice girl, a bit shy like me, which is why we probably took to one another."

"Did Sarah mention something, then?" Prudence leaned forward slightly. Like Selene, she disliked attaching importance to gossip, but it was all she had now.

More tea was poured before Selene answered. "I remember one day; it was spring and the gardens were full of blooms. I had just dressed you for a walk with your mother. I had tea in the kitchen with Sarah while you were outside. We just chatted, not saying anything of any real importance, when Sarah asked me if I planned to visit my family that summer. I replied that I didn't expect to. Then she said that there might be time. Mrs. Tamhill might be taking you away, if Sir Archibald went to London as he usually did before the fleet sailed. Said Mrs. Tamhill had done just that thing the year before. Took you off, no nurse, no governess, just the two of you."

"Did we go away that summer?" Prudence asked, wondering if her mother's mysterious excursion had been to Kent. Trips of any kind usually required at least one servant, and if a child were along, then a nurse or governess was routinely taken as well.

"Not that summer, nor any summer thereafter. It was just the way Sarah said it, as if she knew something I didn't."

Prudence filed the information away. As soon as she met with Mr. Covertly, she'd turn his attention to Helen Barnaby and the scullery maid. "What was Sarah's last name?"

"Hmmm?" Selene gave it a moment's thought. "Hopkins, I think, but she may have married. She was a pretty girl, and she had a sweetheart in the village."

"One last question. Did you ever hear the name Daniel Bartlett? He once commanded a Tamhill ship."

"No. The name doesn't sound familiar. There were visitors from time to time. Some of them worked for your father, but I don't recall a Mr. Bartlett being among them."

"Thank you for being so candid with me," Prudence said.

"It's a quality we both share. You were always an honest child, never pretending you hadn't done something mischievous when you had." Selene turned her attention to Rathbone, who had been content to sit and listen. "Were I able and ten years younger, I'd apply for the position as governess to your children when they begin arriving, my lord. I've always favored her ladyship."

"When the nursery at King's Crossing has a child to visit, then I insist that you do, Miss Hunnicutt. My wife and I will welcome you."

It was with mixed emotions and turbulent feelings that Prudence took her leave a short time later. Once downstairs, she purchased the clock she had admired before going upstairs, and arranged for it to be shipped to Summer House.

Edward Hunnicutt's pleasure at having sold one of

his most expensive timepieces was apparent as he took down the information, promising that he'd see the clock well packed and in a sturdy shipping case before handing it over to the freight wagon.

"All of your clocks are attractive, Mr. Hunnicutt. Have you ever thought of moving your shop to Bond Street? I'm sure your business would prosper."

"This was my father's shop," he said. "And aye, I've thought of renting another building, one closer to the customers I try to please, but having a shop on Bond Street and my sister here alone doesn't suit me."

Prudence hesitated a moment, glancing toward her husband, who, it seemed, already knew what she was thinking. A slight nod of his head was all she needed before pursuing the discussion.

"Your sister is a person I hold in high regard. Had I known of her accident and the hardship it has caused, I would have acted sooner. Now that I do know, may I offer my services in helping you get established in a more profitable neighborhood? I would also like to give Selene a pension, one she earned many years ago. And a maid, if you think she'd allow the generosity."

Edward Hunnicutt stared at her as if she'd just offered him the moon.

"A nice shop, one not too ostentatious, and a few well-placed references would bring customers to your patronage with little effort on my part. It would not be charity, I assure you."

"It would be nice to have someone to help Selene. She does as much as she can, but the cane limits her. I have to carry her up and down the steps. She thinks it a burden, so she doesn't go out much."

"I will set things in motion as soon as possible," Prudence said, sounding very businesslike, as if she would profit right along with Edward Hunnicutt—which she would, but in a different way. "You can expect to hear from his lordship's man of business by next week. In the meantime, I will arrange for a maid to come around. A woman of all work at least three days a week, I would think. Would a cook be helpful, as well? It can't be easy for Miss Hunnicutt to deal with chores in the kitchen."

"Selene will think she's died and gone to heaven."

"I've never been more proud of you," Rathbone said once they were in the carriage and on their way back to Belgrave Square. "At first, I wasn't sure if Edward Hunnicutt would accept your generosity. Fortunately, he puts his sister's welfare above his pride."

"Had he not, I would have stepped back and allowed you to wield your charm. I'm sure it works on men as well as women."

"You have yet to need my assistance, madam."

The truth hurt, though Rathbone was loath to admit it to anyone, even to himself. He had joined Prudence's quest, but he was certain his wife would have persisted without his aid, even traveling to Kent without him if it had come to that. Thankfully, it had not. But now that he enjoyed her full attention in the bedroom, he realized he wanted more of her time.

It was even more shocking to realize that he wanted to be rid of London and on his way to King's Crossing. He wanted to take his wife home.

Unaware of her husband's domestic thoughts, Prudence asked his opinion of their morning visit. "What do you think?"

"Of Miss Hunnicutt? Or of what she told you?"

"Both."

"I think her a reliable source, not overly prejudiced about anyone but you. As for what she said, it fits what you've told me so far. If Sir Archibald knew of your mother's affair, then he might very well dismiss her lady's maid, the most knowing servant, wanting to make an example to the others."

"And the summer trip?" Prudence prompted. "It fits, as well. If mother did take me to Summer House, she wouldn't have taken a lady's maid hired by her husband."

"What about a nurse? I'm assuming you had one at that time."

"I'm sure I did, though I can't recall anyone but Miss Hunnicutt ever being in the nursery." A frown pierced her face. "It isn't unheard of for a woman to take care of her own child, even if it is unusual among the more elite. And it wouldn't have been for long—a few days, nothing more."

"Enough time for your mother to visit her lover."

Rathbone regretted the words almost instantly. Prudence didn't think of her mother and the unnamed man in her diary as lovers, but rather, as two people in love.

The silence that followed the remark was just as he feared—Prudence's way of letting him know she disliked his description.

The truth was, Rathbone wasn't sure what his opinion of love was at this particular point in time. He enjoyed being with Prudence, in or out of bed. The day-by-day, moment-by-moment circumstances of their relationship didn't affect how he regarded her. Until recently, he would have begrudgingly agreed that love did exist, though not as commonly as most would assume. Now, he couldn't be entirely certain he hadn't done the unthinkable and fallen in love with his own wife.

Having the revelation hit him over the head while

riding in a carriage from Finsbury to Belgravia was not the piercing by Cupid's arrow he had expected. Then again, was any man prepared for love? His closest friends hadn't been, but once struck, they seemed to have righted themselves and their lives well enough. Rathbone had no doubt he could do the same once his wife revealed her own feelings.

While he suspected they were strongly in his favor, he couldn't be certain. Prudence was still frowning at him, and still more occupied with her unknown father than with the man she had married.

"You have the maid's name," he said, applying his mind to the business at hand, "and another, that of the scullery maid. When Mr. Covertly returns from Cornwall, we shall set him on their trail."

"That won't be for another five days."

"Captain Bartlett will be coming to dinner this evening," Rathbone replied, hoping to give her impatience something to gnaw upon.

"Miss Hunnicutt didn't recognize his name," Prudence said, wondering why her husband was looking at her so strangely. "Is everything all right, Benjamin? For a moment, you appeared to be gathering wool in Yorkshire."

Shocked by the fact that his feelings had registered even momentarily on his face, Rathbone rallied to the moment with a smile and a noncommittal reply. "Not gathering wool, sweetheart—merely organizing my thoughts."

"Those thoughts being?"

Should he say what he was really thinking? No, Rathbone decided, disliking the creaking of harnesses and the noise coming from the street. This was neither the time nor the place. Soon, he vowed, but not yet.

"I was thinking that once I have deposited you at home, I will pay a visit to the offices of Tamhill Shipping. If

Captain Bartlett once sailed for them, there might be someone who can recall his character at the time. If not, there should be records."

"What would records prove? I doubt he would mention an affair with a married woman in his ship's log."

"For one, the timing of his arrivals and departures," he pointed out. "For another, the circumstances under which he left to captain his own ship."

"I shall go with you."

"To the docks? I think not! The harbor is no place for a lady."

"Frederick took me there once," she argued, not mentioning that she had bullied the poor man until he relented. The visit had been brief. She had waited in the carriage with two footmen and a driver standing guard, while he had dashed inside to pick up a pouch of correspondence and the weekly cargo reports.

"I am not Frederick. Besides, I mean to lunch at the club first. I'll be home in ample time to discuss what I find, if anything, before Captain Bartlett arrives."

Accepting, if not liking, his decision, Prudence decided Miss Hunnicutt had given her more than enough to keep her mind busy for the balance of the day.

"May I make use of your secretary?" she asked. "Finding a suitable shop for Mr. Hunnicutt will take some time. And I should like to have Selene's pension started immediately. I daresay there is need for it."

"I will see the matter taken care of before day's end," he promised. "As to the shop, that will take a little longer. Properties on Bond Street are often spoken for years in advance. Mr. Hunnicutt may have to be satisfied with one of the adjacent streets."

"And the maid?"

"I will have Palrey send one of our staff before supper-time today. She can take things in hand until a suitable woman can be interviewed and employed."

Thaddeus had just halted the carriage when Prudence replied, "I must say, you're being extremely obliging."

"And that surprises you?" Rathbone asked, already outside and on the street, his hand extended to help Prudence down.

Under the noonday sun and a clear sky, heat was already rising from the pavement. It was going to be a wilting day, one to put the best of Londoners in the foulest of spirits.

"Most husbands would not be so understanding, my lord. They think that once married, a woman should keep to her own parlor."

"Most do," he agreed. "However, I have never been a man to agree with the majority simply because it's the majority."

Prudence waited until they were inside, out of the sun. She removed her bonnet and gloves before looking at her husband. "I am quickly discovering you to be very unlike any man I've ever known, my lord."

"Is that good or bad?"

"I'm still deciding." Her husband was looking strange again, his eyes gleaming, but not with the emotion she expected. This was something different, something she hadn't seen before, as if the question he had just put to her was of the utmost importance.

When she didn't answer immediately, he cast his gloves onto the table next to her bonnet.

"Perhaps I can hasten your decision," he said. Taking her hand, he led her into the parlor and nudged the door shut with one foot.

The latch had just come to rest when Prudence found herself being hauled into his arms and kissed with such vigor that she wondered if her husband had taken it into his head to prove the versatility of the parlor chair as he had the chaise longue the previous night. She was just beginning to think it a marvelous idea, when Rathbone set her at arm's length.

"Thaddeus is holding the horses. I have to go."

"What about my decision?" Prudence asked, flushed and somewhat flustered by his unexpected change in attitude.

Shameless or not, she enjoyed her husband's lovemaking. It wasn't as if he didn't care to indulge in intimacy in the middle of the day. In fact, since their reconciliation at Summer House, there wasn't an hour marked on a clock that he hadn't made love to her.

He kissed her again, a quick, hard kiss that in no way compensated for what he'd begun. "I'll make a point of asking you again tonight."

CHAPTER 19

"Are you certain this log is accurate?" Rathbone asked. He looked up from the desk that had been bare on his arrival at the offices of Tamhill Shipping, but was now stacked with cargo ledgers and departure schedules.

"Yes, my lord."

The man making the reply was Mr. Harold Caton. Caton had started out as a shipping clerk in the company's warehouses near the Isle of Dogs, gradually elevating himself during a thirty-two year employment to the respected rank of Cargo Manager. His office now faced Millwork Road, and on a clear day, one could see the opposite bank of the Thames and the old Queen's House, which had been converted into a hospital.

One of Caton's many duties was to keep a complete list of the arrivals and departures of Tamhill ships.

"This log shows Captain Bartlett leaving on the ninth day of September, 1844, and not returning to port until the spring of 1846."

"Yes, my lord. He commanded the *Sussex Marie,* a

clipper bound for the northern ports of China. It was a very successful trip," Caton added, placing a bony finger on the ledger column that had been used to calculate the final profits. "One of our best that season."

Rathbone closed the thick book with its yellowing pages. A simple calculation answered the question he'd come to ask. If Daniel Bartlett had been at sea for eleven months prior to Prudence's birth, he couldn't possibly be her father.

"May I ask why Captain Bartlett's previous employment by Tamhill is of interest to you, my lord? Are you by chance considering the possibility of luring him back?"

"What do you think of the idea?" Rathbone asked offhandedly. He wasn't thinking of Tamhill Shipping now, but of his wife. He disliked the idea of returning home with nothing but another piece of disappointing news for Prudence.

"I think it a splendid idea. Bartlett was one of our best captains. Ran a tight ship. Well respected by peers and crew alike."

"Do you know him?"

"Very well," Caton replied. "I was working the old warehouse when he signed on his first ship. Not much more than a boy, he was tall and lanky, with a head full of sea dreams. But a hard worker. Did as he was told, and then some. Mr. Tamhill always had an eye for a good worker."

"You mean Sir Archibald," Rathbone said, leaving the desk to stretch the kinks from his back. He'd been studying Caton's meticulous recordkeeping for more than two hours.

He walked to the windows that overlooked Millwall Road and the Thames. The sheer volume of goods brought into the empire's capital made East London the busiest section of the city. The men who worked the docks and the women hired by its supporting trades lived in Whitechapel, Spitalfields, Hackney, and Limehouse. Opening the window, Rathbone was immediately assaulted by the sweet smell of the local breweries mixing with the summer odor of the Thames. The result was a perfume that was uniquely the East End's.

"I was referring to old Mr. Tamhill, Sir Archibald's father," Caton said, joining him. Round-shouldered from the endless hours he'd spent bent over a desk, his fingers stained permanently by ink, Caton still possessed the clear, sharp eyes of an intelligent man.

"What was he like?"

"Sly as a fox, old Tamhill was, my lord. Shrewd in business. A man with a vision. Said England's future had to be grasped with long, wet fingers. He believed, and time's proven him right, that China and Africa were the ports we needed to reach. And Australia—it's a booming colony now."

"I can't disagree with his philosophy. Tamhill is one of the most profitable shipping lines in England." He paused to look directly at Harold Caton. "Are you saying that Mr. Tamhill, not his son, promoted Bartlett to the rank of captain?"

Caton gave a firm nod in reply. "Daniel Bartlett was the youngest man ever to command a Tamhill ship."

"Why did he leave? From the figures I have seen, the company rewards its captains for a job well done."

"It's a sound policy, my lord."

"Then why? The ambition of wanting to chart his own course, so to speak?"

The older man's gaze searched Rathbone's face. When it was decided that the new manager of Tamhill Shipping might well be worth his salt, Caton answered the question. "Sir Archibald wasn't like his father, or his grandfather. He had a head for figures and business, a talent close to my heart, but he had no stomach for the sea. Wouldn't even sail from Portsmouth to London—always took to the roads."

"The captains didn't respect him?"

"Not the way they did his father," Caton answered candidly. "Can't blame them. No matter their rank, they're sailors at heart. Sir Archibald always thought he knew more than the men who took to sea."

"In other words, he enjoyed stepping on their toes."

"I've worked close to the docks all my life. Sailors are an independent lot. Got their own code of honor, if you know what I mean."

"I take it Sir Archibald stepped on Captain Bartlett's toes one too many times."

Caton's clear brown eyes began to sparkle. "Bartlett told Sir Archibald he couldn't row a dinghy across the Thames if his life depended on it."

"A epitaph to his dismissal," Rathbone chuckled.

"It was that." Caton shrugged his hunched shoulders. "Will you be bringing him back to the fold?"

"Perhaps."

On his way back to Belgrave Square, Rathbone wondered just how long fate would continue to play havoc with his life. Hopefully, Micah Covertly would have something encouraging to report upon his return from Cornwall. And there was still the matter of Helen Barnaby, Rachel Tamhill's maid, who seemed the likeliest person to name names.

As Thaddeus maneuvered the carriage along Upper Thames Street, then east along the Embankment toward Westminster, Rathbone put the quest for Prudence's father aside. He still had his marriage to sort out, or rather, the feelings that went with his marriage.

While admittedly a passionate man, he had never considered himself an emotional one. Not until recently. Now, he was mired in emotions. What had begun as a subtle attraction, quickly escalating to an unquenched passion, was now the most confusing feeling of all—love.

His marriage to Prudence went beyond the simple sharing of a bed. Amazingly, it was just as satisfying for him to hold his wife in his arms, to feel the warmth of her body pressed close to his as they fell asleep, to take comfort in knowing she would be there when he opened his eyes in the morning. The passion she aroused in him was just as strong as the love she had brought to his life. It was all part of the same thing now, a mixture too well blended to be divided into separate, more easily explained elements.

As the carriage approached Belgravia, Rathbone leaned his head back against the cushions and closed his eyes. A smile came to his face as he thought back, amused by his own behavior since the evening he'd found Prudence in Green Park. Never in his wildest imaginings would he have pictured himself married before the year was over.

Thinking of his wife, of the way they fit together, of her soft body accepting him, of the way she filled his senses with textures and scents and the soft sounds she made when he pleased her, Rathbone vowed that Prudence would never have cause to regret their marriage the way her mother had regretted marrying Sir Archibald.

Strange that falling in love didn't seem all that strange since admitting it to himself. The difficult part would be admitting it to Prudence. He knew now that she wanted to be loved, needed to be loved. But could he satisfy that need? If she didn't discover her true identity, could she be content living at King's Crossing with him? Would the absence of her father's name leave a void that a husband and children couldn't fill?

Late-afternoon sunlight was streaming through the long windows of the library, bathing Prudence in golden light as she sat reading her mother's diary. Rathbone recognized the journal as he entered the room, and knew his wife was diligently searching for a reference to Captain Daniel Bartlett.

She looked up at him and smiled. Putting the book aside, she left the chair, greeting him midway through the room. After she had placed a kiss on his cheek, her expression became curious. "Did you discover anything?"

"I made the acquaintance of Mr. Harold Caton, an energetic employee who keeps the harbor logs," he told her. "He knows Bartlett."

"And?" she asked, her curiosity changing to immediate excitement.

"I do not think the captain is the man you are looking for. In fact, I'm almost certain of it."

"An illicit affair isn't something Mr. Caton would have recorded in a harbor log."

"Granted. But he did record the departure and arrival dates of each of the ships Captain Bartlett commanded. Given those dates, it isn't likely the man fathered any children in England, especially a daughter born eleven months after he set sail."

Prudence frowned in concentration. "Eleven months. Are you sure?"

"I'm sorry, sweetheart, but Daniel Bartlett isn't your father."

When his wife sank into the nearest chair, Rathbone knew just how much hope she had pinned on Daniel Bartlett. Belatedly, he also recognized that she was reaching the end of her tether. While young and full of energy, his wife was working herself toward emotional exhaustion. It was time to return to King's Crossing.

The decision made, he moved to where Prudence was seated in a Gothic-style armchair. Taking her hands, he pulled her up and into his arms. She gave in to the embrace with a frustrated sigh. "I had so hoped."

"I know. But there are other avenues to explore. In the meantime, we will entertain Captain Bartlett this evening. I'm of a mind to offer him the position of fleet manager."

Prudence drew back to look at him. "But he has his own ship."

"Which only means that Tamhill Shipping will increase its convoy. Freddie and I discussed the possibility of dividing the Eastern fleet in half. It's by far the largest flotilla of ships. What do you say to offering Bartlett the Orient trade and assigning Captain Rosedale to the southern ports of Australia and the South Sea Islands? Both routes are lucrative enough to keep their pockets full."

"You're asking my opinion on a matter of business?"

"Tamhill Shipping is your inheritance, not mine."

"That's not the position you took earlier today."

"I will not have you traipsing about the docks, but that doesn't mean I don't value your opinion."

Naturally disappointed that Captain Bartlett was not the man she was looking for, but pleased by her husband's remark, Prudence gave the idea a moment's thought. "Captain Rosedale did marry last year. Freddie asked me to send a note of congratulation to his wife. Her family is English, but she was born in Sydney. She's still there. I'm sure reducing her husband's territory to the surrounding region would aid their marriage. For that reason, I would agree with you. But what if Bartlett isn't interested in returning to Tamhill?"

A crooked smile touched his face as he raised her hand to his lips and kissed it. "You suggested that my charm could be applied to men as well as women. I'll test the theory this evening, by making Bartlett an offer he can't refuse."

Prudence accepted Rathbone's suggestion with a prompt approval, almost surprising herself; she had lost her capacity for high flashes of indignation when it came to remembering how well her husband had plied his "charm" in the past. In fact, she was fast becoming convinced that he was settling into the role of husband more easily than she was fitting into the role of wife.

"I would not be opposed to you offering Captain Bartlett the position of fleet manager," she said. Her husband shifted her back into his arms as another topic came to mind. "Do you think Mr. Covertly will return to London soon?"

"I'm sure he'll be in touch as soon as he returns to the city."

Another frown came to her face. "If Daniel Bartlett isn't my father, then we are dependent upon Mr. Covertly discovering something in Cornwall or finding Helen Barnaby."

"So it would seem."

He kissed her then, and Prudence gave herself to the warmth of his embrace, leaning against the solid strength of his body, willing the kiss to banish the disappointing news he'd brought home with him.

It had been a long day for both of them, but when he would have released her to take up the newspaper Palrey had left on the library table, Prudence moved against him so restlessly that he asked, "What is it, sweetheart?"

"Nothing," she said, unable to describe just how she was feeling. "I was just thinking about going upstairs to take a nap before dinner. It's been a tiring day."

"Then you should rest," he said, wanting to go with her, but knowing she'd get little sleep if he did.

Watching her leave the room, Rathbone was excruciatingly aware that for the first time in a very long time, his first concern was for someone other than himself. Funny how a man could go to bed a scoundrel and wake up the next morning to find his entire life changed.

By fortuitous chance, Rathbone was right to have remained downstairs. He had returned to the library, thinking to attack some of the work on his desk, when a footman carried in a note. It was from Micah Covertly.

Rathbone read the bold, scribbled writing, then glanced at the clock. Knowing Thaddeus had just had the carriage unhitched and was probably taking his ease in the kitchen, he told the footman to have the curricle made ready. It would be an easy matter to drive himself to Piccadilly and the coffeehouse Covertly had named in his note.

Upon entering the Crooked Swan, Rathbone spied Micah Covertly at one of the back tables. A plate of food sat in front of him, along with a steaming cup of coffee and a wedge of pie.

The main room was quiet. Two elderly gentlemen sat in the corner, each nursing a tankard of ale while they studied a chess board. Another man, a merchant by the cut of his coat, was engrossed in a newspaper known for its acrimonious political prose.

"Your Lordship," Covertly said in greeting. He was dressed in a suit of dark brown with a crisp white shirt. Covertly was not handsome, but he was certainly more than presentable with his thick brown hair, intelligent eyes, and strong features. Rathbone accepted his hand when it was offered.

Rathbone agreed to a cup of coffee, then waited until it had been served before asking Covertly if he had anything of value to report.

"Nothing you can sink your teeth into," Covertly told him. "Lady Montague inherited the house in Kent a few months before her marriage to the earl. Seems his lordship had a liking for the tables, so she sold the property to cover his debts. Wretched business, gambling."

"That explains the deed being transferred so quickly," Rathbone said. "What about the man who was supposed to have been seen walking along the beach? Could he be related to Lady Montague?"

"Not that I could find out," Covertly told him. "Lady Montague was an only child. Not much family in either direction, mother or father. She and Lord Montague have two children, a son and a daughter. No connection to Mr. Fenstermaker that I could find, other than the old gent buying the property. Lady Montague listed it with her family's agent. Didn't take more than a week for Fenstermaker to snatch it up." He took a sip of coffee before reaching for the saucer that held a slice of apple pie. "Could have delivered the news directly to Lady Rathbone, but you said you wanted to hear it first. Pity there's nothing more to tell. I'll get back to the servant's ledger first thing tomorrow."

"The ledger can wait, except for whatever reference

you find regarding Helen Barnaby," Rathbone told him. "She was Rachel Tamhill's lady's maid."

He went on to explain what they had learned from Miss Hunnicutt, making sure to include the possibility that the scullery maid, Sarah Hopkins, might know something useful—if she could be found.

"Sounds promising," Covertly agreed. "Ain't no one closer to a lady than her maid. It makes sense that Sir Archibald would dismiss her, especially if she knew more than she should."

"Find Helen Barnaby," Rathbone said, "and I'll wager you'll find the name my wife is seeking."

"Should be easy enough, unless Tamhill turned the girl out without reference. If she took up another line of work, the finding could take longer. Damn shame what some women are forced to do to make a living."

"I doubt that Tamhill tossed Miss Barnaby out into the cold. If anything, he'd give her a glowing reference and a severance bonus," Rathbone said. "Servants with valuable information have been known to turn to blackmail."

"That they have," Covertly agreed. "What about Lady Rathbone?"

"Call tomorrow morning," Rathbone instructed him. "After that, I'll leave word. I plan on returning to my estate in Herefordshire as soon as possible. Again, my instructions hold. You will say nothing to my wife without reporting to me first."

Twilight was spreading over the city by the time Rathbone returned to Belgrave Square. An hour later, he was sitting alone in his room, legs outstretched before him, his dinner jacket at the ready. A bottle of claret sat on the table beside him, a glass poured and in his hand. The house was quiet, except for the occasional sound that came from the room next door, where Prudence was dressing for dinner.

Sipping his drink, Rathbone used the time to reexamine his decision to return to King's Crossing. Prudence would argue, of course, wanting to remain in the city until Covertly brought news of Helen Barnaby. His response would be that these things took time, and they could await the answer as easily in the country as they could in the city. It was the truth, but not the only reason he wanted to put London behind them.

King's Crossing was their home—a place that held no connection to Prudence's past, only her future. Once there, he hoped to be able to convince her to forget the past, at least temporarily. As interesting as their honeymoon had become, it would be nice to have his wife's undivided attention for a few days. And, if the opportunity presented itself, time in which to make his true feelings known.

It was a novel idea to think himself shy when it came to conversing with a woman, but as bemused by love as he was, Rathbone had to admit some hesitation in actually saying the words.

Then again, he was discovering that love wasn't so much a matter of words as it was a reaction. What he felt for Prudence caused him to do things that had once seemed improbable. To feel contentment where he had once felt restlessness.

Reaching for his jacket, he couldn't keep a smile from his face. So this is how Granby felt, and Sterling and Waltham and Fitch. Content, not only with their choice in wives, but with themselves. It was a nice feeling.

CHAPTER 20

They were seated at the dining room table, the silver and crystal sparkling under the chandelier light, when Prudence asked Captain Bartlett to tell her a story of pirates. He was proving to be a very nice man, despite the fact that he wasn't the man she had hoped he would be. He handed out smiles like toffee from a paper bag, immediately removing any strain from the atmosphere.

"Pirates, at least the ones I've encountered in the Orient, aren't what you'd expect them to be," he said, leaning back in the heavily carved chair, which had the look of a judgment seat about it. At the head of the table, in an equally ornate seat, his host smiled. "Ragamuffins, most of them. Small and wiry and as quick as cats. Let one of their junks get within boarding distance and they'll swoop over the side before you can ring the alarm. Hearty little fighters, too. Quite the adversary if you're in a mind to test your wits against them."

A whoosh of warm wind came down the chimney, as rain began to beat at the tall, draped windows in the stop-and-start manner of an untalented child practicing scales at the piano. The fireplace was empty except for the cut flowers that had been carefully placed on the blackened grate.

"Have you ever tested your wits?" Prudence asked.

"A time or two, but there's nothing better for sharpening the mind than dealing with opium smugglers."

"Smugglers!" The word came simultaneously from both host and hostess.

"China has its own set of hostilities," Bartlett told them. "The emperor, along with his mandarins, who constitute the reigning hierarchy—to say nothing of the greedy customs clerks—get highly incensed by the smuggling of Indian opium into the Flowery Kingdom. Any ship pulling into dock can expect a keen eye."

"Isn't opium grown in China?" Prudence asked, recalling something she had read in one of the pamphlets the Duke of Worley would have called "too inciting for the female mind."

"Yes, and the Chinese don't want their prices brought down by smuggled goods. In fact, it isn't unheard of for pirates to be sponsored by the mandarins."

"So something that was once illegal contraband is confiscated and sold as homegrown," Rathbone remarked.

Before the captain could comment on his host's reasonable conclusion, a commotion was heard in the front of the house. The rain was coming down much harder now. The sound of someone cursing the blasted weather made its way into the dining room, along with the hard thumping of the front door being closed against an insistent wind.

"It's Lionel," Prudence said, recognizing his voice instantly.

Rathbone tossed his napkin to the tabletop and came to his feet. "Excuse me," he said, speaking to their guest. He was halfway to the door when it was opened by a footman. Lionel was on the man's heels.

"Sorry to intrude," he said, hurrying into the room.

His boots glistened with rain and his trouser legs were splattered from the mad dash he'd made from the carriage to the front door, but it was the look on his face that alerted Prudence to trouble.

"What is it?" she asked.

"Father. He's taken ill."

Prudence made a sound deep in her throat as Lionel stepped forward to take her hands. "How ill?"

"Seriously, I'm afraid. You know how stubborn he can be. Thinks he can do what he did twenty years ago without complaint. Griswold found him lying at the bottom of the stairs. It's his heart. Dr. Renfro is with him. Freddie sent me to find you." His expression deepened as Rathbone poured a glass of wine and passed it to him. "What the blazes are you doing in London? I rode to King's Crossing. Thank God for the telegraph, or I'd be on my way to Kent now."

She paled at the news of the Duke of Worley being so ill that Freddie was summoning her to North Hill.

Lionel gathered her hands between his own and squeezed. "Father wants to see you. I think he needs to know you're happy."

"Of course," she stammered, trying her best not to cry and failing miserably. She smiled mistily. "I'll go upstairs and change."

"And I shall take my leave," Daniel Bartlett said. "No, don't bother to apologize," he added, seeing the words about to come from Prudence's trembling mouth. "Please accept my thanks for a wonderful evening, and my prayers for the duke's health. I have never had the pleasure of meeting him, but his name draws immediate respect."

The next few minutes were numb ones for Prudence. Rathbone showed Captain Bartlett to the door after a hasty introduction to Lionel, who was now digging into a plate of food, his first since breakfast.

"If we leave now, we can be at North Hill by first light," Rathbone said, returning to the dining room. Beyond the open door, servants were already hurrying back and forth across the foyer, and up and down the stairs, preparing for a hasty departure by the lord and lady of the house.

"Uncle Horace scared me senseless when I first arrived at North Hill," Prudence said, looking up at her husband through tear-dampened lashes. "I always seemed to be in his way when he was rushing up or down the stairs. It wasn't until he played marbles with me one day that I decided he really was a very nice man, and that I was lucky to be under his care."

Neither her husband nor Lionel made any reply. There was nothing to say. The Duke of Worley was dying.

"Help yourself," Rathbone said, placing a bottle of wine within Lionel's reach. "I'll take Prudence upstairs."

Lionel nodded, his expression one of regret that he had burst into the room to deliver unhappy news. "My horses could use a rest. Mind if I share your carriage on the way back?"

"Of course not," Rathbone said, holding out his hand to Prudence. "We'll be down shortly."

Blessedly, the rain had slackened before they were forced to take to the road. The horses' hooves rang against the cobblestones, reminiscent of thunder retreating beyond a distant hill, as Thaddeus made all haste to leave London behind them and gain North Hill by dawn.

Seated next to her husband, Prudence leaned into his warmth. Few words had been said since leaving the dining room. Fiona rode in a following coach with Ferncliffe, Rathbone's valet. The appropriate black clothing had been packed, the seriousness of the trip announced by the haste in which it had been undertaken, and by the knowledge that the duke's youngest son wouldn't have interrupted the couple's honeymoon if there had been another option.

"How is Freddie?" Prudence asked, needing to fill the silence. She had lost one father, and while it hadn't been easy knowing Sir Archibald hadn't cared for her, she cared a great deal for the Duke of Worley. In many ways, he was the only father she'd ever known. Or might ever know.

"Worried," Lionel replied honestly. "Despite his serious ways, I don't think he expected to take up the mantle this soon."

"One rarely does," Rathbone said. He wrapped his arm around Prudence's shoulder and drew her close. "Sleep, if you can."

Prudence did sleep, but only in spits and spurts. By the time the carriage rolled up the graveled drive to stop in front of North Hill Hall, her head was aching.

Griswold stood at the ready by the front door, looking less than robust himself. At the sight of Prudence, his face took on a glow. "Welcome," he said, helping her with her cloak. "It will do the old lord's heart good to see you."

"How is Father?" Lionel asked.

"Resting," Griswold replied. "Lord Roebourne is with him."

Outside, the dawn was adding vague light to a gray sky thick with more rain clouds. Inside, the house was just as somber. Deciding that a cup of tea was just what she needed before going upstairs and seeing the duke—who was blessedly still alive and resting easy for the time being—Prudence made her way into the breakfast room. The cook, having anticipated their arrival, had served up chafing dishes of scrambled eggs and bacon and thick browned sausages. Both coffee and tea steamed on the sideboard.

Dr. Renfro was serving himself a second helping of sausages when Prudence entered the room, followed by Rathbone and Lionel.

With a somewhat awkward bow—the kindly physician wasn't a man designed by nature to bend at the middle—Dr. Renfro introduced himself to Rathbone. "His Grace is resting comfortably," they were assured.

"Is it his heart?" Prudence asked.

"Yes." The physician sipped his tea after lacing it with sugar. He was a roly-poly man with a twinkle in his eye that even the solemnity of the occasion couldn't quite dampen. "His Grace paid me a visit before your wedding to Lord Rathbone. Complained of having more pain than was customary. I suggested that he move the wedding here to North Hill, but he wouldn't hear of it. Said I wasn't to breathe so much as a word to anyone, especially you. Said you had enough worries on your mind. Insisted it was nothing more than too many plum tarts. He said he'd be fine as soon as the wedding frivolities were out of the way and he could spend the summer the way he liked best, here at North Hill."

"He does love the old place," Lionel said, looking around the room with its sixteenth-century walnut furnishings and oil-painted landscapes framed in heavy gilt. "Can't imagine it without him."

The momentary silence that followed the remark

faded as Frederick walked into the room. Dressed in dark trousers and a shirt with the sleeves rolled up and the collar undone, he looked as tired as Prudence felt. She left the table to walk into his open arms, receiving the brotherly hug she so desperately needed.

"Father is awake," he said. "He's asking for you."

The words, kindly spoken, sent a chill through Prudence. The emptiness she was already feeling overflowed as she looked up at the man destined to inherit the Worley title.

"How are you?" she asked in a trembling whisper.

"Tired," he admitted.

"Sit down and eat," Prudence said, walking him toward the breakfast table. "I'll stay with Uncle Horace." She looked at Lionel, who had risen to pour his brother a cup of coffee. "Make sure he gets some sleep. I don't want to worry about more than one of you at a time."

"Do you want me to go with you?" Rathbone asked, feeling slightly out of place, even though he knew it wasn't intentional on anyone's part to exclude him. Marriage might have brought him into the family, but he had no part in its memories. Those belonged exclusively to the two brothers and Prudence.

"Yes, I want you to go, but I think it would be best if I saw him alone, at least for now," Prudence replied.

Rathbone escorted her to the main staircase. When she disappeared from sight, he returned to the breakfast room.

Dr. Renfro had gone outside for a walk, leaving the two brothers to have their morning meal together.

"Lionel said you and Pru had been to Kent," Freddie remarked as Rathbone carried his coffee cup to the sideboard. He refilled it from a French pot with a straight-sided wooden handle. "If that's the case, what took you to London? Not trouble at Tamhill, I hope."

"No trouble, although I would like your opinion on something," Rathbone replied. "Have you ever heard of a ship's captain by the name of Daniel Bartlett?"

"Yes."

"Do you know that he once sailed for Tamhill?"

"Saw his name in the ledgers, but I've never met the man."

"I have. Very impressive. The idea struck me that efficiency might be served by splitting the Eastern fleet. Bartlett has a reputation for dealing well with the Chinese merchants. Rosedale can take the southern islands and Australia. We'd need to acquire some new ships, but the expense would repay itself in three years' time, if not less. Australia is bursting at the seams. Wool, silver, gold—it's a thriving colony with a lucrative future. The more Tamhill ships we put into port, the better."

"It's a sound idea," Freddie agreed. "If you think Bartlett the man to trust, then I say, strike while the iron's hot."

Rathbone intentionally kept the conversation centered on business rather than on the man lying upstairs, knowing Freddie needed the distraction. He could only vaguely recall the days following his own father's sudden death. It all seemed blurred to him now—the funeral, his mother's black veil, the walk down the mossy path to the graveside, the rector intoning the standard verses, including the one about "ashes to ashes."

He hadn't wanted to dwell on the fact that his father was gone forever. Instead, he'd taken up the yoke of title and leadership—although there had been little leading to be done. King's Crossing had gone on, just as it had for generations, the huge house as much an entity as the men who lived under its roof.

"Prudence didn't inherit any property in Kent," Lionel said, quitting the table for one last cup of tea before taking himself upstairs.

"Not from her father," said Rathbone, who had prepared for the question ever since learning Lionel had spoken to his mother, Lady Augusta. "It came from the Gunderson side of the family, a distant cousin of her mother's. Prudence wanted to see it, so we decided to spend some time there."

It wasn't the truth, but Rathbone couldn't think of a way to answer the question without using one falsehood or another.

"You're getting along, then?" Lionel asked, leaning against the sideboard instead of returning to the table. He was almost asleep on his feet, and it showed. "I wondered."

There was no deceit in Rathbone's reply this time. "We're getting along. In fact, I admit to being a contended husband. Surprised?"

"Not in the least," Lionel said. "Pru has a way about her."

Rathbone silently agreed.

"I wasn't wrong to make you marry?" the duke asked, as Prudence sat on the side of the massive four-poster bed, holding his cold hand.

Even though she'd prepared herself before entering the room, the sight of a once-hearty and vigorous man lying vulnerable in his bed brought tears to her eyes. "No, you weren't wrong," she assured him. "Benjamin is a good husband."

"You're happy, then?" he said, his voice a hoarse whisper.

"Yes, I'm happy. I love him very much."

A smile, weak but sincere, came to the duke's face. "I suspected as much. You were never one to do what you were told unless it suited your purpose."

They talked then, mostly of Freddie and his future.

"He'll need a good wife," Worley said. "A woman who can match him in mind and will, who won't let him turn into a recluse. It's his nature, you know. Much rather be off by himself than part of the crowd. His mother was the same way. I had to drag her to London from time to time just to remind her that the world didn't stop at the fence row."

"Then Lionel must take his wandering ways after you," Prudence said teasingly. She felt a strange sense of unreality as she sat talking to the duke, too filled with emotion to allow herself to think beyond the moment.

Worley laughed, if the sound could be called a laugh. It sapped his strength, but he refused to let Prudence summon Dr. Renfro. "Nothing he can do now," the duke said, holding tighter to Prudence's hand. "If I've been hard on Lionel, it's because he is the most like me. Headstrong and wild at heart. I know it's hard to imagine now, but I wasn't always old and set in my ways. There was a time . . ." His voice faded as if he'd stepped into the memories that came to mind.

"Rest," Prudence said. She leaned over and kissed his cheek, then took herself to a nearby chair.

The sun shone bright on the day of the Duke of Worley's funeral. It was a beautiful day, filled with a swelling rapture of the sort that inspired poets and painters. The sort of day that uplifted the human spirit, reminding people that no matter how bad things got, no matter how wearisome life seemed, God and nature together had ways of easing the burden.

As she went downstairs to join Frederick and Lionel for the trip to the church, Prudence couldn't help but remember a day from her childhood when the duke had told her that North Hill had the softest sunshine in all of England.

Now that she had grown up, she thought the best part of rainy days was knowing that afterward, when the sun came out, the world would be put back exactly as it always was, only better, because it would be polished and fresh and new.

But it was different for her as she sat in the pew of North Hill's private chapel, since Prudence knew nothing would be the way it was before. It was as though all the bits and pieces of her life had been put away in the wrong drawer, and she had no idea where to start looking for them. She had truly loved the man who had taken her into his home and heart, and she felt the loss as deeply as she had felt the loss of her mother.

When the time came to leave the church, Prudence walked outside on her husband's arm. She felt justified in retreating behind the black veil that covered her face. Her mind felt dull and unwilling, her body exhausted. The last three days had been worse than the two she had spent by the duke's bedside. To have nothing to do but grieve was the worst sort of torment.

She stared blankly as the coffin was loaded into a gleaming black carriage drawn by four black horses with black plumes attached to their bridles. Frederick and Lionel took their places, walking directly behind the hearse as it pulled slowly away from the chapel, only a short distance from its destination: the Delmont family plot on a knoll west of the stone church.

The funeral procession attested to the prominence and respect of the man being laid to rest. Though the Queen was not in attendance, she had sent her oldest son, Albert, and several members of her court.

Upon reaching the graveside, Prudence was even more thankful for her husband's supporting arm. It wasn't until Frederick and Lionel had paid their final respects, each tossing a handful of dirt onto the casket, that Prudence felt her courage desert her.

"Perhaps a flower," Rathbone whispered, sensing her dislike for the custom which it was now her turn to perform.

He escorted her to the edge of the small rectangular pit that had been dug, then bent down to retrieve a flower from one of the pots that had been carried to the gravesite. Selecting a long-stemmed rose, he handed it to her.

"You will be missed," Prudence whispered as she tossed the flower into the grave.

Then it was over; there was nothing left to do but return to North Hill and the houseful of guests that would gradually dwindle away by nightfall.

"You need to eat and rest," Rathbone said once they reached the house. "I'm taking you upstairs."

"The guests," Prudence protested. "Frederick and Lionel are as exhausted as I am."

"The guests do not expect to be entertained. Most will be leaving as soon as they've taken a meal and paid their private respects to Frederick."

"I don't want to be left alone in my room with nothing but grief for company. Your mother is here. I have barely spoken a word to her—a rudeness I hope she can forgive."

"Mother has done nothing but compliment your stamina. I, on the other hand, know you are close to exhaustion. You will take yourself into one of the parlors. I will bring you a plate and you will eat. The guests can come to you," Rathbone insisted. "I will not have you worn down any more than you are, madam."

"Very well," Prudence relented. She had slept little since leaving London. Despite the exhaustion, she found a smile for her husband. He was looking at her, tenderness in his blue eyes. She could feel the comfort he was trying so hard to offer, feel him willing her to know that he cared, that his first concern was for her. "I promise to eat, and to rest better tonight."

By late afternoon, all but the closest of family friends had taken their leave. Prudence sat in the music room, one of her favorites among the many rooms of North Hill, talking to Lady Augusta.

"Benjamin told me he plans to return to King's Crossing the day after tomorrow," his mother announced. "I admit to being pleased by his decision. The place seems empty since you took yourselves off to Kent."

Prudence saved her comment for her husband, whom she found a short time later.

"May I have a word with you, my lord?"

"Of course." He followed her outside, into one of the small gardens, the black taffeta of her dress rustling and whispering as she walked.

"Your mother informed me that you plan to return to King's Crossing," Prudence said, turning to look at him. He was framed in the late afternoon light, his hair gleaming gilt.

"It's time we went home."

"What of Frederick and Lionel?" she asked. "They need me now."

Rathbone pulled an ungloved hand from his pocket

while he tried to think how to handle the unexpected conversation. He had planned to tell Prudence of his decision to return to King's Crossing that evening, when they were alone.

"Frederick and Lionel are not children. They are grown men who will handle their grief in their own way. Frederick is the duke now. His duties will occupy his time. The same can be said for Lionel. While I understand your distress, I do not believe lingering at North Hill will resolve it. As I said, it is time we went home."

"What of London?" Prudence argued. "Mr. Covertly is certain to have returned from Cornwall by now."

"Mr. Covertly can deliver his report to King's Crossing as easily as he can to London. I left a message to that effect."

"Then you have thought of everything, have you not, my lord?" Prudence declared stiffly.

"You are making an argument where there is no need for one. King's Crossing is our home. I have responsibilities there, responsibilities I have forsaken so that we could traipse from Kent to London in search of your father."

"Traipse!"

"An unfortunate choice of words. I am merely trying to say—"

"I understand precisely what you are saying, my lord."

"No, madam, you do not. You are tired and distressed and in need of a good night's sleep. For that reason, we will postpone this conversation until morning."

"I do not want to postpone it. I do not want to leave North Hill."

Rathbone made a quick bid for patience, and failed. "I understand that you do not want to leave, but you will leave. I am your husband. Your place is with me. Granted, that does not seem to have been the case until now. You have led, and I have merrily followed along. But that is over. We will return to King's Crossing."

When he would have taken her hand, Prudence stepped back. "I have seen two men, each of them my father in his own way, buried." She met his gaze defiantly. "I will know the man I may truly call by that name. You promised to help me find him."

"Damn it, Prudence, you are intentionally twisting my words."

"Am I?" She knew she was being unreasonable, but she couldn't help it. She wanted now, more than ever, to find the answer to the question she had been carrying around for years.

Rathbone stifled an oath. While he told himself reason would prevail once Prudence had rested, her expression told him otherwise. He was about to suggest that she take a nap before dinner when Granby showed himself. His friend, dressed in the appropriate black, had apparently come outside to find some relief from the depressing atmosphere that was ruling the household.

"If you will excuse me, my lord," Prudence said, stepping around him. "I must see to the few guests that will be spending the night."

Rathbone watched her go, knowing the argument was far from over.

"Trouble in paradise?" Granby asked, as he strolled to where Prudence had left her husband standing.

"Trouble, as in a stubborn woman who refuses to admit I know what's best for her," Rathbone mumbled under his breath.

"A problem I've frequently encountered." His friend's

smile wasn't the least bit sympathetic. "I can count on one hand the times Catherine has agreed to my dictates without an argument."

Rathbone continued watching as Prudence entered the house. When she disappeared from sight, he turned to Granby. "Is marriage always this complicated?"

"Only when you think one way and your wife thinks the other. In other words, most of the time."

CHAPTER 21

Rathbone and his lovely bride were still thinking at cross-purposes the following morning. While Prudence dressed and went downstairs, Rathbone took himself to the stables. His mood was less than affable, having spent half of the night wanting to make love to his wife, and the other half rebuking himself for being selfish and uncaring. Prudence was still grieving over the duke's death, a loss she felt deeply.

Thinking some fresh air and distance might clear his head and prepare him for the argument that was sure to ensue the moment he ordered their trunks packed, Rathbone took to the riding trails that circled North Hill.

It was more than frustrating to realize that he was well caught in Prudence's little web, that he couldn't do what he knew was best for her without upsetting her. Equally frustrating was the idea that she actually thought he didn't care. Care! He was obsessed with the woman.

The morning air was bright and clean, and the time spent alone allowed Rathbone to focus on the real problem. If he revealed his true feelings to Prudence, would she do the same? Would she admit that she was truly happy being his wife, that she felt for him as strongly as he felt for her?

If not, if she admitted nothing more than acceptance of her circumstances, what kind of life would they have? While his reputation as a scoundrel had been well earned, he couldn't envision himself as a husband who enjoyed the benefits of a wife and children in the country while he kept a mistress in town.

By the time he returned to the stables, he was certain he'd have to drag Prudence, kicking and screaming, to the carriage.

"Ah, there you be, milord," said one of the grooms, a tall, wiry man by the name of Tipp. "You've got a visitor."

"Who?"

"Said his name was Covertly. Rode in while you were enjoying the trails. I sent him up to the kitchen for a cup of tea."

"Thank you," Rathbone said over his shoulder. He was already making for the house.

As in most English houses, the kitchen of North Hill was below ground. Rathbone walked into the room, which was filled with footmen and scullery maids, bringing the entire staff to a gawking standstill. The kitchen smelled of cinnamon and stewed apples. Baskets and copper pots hung from the overhead beams, and side-by-side china cabinets displayed neat arrays of plates and crystal. Against the far wall, an open range squatted next to a bricked oven. A ruddy-faced maid looked up from a pie crust she was rolling at one of the tables.

The cook, who had been pumping water into a large metal basin, said nothing for a few seconds, as shocked as anyone that the viscount had made his way into the house by a servant's door.

"I'm Mrs. Collins," said the woman when she found her voice. "Is there something I can do for you, milord?"

"I'm looking for a man, a Mr. Covertly. Old Tipp said he was having tea in the kitchen," Rathbone replied, hoping Prudence hadn't somehow become aware of Covertly's presence and rushed him into a parlor.

"I'm here, your lordship," Covertly said, stepping out of the shadows. He was holding a ceramic mug of tea in one hand and a buttered scone in the other.

"Finish your breakfast," Rathbone said, realizing from the man's wrinkled appearance that he had ridden most of the night. "I'll wait for you outside."

"I'm done," Covertly announced, popping the last of the scone into his mouth. He washed it down with tea, then reached for his hat.

As they left the kitchen, Rathbone heard the staff return to their duties, undoubtedly curious as to what had brought Micah Covertly to North Hill and the viscount into their kitchen. Knowing Fiona was sure to hear of it, and knowing he'd be called upon to explain Covertly's visit as soon as the maid made it known to her mistress, Rathbone didn't waste any time getting to the point.

"You have news."

"Helen Barnaby," Covertly said. "She works in London as a housekeeper."

"For whom?"

They were walking away from the house, toward the stables. Before reaching the first of the three buildings, Covertly stopped to light his pipe. Once the tobacco was lit and smoke was curling up from the pipe's wooden bowl, he reached into the inside pocket of his jacket and produced a small envelope. "I wrote down the address."

Rathbone unfolded the paper and read the number and street, then the name Covertly had written underneath. After folding the paper and putting it in his own pocket, he turned and stared at the investigator through narrowed eyes. "Are you absolutely certain you found the right woman?"

"Spoke with her myself, only yesterday. It's the same woman who once worked for Mrs. Tamhill, all right. Turned as pale as a ghost when I mentioned the lady's name. I've got a man watching the house, just in case she doesn't want to be found a second time."

"I don't think that will be necessary," Rathbone said, momentarily stunned by the name of Helen Barnaby's employer, but realizing that everything was finally beginning to make sense.

"Recognize the name, do you?" Covertly said. His tone was faintly gloating. "Thought you might."

Rathbone recovered himself in less time than it took to turn on his heel and face the mammoth house known as North Hill. "I'll instruct my secretary to see that the agreed-upon fee is deposited into your account, along with the hefty bonus my wife promised you."

"Then I found him?"

"I'm certain of it." Rathbone threw the comment back over his shoulder.

Entering the house by the front door this time, Rathbone marched into the breakfast room. It was empty except for Granby, who was relaxing with a second cup of coffee before making his own departure.

"Looking for someone?" his friend asked, dropping the paper he'd been reading onto the tabletop.

"You could say that," Rathbone replied rather cryptically.

Before his friend could ask just who the viscount was in such a hurry to find, Rathbone disappeared in the direction of the library.

The sound of voices coming through the partially closed door told him he'd found his quarry. He entered the oak-paneled room with its cluttered mahogany desk, stopping to look at the Earl of Ackerman, who was sitting in a well-cushioned armchair. "Excuse us, Fitch."

"What's wrong?" Fitch asked, knowing the look on Rathbone's face spelled trouble.

"Nothing that can't be sorted out," Rathbone replied.

As soon as the door closed, Rathbone marched to the liquor cabinet and poured himself a well-deserved drink. He took a sip before turning to face the one guest who stayed behind. "Do you realize that you have turned my honeymoon into a snipe hunt?"

"Whatever are you talking about?"

A tense moment passed. Then, unable to help himself, Rathbone released a short laugh. "When I think of all the times you lectured me about keeping my pecker in my pants, it's ironic to think that you were speaking from experience."

"I beg your pardon," Morland said, coming to his feet.

"You, of all people," Rathbone said, still chuckling. "The one man I never would have suspected."

"Explain yourself, young man."

"Not until you explain an estate in Kent. You do know the property I'm talking about, don't you, Your Grace? The property you had Mr. Fenstermaker buy for you, the land and house he held in trust for my wife—your daughter."

Morland had the decency to blanch. "How did you find out? Fenstermaker didn't tell you."

"No. I couldn't buy the time of day from the old geezer."

While he was waiting for the duke to explain himself, Rathbone poured Morland a brandy. He handed it to him with the words, "It's early, but I think you're going to need this."

"Thank you," the duke said, accepting the drink before making his way to the window. His back was to the room when he asked, "Does Prudence know?"

"Not yet."

"How did you find out?" He turned around as he asked the question.

"I—that is, my wife and I—hired a man of inquiry."

"Why?"

"Because Prudence is as curious as she is lovely, and as stubborn as her father. Bloody hell! The thought of you being my father-in-law is enough to boggle the mind. Did you really think you could gift her an estate and not have her combing every hedgerow in England looking for you?"

"I hoped she would enjoy Summer House, nothing more."

"The estate really doesn't matter. She knew about you before then, or should I say, she knew her mother had a lover."

"How?"

It did Rathbone's spirit good to know he had finally reduced the Duke of Morland to one-word questions. It served the old codger right to have the tables turned on him for a change. "Rachel Tamhill left a diary behind.

She didn't name you, but she did imply that her husband wasn't the man she loved, nor was he the father of her child."

The duke remained silent.

"I think you had better explain things to me first. Think of it as a rehearsal," Rathbone suggested. Now seated, he sighed and sank back into the cushions of the chair Fitch had vacated. "Practice might make telling Prudence easier."

The duke continued to stand. "I'm not sure where to start. My relationship with Rachel wasn't planned. I met her at a party in London. Phoebe had been dead for several years, but I couldn't bring myself to think of marrying again. Didn't have the heart for it . . . until Rachel. But she was already married."

"So you had an affair."

"Not at first." Morland returned to his chair. He looked at Rathbone, but the expression in his eyes said he was looking inward, at the memories he'd kept secret for over twenty years. "Rachel was beautiful, but more than that, she had a zest for life unlike any I'd ever seen. She had a way of making people laugh, of pulling them out of their doldrums and back into the world. I knew the attraction was mutual, and because I didn't want a scandal, for Rachel's sake, I decided it was best not to see her again. I distanced myself from Society as much as possible. Then Gerald died. The death of my son nearly brought me to my knees."

It was Rathbone's turn to remain silent. The only thing he knew of Morland's son was that the boy had died before reaching his tenth birthday.

"Rachel came to me. Tamhill was in London on business. It was the first time I'd seen her in more than two years. I tried to send her away, but she wouldn't go. Truth be told, I didn't want her to leave."

The room fell silent again, each man occupied with his own thoughts.

"When Rachel wrote me that she was going to have a child, I was the happiest man alive, until I realized that I could never be a real father to Prudence. The situation was impossible. Even if Tamhill agreed to a divorce, which he never would have, Rachel would be an outcast. I couldn't allow that to happen. She loved life too much, loved being with people, at parties, at the theater. She thrived when she was in a crowd. My title would have protected her, but only from the outside. And there was the chance that Tamhill would exercise his right to the child, not because he wanted Prudence, but because he had the power to take what Rachel loved most—her daughter."

"So you stayed the man without a name, the unknown lover," Rathbone said, realizing he had never had more respect for Morland than he did at this moment. It took a large heart to sacrifice one's own happiness for the sake of another.

"Yes. I didn't see Rachel again, not until she wrote to me and said she wanted me to at least see my child."

"That's when you took her to Summer House."

Morland nodded. The hold on his cane lessened as he told more and more of the story. "Lady Montague is a distant relative by marriage. When she acquired the property, she wrote to me and asked if I'd inspect the house and grounds. She planned to sell it and wanted to know how much she could expect the property to bring. The moment I saw the place, I thought of Rachel. That was before Gerald died, but I hoped that one day I might be able to take Rachel there, to spend some time with her. It was a foolish notion, but a man in love does foolish things."

"Prudence remembers Summer House," Rathbone told him. "She remembers a man who called her Poppin."

The remark brought Morland's head up. "She was only a child, just past her third birthday. How could she possibly remember?"

"I'm beginning to believe that the mind can be as fickle as the heart," Rathbone said. "She does remember, but more importantly, she wants to know her father."

"I never meant her to know," Morland said. "Not at first, not as long as Rachel was alive. Then she was gone, like Phoebe and Gerald, and my hands were tied. I couldn't walk into Tamhill Hall and take her; I had no legal right. All I could do was hope that she'd grow up as bright and lovely as her mother."

"What about Worley? Did he know?"

"No. We had been friends, at university and later on in London. When I found out he'd been named guardian—"

"You strengthened the friendship."

"Worley was a good man. I never feigned friendship, but I did take advantage of it. It gave me the opportunity to see Prudence from time to time, to see that she was growing into a beautiful young woman."

"You gave Helen Barnaby a job after Tamhill dismissed her."

"Yes. Rachel wrote to me, asking me to help the woman. I hired her as a maid. That was shortly before Prudence was born. Helen's my London housekeeper now. Is that how your investigator found me?"

"In a roundabout way," Rathbone said. "He first

found Miss Hunnicutt, Prudence's governess, who told us that Rachel Tamhill's original maid had been dismissed. We pieced together what might have happened and set Mr. Covertly on the trail. Imagine my surprise when that trail ended at *your* doorstep."

"Not any more surprised than I was the night I found you in Prudence's bedroom."

"I'm amazed you didn't have me drawn and quartered," Rathbone said laughingly.

"I wanted to," Morland glared at him. "Then you walked into the library demanding to be allowed to marry her, and I changed my mind. Tell me, does Prudence still think you were forced to the altar?"

"Yes, and I want her to keep thinking it. At least until I'm ready to confess otherwise. By the way, I never thanked you for intervening upon my behalf. Worley was determined to marry her to Frederick."

"Do you love her?" Morland asked, meeting Rathbone's gaze.

"Yes."

"Have you told her that?"

"No."

"Don't you think it's time you did?"

"I will, in my own way, but not until we're home at King's Crossing. And don't give me that look. This is your inquisition, not mine."

"What more do you want to know?" Morland asked, seemingly pleased that Rathbone had admitted defeat at the hands of love.

"Nothing, actually," he replied. "I understand that you wanted to protect Rachel Tamhill, and that your hands were legally tied after her death. Funny, but I just realized you had to be at least fifty when Prudence was conceived."

"Forty-nine," Morland corrected him.

Rathbone laughed. "I'm impressed."

"You should be," Morland said, refusing to let his "lad" have the last word. "But if you really want to impress me, it's going to have to be with grandchildren. Lots of grandchildren."

"I'll keep that in mind," Rathbone said. "Until then, you can help me convince Prudence to return to King's Crossing. She thinks Frederick and Lionel will see her leaving as desertion."

"That ridiculous. A wife belongs with her husband."

"I'm glad we finally agree on something. Now all we have to do is convince the lady."

"We?"

"You're her father. I expect you to start acting like one."

"Do you think this the time and place to tell her?"

"There's no time like the present." The sound of Prudence's voice brought both men to their feet. She was dressed for a walk, straw hat in hand. "Lord Ackerman said I might find you here," she said, looking at Rathbone. "Fiona told me Mr. Covertly was here."

Rathbone saw the tears she was trying very hard not to shed, and knew she'd heard more than enough to know that she was finally standing in the same room as her father.

She looked from him to Morland and back again.

It was the duke who finally broke the silence. Resting his cane against the chair, he smiled. "Hello, Poppin."

A small cry of joy, and Prudence was in his arms, hugging him around the waist as she buried her face against his chest.

"I'll make sure the door stays closed this time," Rathbone said, doubting they heard him.

* * *

It was later that evening before Rathbone saw his wife again. A knock on the door interrupted him as he was dressing for dinner. Ferncliffe answered it and found the new viscountess standing in the hall.

"I would like a word with my husband," Prudence said, stepping into the room. Rathbone noticed she was looking very pleased with herself.

"That will be all, Ferncliffe," he said, only slightly startled by his wife's arrival. He was becoming accustomed to her doing the unexpected.

The door had only just closed when Prudence asked, "How did you know?"

"Covertly located Helen Barnaby. The moment I saw the address, I knew she was working for Morland. From there, the conclusion was an easy one."

"I should be angry at you for confronting His Grace before coming to find me," she said.

"You could be angry, but I don't think you are."

Prudence shivered as he reached for her hand and drew her toward the bed. Once they were sitting side by side, he brought her hand to his mouth and kissed it. "You aren't angry, are you?"

"No." She smiled, then laughed out loud. "Oh, Benjamin, I have a father. A real father!"

"And I have a father-in-law." He groaned. "Morland. Fate does enjoy playing havoc with my life."

"I have a father, and you a father-in-law, but only in private," Prudence announced. "His Grace insists that we keep it that way. He's afraid there will be gossip, and he's determined that nothing mar my good name. I disagree, of course, but—"

"There's only so much disagreeing you can do with a duke," Rathbone said. He stretched out on the bed, pulling her down beside him. Prudence didn't resist when he drew her close. "It's Morland's nature to be protective. And it really isn't important that the whole world know, is it?"

"No. Not important at all," Prudence agreed. She turned up her face so he could kiss her.

Rathbone obliged with several kisses. He was working on the buttons of her dress when Prudence sat up and pushed him away. "You aren't going to get off that easily, my lord. You should have come to me the moment Mr. Covertly arrived."

"And what of you, madam? Eavesdropping at the library door," he said in defense. "Where have your manners gone?"

"A lady wouldn't have to eavesdrop if her husband was truthful with her." She left the bed to undo the buttons he hadn't been able to reach.

By the time she removed her shoes and stockings, Rathbone was already naked. He helped her with the last of her clothes, then pulled her into his arms. He wanted her so much that his body trembled with the need, and he had to clench his jaw to keep from losing control of the situation.

Prudence gloried in the battle he waged. She broke away from him, then knelt on the bed beside him, pushing him onto his back. Then she began to explore his body with feathery kisses and light caresses, savoring the texture of his skin. She kissed the angle of his jaw, the curve of his mouth, then lower, tormenting him until he promised blissful retribution.

Prudence laughed with joy when he couldn't take anymore and rolled her under him. He loomed over her, his eyes sparkling, his smile as tempting as ever. "Don't think, madam, that because Morland has intimidated me for years that you will do the same."

"Me, intimidate you? I think that very unlikely, my lord."

"Do you?" He traced the delicate circle of her breasts with his tongue, returning to each aroused peak to suck gently.

Prudence moaned deep in her throat as her legs opened to give him access to the rest of her. When he was poised to enter her, she smiled up at him. "Is there something you want to say to me, my lord?"

"Yes, but it will have to wait until later," he said, lowering his body until it was joined to hers. "At the moment, this takes priority."

Sensations rippled through Prudence as he began to move with exquisite slowness, watching her face as she responded to him. "I would like to hear it now," she said, refusing to give herself completely to the pleasure until he said the words.

Rathbone felt as if Prudence was touching his very heart when she moved against him, taking him deep inside her body. "Very well," he whispered as he buried his hands in the loose tresses of her hair. "I love you."

She smiled, then laughed, then moved again, arching her hips. It wasn't until they were both satisfied, resting beside each other, that Rathbone roused himself enough to ask if his wife might return the favor.

"I've loved you from that very first night when you kissed me at the garden gate," she said, propping herself on her elbow so she could look down at him. "I didn't want to, but I couldn't help myself."

Rathbone grinned triumphantly. "I never thought to love a woman the way I love you," he confessed between kisses. "Now, I can't imagine *not* loving you."

"I can't imagine it either," Prudence confessed happily. "I still grieve for Uncle Horace, but I've gained a whole new family. Oh, Benjamin, I can't believe it. You and the Duke of Morland. What more could I possibly ask for?"

"His Grace did mention grandchildren," her husband suggested with his best smile. "And my mother would be pleased. She can't wait to spoil them."

He made love to her again, taking possession of her body and her heart so completely that Prudence was as certain of his love as she was that the sun would rise the next morning.

Experience the Romance of
Rosanne Bittner

Put a Little Romance in Your Life with
Georgina Gentry